Januarius Aloysius MacGahan

Under the Northern Lights

Januarius Aloysius MacGahan

Under the Northern Lights

ISBN/EAN: 9783337250553

Printed in Europe, USA, Canada, Australia, Japan

Cover: Foto ©Andreas Hilbeck / pixelio.de

More available books at **www.hansebooks.com**

UNDER THE NORTHERN LIGHTS.

"A PERILOUS SITUATION."

UNDER THE

NORTHERN LIGHTS.

BY

J. A. MacGAHAN,

Correspondent of the New York Herald;

AUTHOR OF CAMPAIGNING ON THE OXUS, AND THE FALL OF KHIVA.

WITH ILLUSTRATIONS BY G. R. DE WILDE.

London:

SAMPSON LOW, MARSTON, SEARLE, & RIVINGTON,

CROWN BUILDINGS, 188, FLEET STREET.

1876.

PREFACE.

THERE have been about two hundred and fifty books written on the Arctic regions. The reader can therefore hardly expect to find in the following pages anything very new or striking. Those who wish to read detailed accounts of voyages in this interesting part of the globe, will find in the narratives of Parry, Ross, Franklin, Back, Collinson, McClure, McClintock, Osborn, Kane, Hall, and Hayes, a series of fascinating stories; while those who want a short and interesting account of all the voyages that have been made to these regions, and a summary of all that is known about them, can do no better than to read the THRESHOLD OF THE UNKNOWN REGION, by Clements R. Markham, —the only intelligent synopsis of Arctic knowledge ever published.

It only remained for me to give a few pictures

of the pleasant side of Arctic life—pictures hastily sketched on a voyage that was remarkable only for its dash and rapidity. I hope, therefore, that the Reader will not be disappointed to find I have attempted nothing more.

CONTENTS.

APPENDIX.

UNDER THE NORTHERN LIGHTS.

CHAPTER I.

STARTING.

OUR ship is the PANDORA, our commander Captain Allen Young, and we are bound for the Arctic.

We are leaving the homes of men, the swarming cities, the careworn, anxious faces, the toiling multitudes, the smoky, poisoned atmosphere, the fetters of civilization—for a world of pure air and savage freedom, for the frozen regions around the Pole; the home of the reindeer and the walrus, the haunts of the white bear, the land of the Midnight Sun.

The shore, the houses, the steeples, the domes, the tall volcanic chimneys, with clouds of heavy, black smoke hanging over them, and the countless roofs of the great city slowly recede from view.

B

The decreasing roar of the busy streets, the ebbing hum of civilization gradually dies upon the ear like the murmur of the ocean itself, and then is heard no more. We are out at sea.

It is with a feeling of vague sadness we look back at the low-lying land which gradually sinks into the ocean, and think how little we are missed from the great world we leave behind, how well it can get on without us, what a little place we filled in it.

But no matter. If the world can do without us we can do without it, for a time at least. Is not the Arctic before us in all its glory? Are not the icebergs awaiting us with all their weird phantasmagoria of shape and colour, the cold green water dashing around their feet, and gurgling through caverns it has itself worn deep into their icy hearts? Are there not mountains to be scaled, whose snow-capped heads no mortal eye has ever beheld? and continents to be explored, that no mortal foot has ever trod? Are there not cozy little bays and inlets land-locked and hidden away by towering mountains, where we may drop anchor and hunt for seal and walrus? Are there not quiet little rivers, whose waters have never been rippled by prow of boat or canoe, teeming with such delicious trout and salmon as Isaac Walton never dreamed of? Are there not grassy little glades, where the snow has already melted under the steadfast gaze of a midnight sun, on

which reindeer and musk-ox are quietly grazing,
only awaiting the ring of our rifles to turn themselves into savoury steaks broiled over a camp-
fire ? And with such a world and such a prospect before us, shall we regret the chagrins,
crosses, disappointments, and petty annoyances,
the stifling atmosphere of the world we have left
behind ?

We are going to try to make the North-West
Passage ; to pass around the north coast of America,
and come out through Behring's Straits into the
Pacific Ocean—a feat which has been the dream
of navigators for centuries, but only a dream. Our
object is to make this dream a reality. It is our
ambition not only to accomplish the undertaking,
but to accomplish it in a single season. For a
North-west Passage that would require more than
one season would obviously be of no practical use
to navigation. To take a vessel from Southampton
to San Francisco, in a single summer, by way of
Behring's Straits—that is the grand feat which
any true seaman would give his right hand to
accomplish, and that is what we are going to
attempt.

Let it be understood that we are not going to
discover the North-West Passage. That has already
been done by Sir John Franklin, although he
never got home to make his discovery known
to the world.

McClure even made the Passage on foot ; but

no ship has ever yet been able to get through, owing to a barrier of ice, which hitherto has proved to be impassable.

But if we fail in the primary object of our voyage, we may yet reach King William's Island, and there find perhaps some more relics of Sir John Franklin. Or, if we should not succeed in this, we can at least obtain news of the ALERT and DISCOVERY, and learn whether they got safely through the dreaded Melville Bay.

This information alone is of sufficient importance to justify our voyage, should we accomplish nothing else. Melville Bay is a place of evil repute, and formerly many whaling-ships were lost there in attempting to work through the ice. It was in its treacherous waters that the Fox, under McClintock, was caught the first winter she was out, a misfortune which resulted in the loss of a whole year. Should the ALERT and DISCOVERY get beset in this dangerous place, they would simply drift down with the ice through Baffin's Bay into Davis Straits; they would only be released the following April, and they would have . accomplished no more in the way of Arctic exploration than if they had stayed at home. It will therefore be understood that news of their safe passage through Melville Bay is of the greatest importance, and this we hope to obtain without deviating from the real object of our voyage.

Our vessel, the PANDORA, in which we hope to

accomplish so much, was bought from the navy department, by Captain Young, and fitted out by him for Arctic navigation. This was no small matter. Although built for a gun-boat, and therefore much stronger than an ordinary merchantman, her strength had to be materially increased to prepare her for work in the ice. Heavy iron beams and knees were put in amidships to increase her resisting power to a squeeze or "nip," her hull was enveloped in an outer casing of American elm, $4\frac{1}{2}$ inches thick, to strengthen her sides for rubs against the ice. In addition to this, her stem was covered with a solid plate of iron, and her prow, from the stem back over the swell of the waist, was laced with heavy iron cleats, or bars. These changes, while injuring her sailing qualities somewhat, will enable her to work her way with impunity among ice where an ordinary ship would be crushed like an egg-shell.

She is a barque. Her length is 150 feet, her breadth of beam 20, her tonnage (navy register) 438, her engines, though nominally 80-horse power, will work up to 200, and she draws, loaded down as she was when she left Portsmouth, twelve feet of water. As our crew, officers and men all told, only number thirty men, scarcely more than one-third her usual complement, she is very lightly manned for such a vessel. The studding-sails were therefore put aside as being unsuitable and unnecessary for Arctic navigation;

and the great mainsail, the largest sail on the ship, unbent and left behind, as so heavy a piece of canvas would have been very difficult to manage with so few hands.

Finally, provisions were taken in for eighteen months, and 150 tons of coal, which filled her hold and bunkers, besides making a deck load that, I am afraid, would have led to our arrest, had Mr. Plimsoll seen us.

The promoters of our expedition were Captain Allen Young, on whom fell the principal burden and expense; Mr. James Gordon Bennett, whom I had the honour to represent; Lieutenant Innes Lillingston, R.N., who went as second in command; and the late Lady Franklin. She had insisted on contributing to the expenses of the expedition, almost against Captain Young's wishes, who felt by no means confident of doing anything that would entitle him to accept her willing contribution.

The decks of the PANDORA presented a curious topsy-turvey spectacle, and from their appearance alone it would have been easy to guess that she was bound on an Arctic voyage. Boxes, casks, packages, heaps of stores that had not yet been stowed away, were scattered about, together with upturned boats, spars, oars, coils of rope, water-casks, and every other imaginable seafaring object. And everywhere there was coal. Her waist was heaped up with it; the quarter-deck was covered with it; the lower decks and hold were crammed full of it. To move about you had to climb or scramble over huge heaps and sacks of it, that scarcely left room for working the sails. But when we thought of the long, cold Arctic night we might be obliged to pass, buried for months in the ice and snow, with no glimpse of the kindly sun, the sight of all this coal was by no means a disagreeable one. That black, unsightly, despised mineral might be warmth, comfort, cozy fires, and life itself, when the wind and snow were sweeping in terrible whirlwinds through the long, dreary, desolate night around the pole.

When the land had become a mere line along the horizon I went below to take a look at my quarters, and see what sort of place I had to live in for the next few months. I had arrived on board just before we weighed anchor, and had not as yet had time to make a close inspection of my quarters, or to arrange my things. I descended a very steep, narrow step-ladder, at the bottom of which there were two doors. One opened to the left into the navigating room, which was six feet by about fifteen, the long way extending across the ship. It had a bunk and lockers at each end, and was studded around with twelve or fifteen Snider rifles, half-a-dozen heavy revolvers, two or three deep shelves full of books, a fine large brass-mounted astronomical telescope, tripods, barometers, and thermometers, sextants, chronometer boxes, maps, and charts, and all sorts of scientific apparatus. Behind this room, on either side of the mizen-mast and running back to the propeller-well, were two little three-cornered rooms, occupied by the Captain and the First Lieutenant respectively.

The door to the right from the companion-ladder opened into the mess-room. It was of a somewhat diminutive size—only ten feet square; but there was room—oceans of it—for seven people, once you really succeeded in convincing yourself of that fact. True, it did not produce that impression on you at the first glance, heaped full to the ceiling, as it was, of all sorts of strange-looking traps and effects, which had not yet had time to be stowed away in their proper places. It presented, upon the whole, but a damp and cheerless appearance, and it did not at first sight strike the imagination as a place you would choose of your own free will to pass the remainder of your days in.

But it improved upon acquaintance, and developed wonderful resources in the way of lockers which were hid away in nooks and corners, and which received untold heaps of things without ever seeming to get quite full; and there was on one side the merest miniature of a grate, set in a brass fireplace, which was burnished to that extent that it might have served for a looking-glass had it been placed a little higher. Opening into this mess-room, from three different sides, were three little cabins, one of which I found had been reserved for me. It was hardly large enough to swing a cat in, but so large that you could turn round in it if you were very careful. Like every other part of the ship, it was crammed full of effects all topsy-turvy. In an hour or two I had succeeded in stowing everything—books, guns, oilskins, Arctic boots, chamois-leather-lined clothing, heavy woollen furs, and the rest—away in lockers and on shelves, and establishing something like order in my future home.

And now, as it was the hour for tea, we all gathered around the table for the first time. Like the brothers and sisters of Wordsworth's little cottage girl, we were seven. First there was our Captain, Allen Young, who took his place among Arctic explorers sixteen years ago, when in 1857-9 he was navigating officer in the Fox, under McClintock. Fascinated—as everybody who has once seen them seems to be fascinated—by Arctic skies, he ventures to meet the perils of an Arctic journey in command of a ship of his own.

The second in command, Lieutenant Lillingston, I have already mentioned as a subscriber to the expenses of the expedition; and the third was Lieutenant George Pirie, a distinguished young naval officer, whom the Admiralty kindly permitted to accompany us as our navigating officer. Next was Lieutenant Beynen, of the Dutch Royal Navy—whom we called " Tromp," after the old Dutch Admiral who once sailed up the Thames with a broom at his masthead, as a sign and a token unto all the world that he meant to sweep it clean. He was fresh from the assault on the Kratung in Atchin, and was sent out by his government to report on the expedition, and gain experience in Arctic navigation, probably to resume the thread of Arctic exploration where it was dropped by Barents, the old Dutch navigator, three hundred years ago.

Then there was Dr. Horner, a young physician, who had the direction of the natural history and geological department; and our artist, Mr. De Wilde, the first professional artist, excepting Mr. Bradford, who ever visited the polar regions. You are not long in making the acquaintance of your future companions on a voyage of this kind, and in a day or two we knew each other as well as if we had been acquainted for years.

We steamed down the channel until we were well clear of the land; we then hoisted the screw and put out the fires, and the PANDORA became a sailing ship. We could not afford to burn our coal until it should become absolutely necessary, as it was impossible to know whether we would be able to get any more at Disco, on the west coast of Greenland, where it can sometimes be obtained. We were soon out in the broad Atlantic, but were almost immediately met by a nor'-west gale, and from that moment forth we encountered either head winds that drove us far out of our course, or fell into calms that allowed of no progress at all. When we sailed from Portsmouth on June 27th, we expected to reach Disco in twenty days, and with moderately fair winds we should have done so. At the end of a month we were only off Cape Farewell, and still nearly one thousand miles from Disco, which place might be considered only the starting-point of our voyage. When, according to all known laws—even with a falling barometer—the wind ought to have blown from the south-west, it tenaciously held to the opposite point, with an obstinacy that was exasperating. Had it blown from the north, we might have run to the west; had it blown from the west, we might have made northing, and in either case we would have been gaining ground. But it stuck in the nor'-west as though it had been nailed there, and we were obliged to beat the whole distance. From the time we left the channel, we had not twelve consecutive hours of fair wind, and the wonder is that we should have made even the little progress we did.

The time passed somewhat monotonously, but not so heavily as it might have done under other circumstances. We all worked, officers and men alike, in handling the ship, taking in sail, making sail, and hauling at the ropes. This alone would almost have kept the time from hanging heavy on our hands, even without an occasional game of chess or cards, with which we often filled up so much of the day, as eating, sleeping, and a little writing left at our disposal.

There were days when we rolled about, with the water dashing over the decks at every moment, wetting everything above and below, when first one side of the deck was under water and then the other, while the tops of the masts described frightful circles on the low, leaden sky, that made one dizzy to watch; days when you could neither sit still nor stand still, nor even lie still in your bunk without holding on to something; when everybody was cold, wet, half sick, and thoroughly miserable. There were other days when the sun shone brightly, when there was not a ripple on the sea, nor a breath of wind stirring; when the blue water, to the broad horizon, appeared one great circular looking-glass, so still and smooth it lay, and the PANDORA figure-head seemed to be gazing at herself in the dark blue water with a pleased smile. Then some of us would get into a boat, and row off anywhere on the smooth water for miles, until the PANDORA's sails, white and ghostly, seemed to hang between sea and sky like an unsubstantial vision. When we came back we would row around her, glide under her bow, and look up at the figure-head, with her golden hair and her flowing drapery, and find that instead of admiring herself in her ocean mirror, her staring eyes were gazing far away to the horizon with a fixed look, as though the snow and ice of the Polar world were already reflected in them.

On Sundays we had prayers in the forecastle with the men. Lieutenant Lillingston read the Church of England service, to which the men all responded very earnestly; and sometimes he read a sermon from one of the well-known preachers. Afterwards, we often had a hymn or two, accompanied by an organ, of which the reader may have heard before, and which, as compared with its Arctic companions, might look down on them as a veteran upon raw recruits.

This organ was originally presented to the Arctic ship PRINCE ALBERT by the late Prince Consort. It has ever since made a speciality of Arctic voyages, and was now on its fifth expedition to Polar Seas. It is a fine instrument, plays thirty or forty tunes, and was highly prized by our blue jackets. Very pleasant it was to see a rough old tar grinding away, with a long-drawn, serious face, accompanying the rest, who were intoning the " Old Hundredth " or some other old psalm tune. And here I may remark that our crew appeared to have been excellently selected. They were nearly all steady, quiet men; most of them had served in men-of-war, and therefore understood something of the value of discipline. Many of them, too, had made whaling voyages to Baffin's Bay, and four of them were old Arctic explorers; of these, two, Toms and Florence, having been out in the Fox, were old shipmates of Captain Young. Besides, we had " Joe "—heroic Joe—the famous Eskimo, who, together with Hans, saved Captain Tyson's party from starvation. Of him I shall speak in detail by-and-by; at present I will content myself by saying that he is a quiet, good-natured, pleasant little fellow, always ready to do anybody a good turn, and possessing, withal, a grave, stoical face that rarely betrays any emotion.

CHAPTER II.

WHEN I went on deck, on the morning of the 28th
of July, we were in sight of Cape Farewell, and
surrounded on all sides by a field of floating ice.
There was ice everywhere; the horizon was white
with it; while near the ship great pieces, of every

imaginable shape and size, went drifting rapidly
by, in what appeared, to an inexperienced eye, most
dangerous proximity. There were old castles,
with broken, ruined towers, battlements, and loop-
holes; castellated fortresses; cathedrals with the

most fantastic gothic carving and delicate tracery, never equalled in beautiful irregularity of design by anything ever carved by man; and triumphal arches, by the side of which the great Triumphal Arch of Paris would be but a plaything.

The animal and vegetable kingdom were likewise represented. There were huge mushrooms, with broad drooping tops, that were supported on a single slender stem; and great masses of ice-foliage that crowned groups of beautifully-carved columns, like immense bread-fruit trees covered with ice. There were swans with long slender necks gracefully poised on the water; there were dragons, lions, eagles, with spread wings and bended beak. No wild extravagance of shape, no improbable monstrosity of form that one could not have found among the hundreds of pieces that went gliding swiftly by, as they came down from the Arctic world. One example of Arctic sculpture, we all particularly observed and admired; it was an eagle with spread wings, perched on the back of a goose, as though he were trying to carry her away.

The weather, which had been dark and cloudy for three or four days, had cleared up in the night; and now all these wonderful objects appeared gleaming and sparkling in the bright morning sunshine, a most brilliant and animated spectacle.

This was the first ice we had seen, although we had been near the latitude of Cape Farewell for several days.

Icebergs are often seen as far south as the track of the ocean steamers between England and America; but these come down the coast of Labrador, two or three hundred miles further west. This ice was the first sign of our near approach to the Arctic regions, our first foretaste of Arctic scenery, and was hailed with delight after the weary monotony of our long sea voyage.

It was what is called the Spitzbergen ice, which breaks off from the great pack west of that island, and floats down the east coast of Greenland. It drifts up Davis Strait two or three hundred miles, then crosses with the current, and comes down the coast of Labrador. We could, therefore, expect to have it for several days, unless we should get what we had not had yet for more that a few hours at a time—a fair wind.

We soon experienced our first bump. Here and there, great flat pieces or floes, several acres in extent, presented themselves just in our path, and had to be avoided. They grew larger and closer together; sometimes only a narrow channel of water between them. At last we came to a place, where there was no passage at all, unless we went two or three miles out of our route. I was on the forecastle watching our tortuous course with interest; and when I saw the road closed to us, I looked back to the bridge, curious to see what would be done.

Toms, the old gunner who, as I have said,

was out with Captain Young in the Fox, was
there directing the vessel's course, and I soon
perceived that instead of going around, we
were driving straight at the floe. Looking
forward again I saw open water beyond. What
I had taken for a solid field of ice, was in
reality, two large floes, joined together at one spot,
and thus forming a narrow isthmus, only a few
feet wide. It was this isthmus that old Toms was
going to charge. The wind in the course of the
morning, had sprung up from the east, and we
had it consequently on the starboard quarter.
The PANDORA was coming smoothly along under
reefed topsails, at the rate of about five knots.
In a moment her prow plunged into the ice with
the force of a battering ram. There was a loud
crash; the ship quivered and shook, the masts,
with the sails pulling at them, bent and creaked;
the ice rolled up before her in great blocks that
fell splashing into the water, and the PANDORA
stopped quite still, for the moment completely
jammed. But it was for a moment only. Her
sharp iron prow had quite demolished the neck of
ice, and it only remained to squeeze herself between
the floes into clear water beyond. She wriggled
through like an eel, and then shot gaily forward,
as though eager for another encounter.

"That was rather a hard bump, Toms, wasn't
it?" said somebody.

"Oh, bless yer, that's nothing," replied the old

sea-dog with a smile. "We'll have harder ones nor that before we gets through the North-West Passage."

We had several more bumps that day, but they were comparatively slight.

We were now approaching Cape Desolation. The snow had nearly all melted, and the red sandstone mountains streaked with silver lines of snow, lay in the warm sunshine, veiled with a reddish purple mist; here and there were bright yellow patches probably glaciers, that shone like gold, in the bright sunshine, forming a picture, warm, silent, calm, and lovely as a dream.

Not for long could we gaze in quietness on the scene. Seals began to show themselves, quietly sunning themselves on the ice floes, or swimming about our ship, their round smooth heads like plum puddings floating in the water. As we had been living on salt provisions for twenty days, a great longing for fresh meat suddenly came over us. Seal's liver with bacon is a dish fit for the gods, and we determined to have some. We got out our guns, and waited till we saw a seal within range, and immediately opened fire, but although we probably hit him more than once, he managed to wriggle off the floe into the water. The next one we fired at seemed to have been killed, as he lay perfectly still on the floe after receiving our volley.

A boat was lowered, the sails were put aback, and we waited with anxiety the capture of the game.

As soon as the boat approached the ice, we saw one of the men spring on to the floe. We could see him raise the boat-hook, or some other instrument, evidently with the·intention of striking the wounded animal; then there was a splash in the water, man and seal disappeared behind the boat, and for a few minutes we could not make out what had happened. Then the boat put off, and came back to the ship ; but there was no seal !

It turned out that the floe, which had been under-mined by the water, and was besides somewhat rotten, broke off under the additional weight of the man, and he, instead of giving a finishing blow to the seal, suddenly found himself, together with his intended victim, in the water. The seal sunk at once, and was seen no more, while the man scrambled into the boat amidst the laughter of his comrades. So we lost our expected feast. But it was not long before· we saw another seal, and this one we succeeded in capturing. He was a fine large fellow; and it was pleasant to see Joe's satis-fied grin, as he hauled it over the side of the ship, and proceed to divest it of its skin.

The officers took to the seal-flesh most kindly, but the sailors were by far too dainty to feed on such unusual food. It is a curious fact that men on Arctic expeditions will refuse to touch seal or walrus meat, or even preserved or tinned beef and mutton ! The result is that they frequently get the scurvy, which often enough proves fatal.

We had a fair wind all day, blowing pretty strong from the south-east. But we had already lost so much time, that notwithstanding this first fair wind, Captain Young decided to put into Ivigtut, a little Danish settlement on the west coast of Greenland, and get a supply of coal sufficient to steam to Disko. Two days before reaching Cape Farewell, we had seen and boarded a brigantine, the TRAVELLER, bound from Peterhead to that port, for the purpose of getting a cargo of kryolite. The Captain had informed us that there was plenty of coal to be obtained there. To Ivigtut, accordingly, Captain Young decided to go, although it was some forty miles inland, up a deep fjord or inlet, and we would inevitably lose a day by the journey. But that was better than the chance of beating up Davis Straits with a head wind, and so the PANDORA'S bow was turned shorewards.

About sunset, we saw a large floe, almost directly across our course, and the excitement on board was great, when five large seals were observed upon it, apparently asleep. All the men came to the Captain, one after another, for permission to have a shot, which he good naturedly granted; and in a moment the deck of the PANDORA presented the appearance of a man-of-war preparing for action. Thirty gun-barrels were quickly levelled over the nettings, bearing upon the hapless animals, which lay quite still, as the ship moved slowly up, calmly unconscious of their danger.

Joe gave the signal when we were about fifty yards off, by firing his Snider, and then there was a regular volley, followed by an irregular rattling discharge ; each man loading and firing again, when the seals still showed signs of life, by wriggling towards the edge of the floe. Altogether we must have fired two hundred rounds, and yet three of the seals got away ! The biggest of the lot escaped, when we were only thirty or forty feet from the floe, although his body must have been traversed many times by balls ! But seals are hard to kill unless shot through the brain, and as it is difficult to tell just where the neck ends and the head begins, the brain is not an easy mark to hit. They might have all escaped, I believe, but that they were at first partly bewildered by our fire, and partly curious to see what we were driving at, and this curiosity proved fatal to them.

In a few minutes we had moored the ship alongside the floe, and were out on it to secure our
game. It was like going ashore. The floe was
just like a little island, two or three acres in extent. There were little hills and hollows on it,
covered with snow, of course; and what made
the resemblance still more complete, we found a
little lake of water, quite fresh and pure. We
had been on a short allowance of water for several
days, and had been obliged to wash in sea water,
which is of little or no use as regards cleanliness.
We hailed the sight of this lake with delight, the
more as the little water remaining in our casks
was bad. We had a long drink first of all, then
a run over the island, and finally, a good roll
in the snow—a luxury, which in the beginning
of August, when the denizens of great cities are
sweltering and panting with the heat, is not to
be despised. Talk of iced drinks, and cooling
draughts! Here we could take a drink of pure,
sweet, clear water, from a lake whose bottom and
shores were ice!

The Captain decided to stop long enough to
renew our supply of water; and soon the island
of ice presented a lively spectacle; officers and
men running backwards and forwards, some
dipping up the water, others carrying it in buckets
to the ship, now moored against the floe. Lillingston and Pirie were sitting down by the snow
at the edge of the water, filling the buckets by

means of wooden ladles, and splashing it about like children. Everybody was laughing, shouting, singing, rolling over the snow. It was so delightful to be able to stretch one's legs, after the confinement of our deck-encumbered ship.

Very pretty everything looked in this icy world. Behind us was the rugged, lowering coast-line, looming up high and dark against the eastern sky ; before us the tall, slender, raking masts, and light, airy spars and thread-like cordage of the PANDORA, that rose up black as ink against the fiery western sky, which was a blaze of crimson flame.

CHAPTER III.

BANKO.

At ten o'clock we were again under way, steaming,
—for we had lowered the screw, and lighted fires
—towards the mouth of the Arsuk fjord or inlet,
on which Ivigtut is situated.

The next morning we were surprised to find
that the Traveller, which we had not seen for
three days, had arrived before us. She was be-
calmed, however, and might have been two weeks
getting up to Ivigtut had we not taken her in
tow. The Arsuk fjord is a narrow, crooked
inlet, extending inland about fifty miles between
precipitous, rocky mountains, that for the
most part come so steep down to the water
that there is not footing for a goat. The de-
clivities were covered here and there with a little
grass or vegetation of some kind, which might
support many a flock of sheep and goats, were
it not for the long, cold, dark winter night.
It was a bright, warm day, and our progress up
the wild, rocky, little gorge—it could be called

nothing else—was far more pleasant, I thought, than a sail on the lake of Como.

Steaming around a little point, we suddenly found ourselves before a collection of fifteen or twenty wooden huts, scattered over a rocky slope; this was the settlement of Ivigtut. Three ships were anchored before it. One of these proved to be the Fox, Captain Young's old vessel, which is now in the Kryolite trade.

While the ship was coaling, some of us went ashore, and were rather disagreeably surprised by a sudden onslaught of flies and mosquitos that instantly settled on our faces. They did not seem disposed to sting, but the feeling they produced was maddening. As there was absolutely nothing to be seen here but a few Danish houses—there were only three or four Eskimos in the place—and two or three heaps of kryolite, we were glad to accept the invitation of the doctor of the colony, to enter his little house, and thus escape our tiny persecutors. These insects seem to be too wild as yet to come inside a house, and once we had passed the threshold of the doctor's door we were at peace.

But such is the lot of man! We had no sooner escaped one danger than we were beset by another. Our enemy in this case was a pleasant and insinuating one; it came from Sweden, and its name was " banko."

The doctor first gave us cigars and a glass of

sherry. When we had drunk this, he poured out some "banko:" then we put a layer of banko on the sherry, and then a layer of sherry on the banko, the doctor insisting, that was the only proper way to drink it. We afterwards went on heaping up alternate layers of sherry and banko, until they had acquired a height I would be afraid to mention, partly because I might not be believed, partly because I am not quite sure about it myself.

Then the Governor of the place came and invited us to take a glass of punch with him, an invitation we readily accepted. He was a large, fat man—one of the fattest men I ever saw. He wore sealskin trowsers, and a reindeer-skin jacket with a fur collar; and was as like Falstaff in his uncontrollable jollity as in his portliness of person. The punch was made of sherry and claret and banko, and had a mild, pleasant taste, quite disproportionate to the powerful effects it produced. The Governor had entertained the officers of the TIGRESS when she came here in search of the crew of the POLARIS. They, he said, had also drunk banko punch until some of them had been observed to stir it up with their cigars for teaspoons, and then to express astonishment at the cigars appearing damp.

A good many events of that night I do not remember; but I cannot forget the wonderful way in which one of our party went a-board ship. There was a very narrow gangway, fifty or sixty feet long, and without any handrail, leading from the shore, first to one of the ships which were lying there, and from her deck to ours. There was nothing at all by which to hold on to, and it looked exceedingly dangerous to me, although I had not remarked the fact upon coming ashore. "Sh' all right," he said, as he poised himself, took a careful aim, and shot off like an arrow over the high narrow plank. He brought up safely on our ship, a feat which I remember thinking at the time, one of the most brilliant and daring I had ever witnessed. Once started, he could no more have changed his course than a bullet, and the slightest deviation in his original aim would inevitably have sent him into the sea. He brought up, however, quite safely on our deck. The rest of us got on board somehow—I do not remember exactly how I myself got on board, as it was somewhat dark at the time, and this seems to have affected my memory. The last thing I recollect seeing, before turning in, was a figure in the obscurity, that strangely resembled our Doctor, leaning over the nettings, and gazing moodily down into the water. What he could have been looking at I cannot imagine, as it was too dark to see anything.

There are about 150 people in Ivigtut in summer, while in winter there are only fifty, the rest going back to Denmark. They are employed in getting out the kryolite, for which purpose the colony was established. The kryolite mines produce about £20,000 a year, and are worked by a Danish company, with a concession from the Danish Government.

Buried in complete darkness for three months of the year, and in snow for eight, it would be but a dreary spot for a European. Dr. Arctander, who entertained us, proposes to stay another year here; and one of the engineers, who showed us a great number of geological specimens, and most kindly allowed us to choose any that took our fancy, had been there two years already.

With regard to the kryolite trade, I find I can do no better than to make the following interesting extract from Captain Young's journal:—

" Ivigtut is situate about sixteen miles up the fiord named Arsuk, after the lofty island of that name, which borders the left or rather northern side of the fiord. It is here the kryolite is found; the name Ivigtut was given to this place by the natives, on account of its fertility. It was first frequented by them for the purpose of fishing and drying the Arctic salmon, but was deserted on account of the increasing floating ice. We owe the discovery of kryolite to a peculiar circumstance. The Greenlanders employed the water-worn fragments of this mineral as weight for their fishing-lines, and in this shape the first specimens were sent by the missionaries to Copenhagen as ethnographical curiosities. The kryolite is found near the shore, resting immediately upon the gneiss. The purest is of a snow white colour, without any intermixture of foreign substances. The greyish white variety, which lies on the surface, is considered the second quality of commerce. The kryolite mines are now regularly worked by a company in Copenhagen, which employs a manager to superintend the works; and sufficient men are sent out annually to load the ships, which generally obtain a freight—£2 per ton—to England or Philadelphia. These workmen are relieved at fixed periods. They do not bring any of their families with them, and generally contract to remain three years, the mines being worked both winter and summer. The kryolite is used for a variety of purposes, but principally for making soda, and also in the United States for preparing aluminium. The Fox, so celebrated in Arctic history, is now in the employ of the company, and is used for bringing out supplies and relief of workmen to the colony. The kryolite is all brought from the mine—which is, perhaps, 200 yards from the sea —to the beach, close to the shipping stage, and is stacked in large square heaps, as being the most convenient for measuring it both for shipment and for the royalty to be paid to the Royal Danish Greenland Company."

CHAPTER IV.

THEY were all very kind to us, and we were especially indebted to Mr. Fritz, the head engineer of the mines, for his extreme kindness in furnishing us coals and putting them on board.

We got under way next morning at three o'clock, and not having another ship in tow, steamed down the fiord much faster than we had gone up. We ran along the coast a short distance but we soon found so much ice that we were obliged to put out to sea. Next day we got quite out of the ice, and all the way up the coast to Disco had clear water, with only here and there a small floating berg. Our old friends, the head winds, clung to us with the greatest fidelity, so that we had to steam nearly all the time.

The coast of Greenland at this season of the year is beautiful in the extreme. It is a broken, serrated line of high, rugged mountains, that rise abruptly out of the water, in lowering perpendicular masses, to a height of 3000 feet. Over

these the sun and atmosphere combine to produce
the most fantastic effects of colour. A thin veil
of mist gathers over them, as if to drape and hide
their savage nakedness—a kind of spider-web, of
gigantic proportions, that catches the sunlight,
and holds it prisoner in the meshes of a fairy net;
that folds itself caressingly around the stern and
rugged heights in a luminous film of purple rosy
light, and blends here and there into the yellow
trembling glimmer of a glacier. Here and there

are sharp, needle-like peaks, behind which may
be seen, gleaming white in the sun, the mighty sea
of ice, 4000 feet deep, which has overwhelmed
Greenland.

The whole of this great continent is, in reality,
nothing but one immense, deep glacier, with a
fringe of mountains around it, forming the coast-
line. This glacier has never been explored, never
been crossed, and probably never will be; for
yawning gaps and fissures, many hundred feet in

GREENLAND.

[Page 33.

depth, traverse it in every direction, and intercept for ever the traveller's way.

The interior of this great continent is an icy solitude that is a secret unknown to man, and it will probably always remain so. Its surface is 4000 feet above the sea, and when you ascend to it, you will probably perceive somewhere on the plain which rises before you in a slight ascent till it touches the sky, two or three little sharp conical hills, a few feet high, that pierce through the ice; and you will be astonished to learn that these insignificant mole-hills are in reality the tops of lofty mountains, that have been submerged beneath the mighty inundation of ice.

Somebody has said of Switzerland, that if it were ironed out, it would be a very large country. If Switzerland were about ten thousand times larger than it is, and ice were then poured into it until it should be full up nearly to a level with the highest mountain peaks, it would present just the appearance of the interior of Greenland.

And yet the whole of this vast continent was, at one period of the earth's history, green and fertile.

There have been found here, forests of carbonized trees and plants, and the fossil remains of many animals that could only have existed in a warm climate. Fossil corals and sponges are often picked up now in Lancaster Sound, and on the shore of Beechey Island. It is very certain that the climate was soft and mild, and that the country was covered with trees and verdure, and it is equally certain that this terrible inundation of ice came and buried every vestige of it, as Herculanæum and Pompeii were buried beneath the ashes of Vesuvius.

But, instead of the two poor little villages, and perhaps a few square miles of the adjacent country, that Vesuvius covered with its fine ashes as with a soft warm blanket, here is a continent larger than the whole of Europe, buried beneath a massive sea of ice. It is as though the waters of the flood had suddenly frozen to the very bottom, and had never thawed.

What terrible convulsion of the earth's crust, what mighty effort of the forces within her bosom, has wrought such stupenduous changes in this great continent ?

The scientific men peering continually into the depths of ages, would fain believe they have discovered the secret, that they have torn aside the dark curtain of the past, and dragged the mystery forth to the light. In order to explain the theory as set forth by Professor Geike in his GREAT ICE AGE, it will be necessary to begin by saying that the " glacial period," of which we continually hear, in discussions about geology, was a period when Britain and the whole of Europe and Siberia were in exactly the same condition in which Greenland is now, but long before the time when this continent is supposed to have been enjoying a mild climate. These changes, it would appear, are in great part owing to the following cause :—

For the last seventy or eighty thousand years—the difference of a few thousand more or less does not matter—the inclination of the axis of the earth to the ecliptic has been slowly increasing. In other words, the North Pole is gradually leaning outward from the sun, so that if it should keep on long enough, say a few billion years, the earth would take a position in which the axis, if prolonged far enough, would pass through the sun. The consequences of such a change in the climate and seasons would be incalculable. The poles and Equator would, to a certain extent, change places. The Equator would, twice during the year, have an Arctic day, when the sun would go around the whole horizon without setting, but it would never have an Arctic night. The poles would each have successively six months day and six months night, as at present; but the day would be the day of the tropics, with a burning, fiery sun directly overhead; the night would be the night of the Arctic, with results upon the climatic conditions of the globe that are beyond computation. It is unnecessary, however, to consider these results further, as they could only have an actual interest for our descendants, of some millions of years hence.

Besides, it would appear that the change in the

inclination of the earth's axis will never be so great as I have supposed. This inclination goes on increasing for about a hundred thousand years; then it commences to decrease, and the axis begins to resume its former position, approaching the upright. In other words, the North Pole, as the earth goes spinning around the sun, sways back and forth, like the stem of a top that is gaining or losing its perpendicular. It is a kind of gigantic pendulum, whose oscillations each mark a hundred thousand years. Slight as these oscillations are—they are only a few seconds—their effects, nevertheless, upon the earth, owing to the fact that different regions are brought successively under the more direct influence of the sun, are enough to appal the imagination. We have not yet reached the extreme limit of our present swing; and already one immense continent, larger than the whole of Europe, has been engulfed.

England and Europe must inevitably follow and become as Greenland now is, and, indeed, as they once were, if Agassiz is right. All our great cities, our churches, our temples, our monuments that we raise with so much care, London, Paris, St. Paul's, Notre Dame, will be ground to sand beneath this mighty, moving mass of ice. Even the Pyramids would be swept away, and the huge blocks of which they are built ground down to the size of marbles by this terrible mill-stone. The millions of people, our

boasted civilization so hardly acquired, our progress, gained at the expense of so many thousand
years of painful effort and suffering, our art, our
science, our literature, all the efforts of mind,
even Homer and Shakspeare, will disappear, and
leave not a wrack behind.

Then, after the destruction has been accomplished, when the ruin is complete, the pendulum
will swing back again, the ice will melt, vegetation
will again spring up, and there will be room for
another race of men, who will know as little of us
as we know of our predecessors. In the course
of fifty thousand years perhaps, at a cost of five
hundred centuries of suffering and toil, a fifty
thousand years' combat, during which untold
millions must suffer and die, they will perhaps have
reached our present proud position ; to be in their
turn wiped out, like the sum on a schoolboy's slate,
as the pendulum swings back again!

How pleasant are the ways of science, and how
cheerful and encouraging the prospects she opens
up to our anxious vision !

Here and there the coast-line of Greenland is
broken by deep narrow fjords, extending from five
or six to sixty or seventy miles inland, so that
they may easily be mistaken for rivers. They
often take rise in the glacier itself, and they
teem with the most delicious salmon and sea-trout
in the world. Their banks and the adjacent
mountains and valleys, are full of partridges, ptar-

migan, reindeer, that are scarcely ever disturbed by the presence of man, and they offer the most delightful hunting-grounds it is possible to imagine. But unfortunately, we had lost so much time with those exasperating head winds, that we dared not stop even for a day. And so we glided past the silent, dreamy coast which lay asleep in the purple sunshine, content to feast our eyes alone on its wild and glorious beauty.

But we got a taste of the delicious sea-trout, nevertheless. One evening, towards sunset, when fully fifteen miles from shore, we were greatly surprised to see three kyaks approaching us. The kyak is the lightest of light canoes. It is made of a light framework of wood, over which is stretched a covering of seal-skin. It is about eighteen feet long, fifteen to eighteen inches wide, eight deep, is beautifully proportioned, and all covered in, so as to be water-tight, except where there is a round hole, just large enough to receive one man. In such frail crafts had three Esquimaux advanced fifteen miles out to sea, with a few trout, which they wished to barter for biscuit, coffee, and tobacco.

Imagine a man getting into a canoe and paddling across the English Channel, from Dover to Boulogne or Calais, in order to sell half-a-dozen trout! They came skimming along over the surface of the water like sea-gulls, and in a few minutes after we first perceived them, shot alongside. We hoisted

them on board, one after another, kyaks and all.
Before we had seen them, we had stood out
farther to sea with a change of wind, but they,
nothing daunted, paddled after us, although we
were under steam and sail at the time. As soon as
we had caught sight of them, we of course tacked,
and ran in to meet them.

They were thoroughly drenched with the water
dashing over them, but they had got very little in
the kyaks, so closely
does the jacket they
wear fit the round
hole in the top of the
kyak. They were un-
der the medium size,
and had great shock
heads of black, coarse,
uncombed hair, with
very black eyes, and
such big, round, good-
natured, half-foolish faces, that we were instantly
prepossessed in their favour.

We brought them below, gave them a glass of
rum round, which they took " straight," and
without winking, as though it were the most
natural thing to do in the world.

The services of Joe were brought into requisition
as interpreter, and we proceeded to trade with
them. They had fifteen beautiful trout, that
weighed about three pounds apiece, which they

had just caught, and half-a-dozen fine smoked salmon. They seemed to have no idea of driving a bargain, but accepted thankfully whatever we gave them, without asking more. We got altogether fifty-five pounds of delicious fish, in exchange for about two dozen small sea biscuit and half a pound of tobacco, and they seemed delighted with their bargain.

It was about nine o'clock when we put them down over the side, after having given them another glass of grog, and they started off on their return voyage of fifteen miles as merrily as if it were the merest trifle in the world. It would take them about two hours and a half steady paddling to reach the land, and as it does not get entirely dark here at this season of the year, they would have no difficulty in finding their way.

We continued our course along the coast, keeping much nearer in shore than the ordinary track of vessels. About noon on the 4th of August, when just outside of the Arctic circle, we were all brought to our feet by a sudden thump, which made the dishes on the table dance and jingle. Had there been any ice near, this would not have been alarming, but as there was none in sight it could only have been a rock. The sensation of striking on a rock at sea is a very unpleasant one, and we all rushed on deck to see what was the matter. We saw on the starboard beam a long line of reefs, over which the breakers were dashing in white wreaths of foam and spray. We had given these reefs a wide berth, but they were continued a long way under water, and it was on a sunken rock the PANDORA had struck. Fortunately she had, owing to her solid construction, suffered not the slightest damage. In this she was more lucky than the VALOROUS which, just outside of Holsteinburg, struck a rock and knocked a hole in her bottom, obliging her to put into that place to repair the damage. These reefs were in latitude 66° 12′, and were not laid down on any chart. They were the first of our Arctic discoveries, and we named them the " Pandora Reefs."

On the morning of the 5th of August, we crossed the Arctic circle with a fair wind, which, however, only lasted a few hours—a bright day, and a sea as smooth as glass. It is a peculiarity of navigation in these seas, that the water is always smooth. There is never any swell nor waves, and the ship is as steady as if she were on some little inland river; a fact which makes sailing extremely pleasant. This smoothness of the water is caused by the great quantities of ice, which seemed to prevent even the slightest swell. On the morning of the 7th of August—just forty days after leaving Portsmouth, we dropped anchor in the little bay of Godhavn, in the island of Disko.

CHAPTER V.

DISKO.

A LITTLE land-locked bay large enough for two or three ships to swing in, shut in on one side by towering red cliffs, between whose tops may be seen the edge of a glacier; on the other by a rocky slope surmounted by a flag-staff without a flag. Lying in the bay are two small schooners, and a vessel with a long, low, dark hull, and slender masts stepped back, that give her a rakish, jaunty air, as she lies reflected with the tall cliffs in the clear smooth water of the little bay. Scattered over the rocky slope are ten or fifteen half-wooden, half-earthen houses, standing about in a loose, free, and easy manner, quite independent of each other, as though despising the restraint of streets, to which they do not make the slightest pretension.

The rakish-looking vessel is the PANDORA; the little bay is that of Godhavn, and the collection of houses scattered up the slope is the town of

Lievely, in North Greenland, usually known by the name of Disko.

The Danes, by the way, seem to be ruinously extravagant in the matter of nomenclature. One would almost think they had resolved that this country, so poor in inhabitants, should at least be rich in names. Thus, the island on which the above-mentioned town is situated is called Disko, the name of the little harbour is Godhavn, while the collection of fifteen or twenty houses, which makes up the village itself, is called Lievely. They are evidently determined that no error shall be committed in regard to it, and that there shall be no danger of the town being mistaken for the harbour.

A sunny pleasant little spot it is just now during its few short weeks of summer, when the grass is peeping out timidly between the rocks, and the great round smooth boulders exchange their winter dress of snow for one of moss, deep, green and soft; when the melted snow comes tumbling down the ravines in white fleecy torrents, and the tall, rugged cliffs in the glow of the summer sun turn a warm reddish purple, like a great red curtain drawn across to shelter the little bay from the biting northern blasts. Altogether the little place has a warm and comfortable look, very agreeable after the chilly winds and icy air of these northern seas.

But there are no trees; and of vegetation,

properly speaking, there is none; only a little grass and moss and a little yellow flower that shoots up almost as soon as the snow disappears, and smiles, and waves its tiny head in the afternoon sun, as gaily as do any of its sisters in the tropical air of the south.

The world has probably a very exaggerated notion of the size and importance of Disko or Lievely. One continually reads of it in Arctic books of travels. Arctic ships are always putting into it, or going out of it, or touching at it, or getting a fresh start from it, or having some other relation with it; and, in short, Disko plays so important a roll in Arctic discovery that one very unreasonably, perhaps, gets an idea that it is a rich and thriving metropolis with thronged streets and busy marts, where all the luxuries of the Arctic world, all the commodities of the Polar regions are to be found in unlimited quantity. But it is in truth just the kind of place I have described; so small, so primitive, bearing so little resemblance to anything approaching civilization, that it is difficult to bring one's self to believe it is the Disko of which we have heard so much.

The Danish Governor of the place, Mr. Elberg, called on us soon after we dropped anchor, and from him we learned that the ALERT and DISCOVERY had proceeded on their voyage north, ten days previously, and that the VALOROUS had sailed for England about the same time. It was with the

VALOROUS we had expected to send home our first letters, and we were considerably disappointed to hear of her departure, as our letters would now have to go to Denmark by some Danish merchant ship, to be mailed at Copenhagen.

We all went ashore in the course of the fore-noon, and returned the Governor's call. He was living in a neat little wooden house, which was pleasantly situated overlooking the bay. He offered us wine and cigars, and introduced us to his wife, who is an Eskimo lady,—in the days of her maidenhood one of the belles of Disko.

The men who come out here from Denmark to take charge of these trading colonies, seem to resign themselves to passing their lives here. They leave the world behind, and completely identify themselves with the interests of the little colony around them. Some of them have been in Greenland for twenty years, having only returned to Denmark once or twice during that time. When a man has passed so much of his life here, he would probably find that even if he should go back to the world, he would only be a stranger in a strange land. Some of them marry Eskimo wives, others go back to Denmark and induce a Danish girl to share their lonely home, and some-times a girl comes out alone to her betrothed, and gets married here.

We took a walk about the village. The people, young and old, men, women, and children, turned out to see us, and greeted us with pleasant smiles; many of them giving us a "Good Morning," in English, which they pronounced very well.

The girls were all dressed in their best finery, and some of them, especially those who had Danish blood, were very pretty; only it was rather difficult at first to bring oneself to believe they were girls at all.

This is the country for Mrs. Bloomer; the women all wear trowsers, and would scout the idea of anything else as absurd and probably indecent. I should pity the girl who tried to introduce the fashion of petticoats in Greenland. A fashionable West End beauty who should walk down Regent Street in knee-breeches, top-boots, and a gentleman's shooting-jacket, with a cigar in her mouth, would not be more utterly lost in the eyes of Society, than a Disko young lady who ventured to walk about over the rocky slope, in a fashionable hat, ribbons, long skirts, and a crinoline. "Oh, the shameless huzzy!" "the brazen-faced thing!" would be the verdict of every Disko woman; and Disko Society would know her no more.

The Disko costume appears very funny until you get accustomed to it, but rather pretty, nevertheless. The hair is done up in a kind of top-knot on the crown of the head, a loose-fitting jacket, made of any kind of light thin stuff and of any colour, trimmed with a fur collar, reaches to the waist; a pair of sealskin trowsers with the hairy side out descend nearly to the knee, where they are confined with a garter; a pair of top-boots meet the trowsers at the knee, the feet and ankles being of red leather, the upper portion of white linen, trimmed with fur around the tops. Imagine a pretty girl clothed in this costume; with the darkest, demurest eyes, and the sunniest brown complexion ever painted by sunshine and sea breezes and ocean spray, and you have a faint idea of a Disko girl. You should see them tripping about in their little red boots, that scarcely seem to touch the ground, so soft is their tread, or springing over the rocks like young antelopes, to know how charming a girl may be in boots and breeches. And they have the daintiest little feet and hands too; feet and hands that would make the prettiest English or American girl burst with envy, so finely shaped, so small, so delicate, and yet so strong.

. These girls dance like sylphs, a fact which we soon discovered. It is the custom in Disko to give a ball to every ship that comes there, and the PANDORA, of course, could not form an exception to the rule. The entertainment proved to be a very great success.

The ball-room, it is true, was rather small for forty or fifty people to dance in, being only twelve feet by fifteen. It was also perhaps a little dark, being lighted by only one small window, for, as it was broad daylight at ten o'clock in the evening, it was not thought worth while to bring in candles. In fact, there was no place to put candles, even had they been necessary; the ceiling was barely six feet high, so that most of us had to be very careful not to bump our heads, and the room, besides, was crammed full of people, excepting a little space in the middle four or five feet square, where the dancing was done.

The festive hall was no other, in short, than the workshop of Disko's lonely carpenter, which had been cleaned out and transformed for the occasion; although the following legend, inscribed over the door in chalk, would seem to indicate that its natural and normal state was something far removed from the stern realities of carpenter life.

"MUSI CHAL DOR E OPE NAT 8 CLOCK."

This inscription naturally excited the curiosity of our learned and erudite Doctor, who having in the beginning pronounced it to be a first rude attempt of the Eskimos at a written literature, finally deciphered it to mean "Music Hall Door open at 8 o'clock." Further investigation proved that this was the only record the ALERT and DISCOVERY had left of their visit here.

I will not deny that this hall was perhaps a little warm and close when twenty of our blue-jackets and the whole population of the village had crowded into it, and that a little more room might have been desirable. But then there were no petticoats, no crinoline, no long trains to be trampled upon; a woman took up no more space than a man, and that made a vast deal of difference. You have no conception of the small space you can dance in when you have no petticoats to deal with. I found that three feet square was oceans of room to waltz in, while for a polka I was quite lost in so much superfluous space. After a while, however, we found the place so oppressively hot that we decided to adjourn to the open air.

It was now eleven o'clock. The sun had just set, but there was a pleasant twilight, which would last all night. As we went forth we gave a glance at the PANDORA, that lay asleep in the little bay, looking like a mere toy-ship beneath the towering cliffs that rose above, threatening to fall and crush her like an egg-shell, beneath their tremendous masses.

The dancing was continued outside with renewed enthusiasm, and I am ready to aver that I never enjoyed a dance more in my life. Officers and blue-jackets all mixed together on equal terms, and went through waltzes, polkas, and cotillions, with a vigour and good will only to be acquired by forty days at sea. The girls were not acquainted with all the forms of cotillion, which we, in the exuberance of our imagination, adopted for the occasion; but they were quick to learn, and got through the most complicated figures very readily.

My partner was a demure little beauty, with
dark, slightly almond-shaped eyes, a skin as

brown as that of
the nut - brown
maid herself, the
reddest, ripest
lips, and the dain-
tiest little feet
that ever were
seen. A greater
pleasure even than
to encircle her
slender waist or
to gaze into her dark eyes, was to watch her
little red-booted feet as they skimmed over
the ground like the wings of a sea-bird over the
waves—a pleasure quite lost when you dance
with a girl who wears petticoats. And then what
a hand she had ! So small, so delicate, so soft
and brown, it dropped in mine as lightly as the
falling of an autumn leaf. The motion of
dancing had caused her boots to settle down,
leaving just above the knee a bit of the leg exposed, which, contrasting with the white starched
linen tops of the boots, appeared as brown as a
walnut.

This peculiarity of the costume is a bit of coquetry
with the Disko girls, by which they probably in-
demnify themselves for not wearing low-necked
dresses. But a girl who should expose her bust

as a European lady does at a ball or theatre would
be hooted out of the village.

My partner's queer little top-knot, planted
perpendicularly on the top of her head, and
tied up with a red ribbon, just reached to my
mouth, so that I must have looked as though I
had an enormous imperial, with a girl suspended
to it by a red ribbon.

Young girls, by the way, tie this top-knot up with
a red ribbon; married women, with a blue; widows,

REFRESHMENTS.

with black; while those who are neither maid,
wife, nor widow, are restricted to green, or to a
simple handkerchief, tied around the head.

I could not talk much with her, but I had been studying Eskimo with Joe, and could say a good many things, though, as is always the case, not the things I most wanted to say. I opened the conversation during one of the pauses in the dance, by uttering the following easy little word, which I had learned from Joe, for the occasion,—

"Audlarhatiguemangilyarmaamerica?" I asked, in as carelessly natural a voice as I could assume.

She looked at me in doubt.

" Nuliaginga ? " I continued gravely.

She evidently regarded it as a somewhat abrupt way of opening the conversation ; but she grasped the situation instantly, smilingly kissed her hand to me, and with a merry little laugh, replied, " Ukharluguangutil," which would be equivalent in English to " You must ask Pa, please."

But her Pa was away on a fishing expedition, a distance of three or four days' march, and as the PANDORA steamed out of the little bay an hour after our dance was over, that match was untimely broken off.

While the younger and prettier portion of the female community were thus " chasing the glowing hours with flying feet," their elders were doing a thriving business with those of the sailors, who were not for the moment dancing. The old women came loaded down with sealskin slippers, sealskin needle-cases, sealskin pin-cushions, sealskin tobacco-pouches, sealskin boots, breeches, jackets, and a hundred other things made from the skin of this useful animal, which they exchanged for old coats, trowsers, hats socks, handkerchiefs, pocket-knives, beads, needles, brass, jewellery, and sometimes a little money. This ball was therefore a combination of business and pleasure in the strictest sense, and was equally successful, whether considered as a ball or as a mart. The language in which business was transacted was, it is true, of a somewhat laconic and restricted kind, and

the commercial terms were of the fewest, consisting chiefly of "You truckum?" "No!" "Yes!" "How much you wantum?" "How much you givum." But these, with the use of the fingers for counting, and an astonishing variety of signs and gesticulations, very remarkable for their expressiveness, made the transaction of business a pleasant and easy matter.

As these people cannot cultivate cotton, nor flax, and can raise neither sheep nor silkworms, all kinds of woollen, cotton, and silk clothing are more highly prized by them than the finest furs are by us. Our men drove some very profitable bargains by exchanging their old clothing for furs and skins. No more valuable present can be made, for instance, to a Disko lady than an old coat or a pair of trowsers. Old clothes were found to be so very acceptable to the fair ones, that if the PANDORA had lingered a few days longer at Disko I am afraid several of our officers, including "Tromp" and myself, would not have had a whole suit of clothes left.

The poet has sung that it is the nature of man to drink. I think it is the nature of a Dutchman to waltz.

"Tromp" seemed to throw his whole soul into the dance, and went flying over the ground with a grace and smoothness which are only acquired by people of his nation. He told me afterwards, that never, even with the most beautiful and refined European lady, had he enjoyed a dance so much, and that he had never seen a waltzer that even approached this Disko girl. "Why, she does dance so lightly as a feather," he said. "You feel as though she would escape you from your fingers and fly away very quick. It is like waltzing with a butterfly."

The truth is that "Tromp" had fallen desperately in love with his partner. From the moment he discovered her, he refused to dance with any other girl, and so monopolized her that nobody else had the ghost of a chance. She was, in fact, the acknowledged belle of Disko, the prettiest girl in the place, and well the little coquette knew it.

Her tiny red boots showed some very pretty needle-work done in different coloured thread by her own dainty fingers; the white starched and ironed linen of her boot-tops was embroidered with some kind of open work, resembling that sort of thing you continually see civilized ladies working upon, but which always mysteriously disappears just when it is ready to be worn, and is henceforth lost to the vision of man.   Above this was a band of white fur, a circlet of brown flesh and blood, a red garter fastened with a buckle, then a pair of sealskin trowsers of a soft, mouse colour, above which, puffed out around the waist, was a red che-

mise covered by a sort of jacket, fitting close around the throat and loosely over the bust. This jacket was trim-med around the neck with a white fur collar, and out of it arose a soft, rounded throat and chin, a pair of pouting lips, a little, slightly turned - up, saucy nose, and such

eyes ! It was no wonder the susceptible " Tromp " fell in love at first sight. So large and brown and soft, and they cast upon him now and then such a timid, half-tender, half-saucy glance that it was enough to drive a hardened old bachelor mad, let alone a young and enthusiastic adorer of the sex like " Tromp."

And how divinely she danced! It was a pure delight to watch her little feet flitting over the ground like butterflies, or humming-birds, or rose-buds, or anything else that is delicate and sweet and delightful. It was not dancing at all, it was flying, it was floating through the air on a wave of rhythm without ever so much as touching the ground.

Her name was Darwa, and she appeared to be about half Eskimo, half Danish. Her father, the pilot of the little harbour, was by far the richest and most influential man of all the Eskimos of Disko, and we had an opportunity of seeing the young lady in her own home, which was a fine large residence, built partly of wood, partly of earth.

There were two rooms in this house, one of which was fully fifteen feet square, and lighted by a large glass window, that filled up nearly one whole side; the other, smaller and less pre-tentious. The house was warmed by a stove, and on the side opposite the window was a kind of wooden stage or platform, raised two feet above the ground, and running across the room. On this were arranged coverlets, blankets, and furs, and here it was the young lady slept, with brothers and sisters, all together, higgledy-piggledy, like a nest of young squirrels. There were four or five guns hung on racks on the ceiling, a few religious prints around the walls, together with cooking utensils, and all the fine clothes of the family.

We had ample opportunity to examine the whole of the young lady's wardrobe, which we could easily distinguish by its superior fineness from that of her younger brothers and sisters. We learned that her father had dogs and *kyaks* and an *umiak*, or large boat, besides men employed in hunting and fishing for him. He also had some gold pieces stowed away in a bag, among which I saw some American half eagles. Miss Darwa was therefore a very great heiress. This, together with her beauty, of which she was as well aware as any other pretty girl would be, made her somewhat proud, disdainful, and disposed to queen it over the rest of the girls.

But "Tromp" was so desperately in love that he found even this grave defect of character charming, and defended her hotly. In spite of the fact that we were all, officers and men, dressed very much alike, she early detected the difference and refused to dance with anybody but officers. "Tromp" encouraged her in this odious distinction, and at last, with a subtle and malicious cunning which I cannot too strongly reprehend, persuaded her to push her exclusiveness to the extent of dancing with nobody but himself. Fortunately for the peace of the PANDORA's wardroom, Miss Darwa had three or four dangerous rivals, who, if less wealthy, were far less proud and haughty; and if less beautiful, far sweeter and more charming.

For my own part, I early concluded that I preferred the sweet and gentle style of beauty, to the proud and scornful, and inwardly decided that Miss Darwa was a spoiled, ill-natured, disagreeable young lady, and wished "Tromp" joy of her with all my heart.

Her pride and arrogance may have been augmented by the circumstance that her uncle played the violin, and was the musician of the ball. It was he that directed the festivals; and in truth he did it very well. He gave us a waltz, or a polka, or a reel as we in turn demanded them, although he spoke only a word or two of English, which  he had picked up from an occasional English whaler, or a still rarer Arctic exploring ship.

It must not be supposed, however, that "Tromp" was the only one who was susceptible to the charms of those fair ones. Our navigating officer appeared to be just as badly smitten, and devoted himself to a young lady who wore a very high top-knot, with an assiduity which, I am afraid, would have rendered some fair English lady highly indignant could she but have seen him.

When the dance was over he went walking about the village with her on his arm, smiling down upon her, in a way which must have stirred her little heart to its very depths ; carrying on a conversation by means of signs, nods, and winks, and from time to time making what to a perfectly unprejudiced spectator, seemed to be idiotic gesticulations, but which were intended probably as passing remarks about the weather.

It should not be forgotten with regard to these girls, that they were all very well behaved. They allowed the men not even a kiss nor a squeeze of the hand, and knew as well how to maintain their dignity and keep people at a proper distance, as any other young ladies. They are all good Christians and church-going people, belonging, as do all the Eskimos of Greenland, to some form of the Lutheran faith, to which they have been converted by the mild and beneficent influence of the kindly Danes. They have a neat little wooden church, where they have religious service every Sunday, and a pastor, who goes the rounds of a district and appears among them three or four times a year, and they lead a quiet, innocent, virtuous, and to all appearances a happy life in their little ice-bound world. The summer is probably the most lonesome time for them, as nearly all the men are away then on the hunting and fishing grounds.

We only saw five or six about the village, but they took no part in the festivities, and the girls look for ships touching here—a very rare occurrence—as the great event of the summer.

At length, about 12 o'clock, we saw the signal to come off flying from the PANDORA'S masthead, and after one more waltz we took an affectionate leave of our fair friends, thanking them as well as we could for the pleasant evening they had given us. They accompanied us down to the water-side, and we then scrambled into the jolly boat, while they stood on the shore in a group, watching us with smiling though saddened faces.

As we pushed off they set up a kind of half-laughing, half-tearful cry which followed us far out into the bay, and came to us over the widening water, softened into a strain as sweet and musical as the sighing of an Æolian harp. It was so sad withal, that the dogs of the village, that had likewise followed us down to the water's edge, joined in with a mournful howl, and made up a sorrowful chant that sounded strangely wild and weird in the dim twilight of the Arctic summer night. It was a pretty and graceful farewell, and added one more kindly souvenir to our memories of Disko.

The dear girls! we shall never see them again, but we shall not soon forget their happy mirth and smiling faces that made the dreary desolation around them blossom as with roses.

CHAPTER VI.

A BALL ON BOARD SHIP.

WE had not lost much time in Disco. Eighteen
hours after we dropped anchor in the little bay, the
PANDORA suddenly awakened, as if from a nap in
which she had overslept herself, slowly turned

around, looking all about the harbour, trying to
find out where she was; and then, having apparently discovered the right way, spread her wings
and darted out to sea.

But, instead of directing her course out into
Baffin's Bay, she turned up the Waigat Strait,

which separates the island of Disko from the mainland. For the PANDORA was hungry again. In spite of her delicate lines and light, jaunty appearance, she had an insatiable maw, and having already consumed nearly all the coal we supplied her with at Ivigtut, was greedily demanding more. We did not choose to let her encroach upon our winter supply just yet, and so we steered up Waigat Strait, on whose shores coal could be obtained for the trouble of putting it aboard ship.

We were no sooner fairly out of the little harbour than our old friends, the head winds, greeted us and intimated that we might count upon them all the way up the strait. So we had to commence our old business of beating again, which at last began to appear to us the natural and normal way of sailing, so long had we been at it.

We kept the screw going at " easy," as we had now but little time before us and could not depend upon the persistently obstinate winds for getting forward. All that day and the next, until noon, we worked up the strait, either shore of which was visible nearly all the time. We met a good deal of floating ice, but not enough to interfere with our progress, except when we ran into great, thick, heavy curtains of fog, which at times prevented our seeing more than a few yards ahead of the vessel.

Navigation under such circumstances is exceedingly dangerous, as it is almost impossible to see the heavy pieces of ice in time to avoid them, and it becomes necessary to proceed very slowly in order to prevent a dangerous collision. During the whole forenoon of August 9, we were most of the time in one of these fogs, which effectually hid the western shore from view. This was very annoying, as we were on the look out for an Eskimo village where we were to get a number of the natives to show us the coal and help us to put it on board.

We felt our way along the shore, blindfold as it were, until one o'clock, when Captain Young decided that we must have passed the place, and he therefore put the ship about. He had scarcely done so when the fog lifted and we beheld the coast but a few cables' length distant, and we were not long in making out the village, which we had already passed two or three miles back.

We were soon opposite; the ship was hove to, and the Captain went ashore with a letter to the Danish Governor which had been given him by Governor Elberg at Lievely. By this time the fog had quite cleared away and we saw the eastern shore about ten miles distant, which rose in a steep, rugged wall that appeared to be scarcely broken by a single crevasse, and curving around to the north and south seemed to meet our shore and form a large and beautiful inland sea. It was full of floating ice; not in sufficient quantities, however, to impede the progress of a ship, and there were many icebergs which rose in huge masses here and there, displaying beautiful tints of blue, green, and white that became so brilliant as to dazzle the eyes in the warm bright light of an after-noon sun. The wind, now that we were no longer moving, had quite died out, and the water, undis-turbed by a single ripple, was as smooth as glass; while from time to time there was a deep, dull report like the distant booming of a heavy gun, fol-lowed, perhaps, a long time afterward, by a gentle swell, telling where an ice-berg had split asunder and turned over. These reports are heard con-tinually among icebergs, and so resemble a distant cannonade that Dr. Kane named them very aptly ice artillery.

The place off which we had stopped is called Yu-yarsusuk, and consists of four or five houses jumbled together and inhabited by perhaps thirty or forty people, young and old. The Captain soon came off with the Governor, who spoke a little German, by means of which language we communicated with him. To our great satisfaction we learned that the coal was dug out for us and all ready to be put on board. For this we had to thank Captain Nares, who had promised Captain Young to have the coal got out, and had faithfully kept his promise in all the hurry and trouble of making the final preparations for his own departure.

Closely following the Governor came an *umiak*, or " woman's boat," loaded full of women and

children.   They had come partly out of curiosity
to see the ships, partly to bring off four fine dogs
that Captain Young had bought.   Dogs, women,
and children were taken on board, and they all
seemed about equally frightened at everything
they saw.   The dogs were tied up, and the women
and children given something to eat, which very
soon put them at their ease.

The Eskimos have always shown so much kindness to shipwrecked whalers and distressed Arctic
explorers who have fallen into their power, that
Arctic navigators always make a point of treating
them kindly and giving them little presents, which
are highly prized.   The women were nearly all
old and ugly, and there were no pretty girls
among them, except two children with fair flaxen
hair and blue eyes, who looked very odd in their
little boots and trowsers.   They turned out to be
the children of the Governor, who was married to
an Eskimo woman, and he had, as we afterward
learned, several more.

He informed us that all the men and several of
the women of the village were up the strait, somewhere in the direction of the Kudliset, or Ritten-
bank, coal-mine, in a boat, and that if we went on
we should find them.   We accordingly turned the
ship's head again to the north, and proceeded up
the strait.

In an hour we perceived a little sloop coming
lazily down before the wind, the crew appa-

rently, all except the man at the helm, asleep in the warm sunshine, as indolently as if they were drifting on some sunny Southern sea, instead of among the ice mountains of the Arctic. In a few minutes they were within hailing distance. The Governor spoke to them, and about twenty of them tumbled into a boat that was towing astern, and came off to us. He gave them their instructions, which were to go with us, help us coal, and bring back any letters we might want to send to Europe, and then went aboard the little sloop, after wishing us a hearty God speed on our voyage.

Arctic navigators owe a great deal to the kindness of these simple, honest Greenland Danes, and the courtesy of the Danish Government. Year after year Arctic explorers and whalers are indebted to them for assistance in a number of ways, which they always offer with the most hearty and friendly cordiality; and seamen of nearly every nation have to thank them for many acts of kindness. They rendered us every assistance in coaling, and we had to rely upon them to send our letters to Denmark, where they are always carefully mailed by the courtesy of the Danish authorities.

With the addition of sixteen Eskimo men and six women to our crew, we continued our course up the coast toward the Kudliset coal banks. We were not very long in learning

that five of the six women were girls, two of
them pure Eskimo, three half Danish, and very
pretty ; while the
other was a vigorous
and muscular old
woman, sent along
with them, as is al-
ways the custom, to
look after their mo-
rals — a precaution
which, I would has-
ten to observe, was
altogether superfluous
on board the PANDORA.
As soon as it was dis-
covered that the girls

were pretty, a place was cleared away on the
deck, and a dance organized upon the instant to
the music of a plaintive accordion, played by
one of the blue jackets, while the ship steamed
slowly forward.

The deck of the PANDORA now presented one of
those strange, pretty scenes often represented
upon the stage, but which one rarely looks for in
real life, least of all upon an Arctic ship. She
was still encumbered with the great heaps of
sacks, full of coal, we had brought from England,
in addition to which there was heaped up in bulk
on either side of the funnel a part of that we had
taken in at Ivigtut, and which, continually trampled

over by everybody running back and forth, had blackened the rest of the ship, until she looked like a collier.

It was useless to try to keep her neat and clean under such circumstances, and the result was that she had been allowed to go to the dogs in her own way, and now presented a disreputable, disorderly, vagabond appearance, reminding one of a stray dog without an owner. In fact, the PANDORA, instead of the trim, neat, jaunty, well-dressed thing she used to be, began to have a very dirty, slip-shod, draggle-tail look. But she had gained so much freedom in exchange for her lost respectability, and had such a jolly, reckless, happy air, that you could not find it in your heart to blame her.

On what proper, well-behaved ship, for instance, could you have witnessed such a scene of mirth and fun as her decks presented this evening? Dogs, a pig, and cats we had obtained in Ivigtut, by way of insuring fair winds, were running loose about the decks. Music and dancing; the men gathered around the dancers, some up on the heaps of coal around the funnel, some up on the shrouds, one man standing on the nettings playing the accordion, while six or eight dancers kept up a patter on the deck like the rattle of a drum, amid shouts of laughter and a cross fire of cheers and exclamations. The great, strong, iron heart of the PANDORA, deep down below, seemed to throb and pulse with a new delight as she swept along through the masses of floating ice, breaking through their cold embraces as they closed around her, and rejoicing in her freedom and wild dissipation.

From time to time she glided past some towering iceberg, in which you could see a kind of indistinct resemblance to a gigantic human face, as though some mighty old giant shut up in there were glowering down upon us through his ice window. Sometimes one of these icebergs would suddenly commence to crumble and break when we glided past, as though the PANDORA's wild behaviour were too much for the old fellow inside, and as if, taken with a sudden fit of rage, he were struggling and writhing through the walls of ice to get at her. Then there would be a report like a clap of thunder and a terrible splash, as a great mass would drop off, and, having lost his balance, the old giant inside would pitch over, head foremost, and disappear in the cold green water with a roar.

How big and round and red the sun looked as he rolled along the tops of the purple mountains and cast a crimson glow over the pure blue, green, and white of the towering icebergs ! How weird and sad and lonely looked the silent, desolate coast ! How the water shimmered and glistened in the white, icy glare of the evening, and how warm and merry and cozy looked our little ship as she lightly

threaded her tortuous course among the icebergs! Who would have expected to behold
such a scene in the Arctic, of all other places
in the world?

CHAPTER VII.

A TEA-PARTY.

At length, about nine o'clock, we dropped anchor off a steep, high bluff, that came sheer down to the water's edge, behind which, at the distance of two or three miles, rose the sharp ragged summit of a mountain. Along the face of this bluff, which was 150 feet high, we could see two or three dark streaks, that Captain Young recognized as the coal seams. It was too late to begin coaling, but everything was got ready for an early start next morning, with the hope of getting in thirty or forty tons. In the meantime the dancing had ceased, and we had all gone below to take tea.

We had just sat down to the table when the girls came aft, and we invited them all down into the wardroom to take tea with us, an invitation which they accepted without the slightest hesitation. This we considered a touching proof of the confidence with which the polite and kind treatment of the officers had inspired them—a confidence which we endeavoured to persuade ourselves was not altogether disconnected with our prepossessing looks and superior accomplishments! We, therefore, made room for them at our little table and invited them to sit down; but, although they had come below fast enough when invited, once there, they stood timid and abashed, with downcast eyes before the splendour and magnificence that burst thus suddenly upon them. They had probably never seen but one or two such ships before, and certainly had never gone aboard one, and our little wardroom, ten feet square, possibly appeared to them as the very height of magnificence and splendour.

It was amusing to observe their timid, half-frightened looks as they watched us pour out their tea and heap up their plates with strange-looking viands, such as they had never seen before, and which, perhaps, even appeared to them very unsavoury. Indeed, their position must have been altogether very embarrassing.

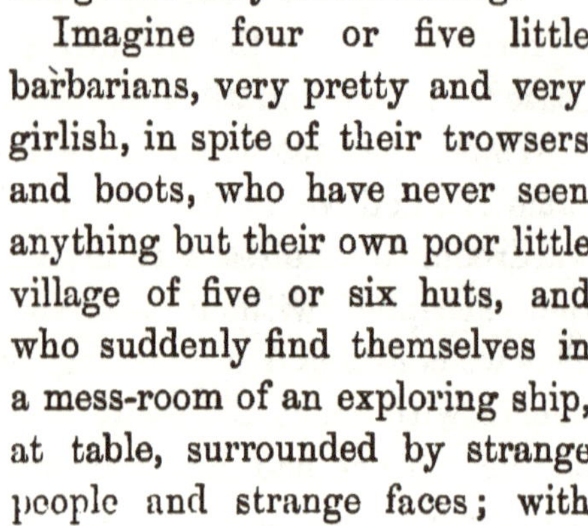

Imagine four or five little barbarians, very pretty and very girlish, in spite of their trowsers and boots, who have never seen anything but their own poor little village of five or six huts, and who suddenly find themselves in a mess-room of an exploring ship, at table, surrounded by strange people and strange faces; with five or, six polite, affable, and distinguished, but strange young gentlemen, who flatter themselves that their blandishments are not, as a rule, altogether thrown away upon the fair sex, and all heaping up their plates and doing the polite in the most approved style, and you can form some idea of the position of these poor little girls.

Nevertheless, I must say that they got on very well, considering the circumstances, and showed themselves remarkably quick to learn. They had never even used a knife and fork before, and declined to touch the ones we gave them until they saw how we managed these symbols of civilization. It was amusing to see the sly way they watched us out of the corners of their eyes; and when one of them, having apparently mastered the theory of the use of these implements, took up a fork and carried it to her mouth, the others looked at her with a droll, inquiring expression, as though asking her if it was a success. Apparently, the result of this eye telegraphing was satisfactory, as two or three more of them proceeded to imitate her in a very grave and demure way, and, to tell the truth, acquitted themselves very well indeed.

Please do not, reader, turn up your nose at these pretty little barbarians and imagine yourself vastly superior to them simply because you know how to eat with a knife and fork. Do you think Cleopatra used a knife and fork? or the cold, pale Octavia, the sister of Augustus? or the Queen of Sheba? or Rebecca? or Rachel? or Ruth? Just remember that there is a people who once were nearly masters of the world, distinguished alike for their refinement, music, poetry and architecture as well as their chivalry and feats of arms, and princes before whose splendour and riches the magnificence of modern western monarchs pale and grow dim, who never knew the use of these weapons. Do not, therefore, think you have any right to look down on our little friends simply because you know how to use instruments that by seven or eight hundred millions of the earth's inhabitants are considered ridiculous and absurd inventions.

To return to our friends, we found they were very fond of tea, sugar, biscuit, and pickles. Preserved meat they did not seem to relish much—a fact we did not find at all strange after having ourselves learned to like seal and bear. As soon as the one who sat beside me had somewhat recovered her presence of mind, I proceeded to open a conversation with her and she told me her name was " Akushta," which we soon discovered to be only the Danish for Augusta. The names of the others were Carolina Wilhelmina, Julietta, Marie, and so on, which rather disappointed us, as we would have preferred to hear unpronounceable Eskimo names.

Julietta was the prettiest of them, and, it may

have been quite accidental, but it struck me as singular that she should have taken a place at table beside "Tromp," and that Carolina Wilhelmina should have gone straight and sat down beside our navigating officer.

The truth is, I was considerably grieved and pained at the conduct of these young gentlemen, and must say that their levity and inconstancy were really shocking. No sooner had they discovered that the girls were pretty, than, forgetting all about Disko and the tender glances given and received there, and the gentle squeezing of hands, and mute but eloquent protesta-  tions of attachment, they commenced making the most violent love to these girls with a cynicism worthy of Don Juan himself. Before the evening was half over they had wormed themselves into the good graces of the old woman, by plying her with rum and tobacco, and she now sat there complacently smoking a pipe, with her legs crossed like a man, and a grim smile on her bull-dog face, while these two double-dyed Don Juans sat each beside a girl, with her hands clasped in his own.

It is true that some palliation may be found for

their conduct in the fact that the hands in question were very soft, small, and delicate, and they nestled in yours so gently and softly that it was almost impossible to resist their charm; and I would not have been, upon the whole, inclined to look with disfavour upon this behaviour, had it not been for the proceedings of those same young gentlemen at Disko only two days before.

We had some music during the course of the evening. The old wheezy accordion was brought aft and produced much satisfaction and delight. The girls even favoured us with some songs, very sweet and plaintive, to which the Doctor played a lamentable accompaniment.

It was now eleven o'clock and we went on deck. The sun was still shining brightly above the horizon, and it was broad daylight. The Moon had risen, but she was only the faintest shadow. She had faded away to the merest ghost of a moon, as though, seeing herself supplanted by the Sun and finding she was of no use, she had determined to pine away and die. It seemed to me that Tweedle Dee must have had this scene in his mind when he wrote his immortal poem of the " Walrus and the Carpenter," where he says,—

> " The sun was shining on the sea,
>   Shining with all his might.
> He did his very best to make
>   The billows smooth and white,
> And this was odd, because it was
>   The middle of the night.

> The moon was shining sulkily,
>   Because she thought the sun
> Had no business to be there
>   After the day was done.
> ' It's very rude of him,' she said,
>   ' To come and spoil the fun.' "

It was now bed-time. The women brought their blankets aft and spread them down on the floor of the chart-room. We improvised pillows for them out of cushions and overcoats, tucked them in amid much laughing and giggling on their part, and then retired to our own cabins in order to get a few hours' sleep before commencing to coal the ship.

CHAPTER VIII.

COALING.

At five o'clock next morning we were all called up to commence coaling, and after the unusual luxury of a cup of coffee, a number of us got into the boats and rowed off to the beach, 300 or 400 yards distant.   A bright, unclouded sun, and the soft, warm air, reminding one of the approach of spring in more southern latitudes, gave promise of a beautiful day; and as the boats touched we sprang ashore on the wild, strange coast, with a keen feeling of delight, only to be understood and appreciated by those who have been a long time on board ship.

We found a smooth, sandy beach, very favourable for the boats.   It was thirty or forty feet wide, and extended like a narrow shelf along the foot of the rugged, perpendicular cliff, which appeared to be 150 or 200 feet high.   At one place there was a break in this gigantic wall, where an avalanche had torn over it, carrying away a mass of loose stones and earth, and here a cascade of the purest, clearest water now came tumbling down, foaming and sparkling in the bright morning sunshine. Out on the still, shining water lay the ship, looking, among the white, glistening icebergs, like some dark, unnatural monster that had wandered out of its own world and lost its way here. It was a delight merely to live and breathe the soft, spring-like air, to run along the beach or scramble up the face of the steep, rugged cliff, and trace the opposite shore of Waigat Strait, that stood up dim, distant, and misty in the shifting vapours of the morning.

From the top of the bluff the ground, which appeared to be covered with a rich carpet of grass and flowers, rose in a gentle incline to the foot of some mountains about three miles distant. Behind these, again, a glacier could be seen; for the interior of the Island of Disko, like that of Greenland itself, appears to be, summer and winter, one solid mass of ice and snow.

The coal lay in three or four different seams, which could easily be seen at some distance out to sea. The first was nearly on a level with the water; it was about eighteen inches thick, very black and hard, and as it was immediately covered by a sandstone rock ten or fifteen feet thick, was difficult to get at, although the VALOROUS, which had been here only a few days before, had evidently been working it. The next seam cropped out of the face of the bluff sixty or seventy feet above the level of the water, and it was on this seam the Eskimos had been at work; while still above this could be seen two more black streaks that appeared likewise to be coal. The cliff seemed to be composed, as nearly as we could judge, of alternate strata of coal, sandstone rock, containing in many places iron, slate, soapstone, and irregular layers of loose earth and stones.

The Eskimos had simply uncovered the coal by cutting away the soapstone and loose earth that overlaid the second seam, leaving a bench or shelf from two to six feet wide, running along the face of the bluff a distance of a quarter of a mile or more. We had only to plunge a crowbar into the cracks and crevices, and pry it out in great blocks and lumps, and roll it down the face of the bluff to the water's edge.

Never was coal more easily got. The only difficulty was in climbing up to it in the first place; but after that was once accomplished, we ran up a couple of lines, which we fastened to crowbars driven into the ground, by which means we were enabled to scramble up without much difficulty. The getting down was easy enough. We had soon thrown down a great heap of loose earth and rubbish, which formed a moving inclined plane that slid down with each step so rapidly that only about two steps were required to reach the bottom. The fine coal was filled into large sacks on the ledge where it was got

COAL MINES OF KIDLISET.

[Page 81.

... and tumbled over the precipice, while the ... that came out were rolled down.

Coaling, such hard work under ordinary circumstances, here afforded the greatest sport. There would be a cry of " Heads!" as a mass of half a ... perhaps, was launched on its mad course, down ... in ... every- ... block ... ... it was ... ... to ... and more than one of them below received a piece of coal about the ... that made them call down ... on the heads of the guilty ...

As fast as the boats were loaded they were towed off to the ship by the steam launch. and the work progressed so rapidly that at noon, when we went to dinner, we had already got in twenty tons. It was not, however, very good coal, and although it burned very readily and made little smoke. it produced scarcely more than half ... produced by an equal quantity of ... ... it had every appearance of ... ... worked deeper into the ...

COAL MINES OF BELIZE

out, and tumbled over the precipice, while the blocks that came out were rolled down.

Coaling, such hard work under ordinary circumstances, here afforded the greatest sport. There would be a cry of "Heads!" as a mass of half a ton, perhaps, was launched on its mad course, down the steep, while the crowd below, engaged in getting the sacks into the boats, would drop everything and scatter in all directions, and the block rushing down the steep bank, gathering new force at every instant, would suddenly strike the bottom, break to pieces and fly in all directions like an exploding shell. It was not altogether unattended with danger either, for sometimes those above maliciously delayed singing out, "Heads!" until it was almost too late to escape, and more than one of those below received a piece of coal about the legs or shins that made them call down loud maledictions on the heads of the guilty ones.

As fast as the boats were loaded they were towed off to the ship by the steam launch, and the work progressed so rapidly that at noon, when we went to dinner, we had already got in twenty tons. It was not, however, very good coal, for although it burned very readily and made little smoke, it produced scarcely more than half the steam produced by an equal quantity of Welsh coal. But it had every appearance of growing better as it was worked deeper into the hill. And as we really could only get that which, cropping out of the steep face of the bluff, had been exposed to the action of the frost for centuries, and had, of course, been more or less decomposed, we had no means of seeing what it was really like. But I believe that if worked in from the face of the cliff, say ten feet, coal would be found of excellent quality.

The girls employed themselves in picking up the pieces and filling them into the sacks, and they appeared to enjoy the sport as much as anybody, evidently regarding it as a grand holiday. I must say that I think that everybody was greatly astonished at the neatness these girls displayed in their dress, and the trouble they took to keep from getting stained and soiled with their work; for we had generally heard the Eskimos accused of want of cleanliness.

These girls, like those of Disko, wore white starched linen tops to their boots, and as it was impossible to keep them from getting blackened with the coal-dust, they changed them, and put on clean pairs no less than three times during the day—a fact which is alone a sufficient refutation of the slanders that have been heaped upon their devoted little heads.

About seven o'clock in the evening a slow, drizzling, disagreeable rain set in, giving promise of bad weather for the next two or three days. But we had, fortunately, got in nearly forty tons of coal, as much as the Captain wanted, and we accordingly stopped, tired, but well satisfied with the result of our day's work. Had we not been favoured with fine weather, we might have been here four or five days without accomplishing so much. We did not get up anchor till next morning, having in the evening taken leave of our Eskimo friends, who had set up a tent on shore, where they passed the night before returning to Yuyar-susuk. We gave the girls a number of little presents, with which they seemed much pleased, before bidding them adieu. Among other things, I observed that Juliet had received a prettily embroidered white linen pillow-case, but could not find out who had given it to her, although I am pretty sure I had seen it in Tromp's cabin. It is probably long ere this worked up into boot-tops.

As we shall meet with no more pretty girls in the course of our narrative, I would like, before finally taking leave of these, to assure the reader that I do not think I have exaggerated the charms of the fair girls of the Arctic in the least. Nor am I alone in my appreciation of them, for I found that all my messmates were of the same opinion as myself. Perhaps it was because these people have been so persistently misrepresented by travellers as " dirty " and filthy " that we were agreeably astonished to find them otherwise, and all the more disposed to do them justice; but certain it is that my companions were even more enthusiastic in singing their praises than myself.

Soon after leaving England we had established a little weekly paper, called the PANDORA'S BOX, to which everybody was expected to contribute; and the week succeeding our visit to Disko and Yuyarsusuk the editor was considerably amused to find that every contributor had chosen one subject with a unanimity that was somewhat embarrassing. The consequence was that the PANDORA'S BOX for August 17, 1875, presented a funny succession of articles about the Arctic girls, one of which I herewith present as an evidence that I have not been exaggerating. It was signed " Tromp."

" It is a truth old as the hills that the sailor stops just long enough in every harbour to feel the true value of those whom he is obliged to leave behind him. Untrue it is, however, that he forgets those good fairies who throw now and then a warm sunbeam on his troubled path as quickly as he does the privations which he often has to bear. On the contrary, once returned on board of his ship, he often quietly remembers the lovely beauty to whom he was obliged (perhaps for ever) to bid farewell, and he remains a long time thankful for the moments which were so dear to him. Let us then, too, in our PANDORA'S BOX reserve a little room for the commemoration of these simple children of nature of the high north, who, during two days, have shared with us the joy and grief of our life; for it is impossible for us to see in those kind pretty sisters

from the unknown homes of Yuyarsusuk, common workers of a coal-mine. There is no resemblance at all between these healthy, merry children of Kudliset and the poor, worn-out faces of the miners of old Europe. Without being aware of it, they possessed all the virtues which we admire in a high-bred woman—simplicity, modesty, intelligence, and refinement—and when we compared them with the ugly old woman who guarded them with the eye of an Argus, we regretted very much that these lonely flowers were planted in the cold, barren ground of this bleak shore to prematurely wither beneath its long and bitter winter. More utterly forgotten in the world none can live; but as we recall those sweet, melancholy tones of their native land, we are unable to forget that fellow-creatures were never more misplaced. Let us, then, finish with wishing them all possible good, and let our thoughts sometimes return to those pretty little flowers who flourish utterly forgotten in the snow-covered mountain homes of Disko Island."

CHAPTER IX.

THE ESKIMOS.

A PEOPLE who live neither by agriculture nor the pasturage of sheep and cattle, nor yet, properly speaking, by the chase, as the chase is ordinarily understood: a people who have for food neither beef, mutton, nor pork; neither fruit, bread, nor vegetables; neither sugar nor salt; who have for drink neither tea, coffee, wine, beer, nor spirits of any kind; for clothing neither silk, cotton, flaxen, nor woollen stuffs; who have neither iron, nor steel, nor lead, nor copper, nor gold, nor pottery; who have for fuel neither wood, nor coal, nor peat—such a people are the Eskimos, or, as they call themselves, the "Innuits," of the Arctic.

In the barren, desolate world they inhabit the frozen earth brings forth no fruits, and there is no food for the animals that in a softer clime supply man with food and clothing. There are here no forests of trees, no smiling orchards, no fields of waving grain, no hill-sides covered with sheep and cattle; and consequently there are none of those things which we, of another world, think necessary for the existence of Man.

It seems at first sight impossible that men should live amid such conditions. The things I have enumerated appear to include all the possibilities of food, clothing, and fire, found on the

Earth; and the question which unconsciously arises to our lips is, Can a people, then, live without either of these three first necessities of life—food, clothing, and fire?

But the Innuits, deprived literally of everything which in our clime makes life possible, have nevertheless found in the world they have chosen, or into which they have been driven, the means of existence in a very different shape from that in which they abound in our southern clime. They have found them all—food, fire, light, clothing, arms, implements, everything—combined in one single animal.

That animal is the seal.

Without it, the existence of man in these regions would be an impossibility, for there is no other animal here, sufficiently numerous and easy of capture, to supply him with sustenance. This one animal alone furnishes him with everything.

Its flesh supplies him with food; its blubber with light and fire; its skin with clothing and shelter.

It is astonishing to see the multifarious uses to which the Innuit has put this animal, the extra-ordinary number of things he has obtained from it. Its skin supplies him not only with the boots he wears on his feet, the hood that protects his head, the coat that covers his back, but the thread or thongs with which these articles are sewed; and its bones supply the needles with which he sews them. In its skin he finds not only the covering for his bed, but the material with which he makes his summer tent, and the hangings or tapestry which clothe the walls of his winter habitation. In the absence of wood, its bones furnish him with the framework of his kayak and umiak, his hunting canoe and his large boat ; while its skin supplies the shell or covering. From its bones he makes the runners of his sledges; from the skin he cuts the lashings that bind the different parts together. From the bones he fashions his arms, knives, axes, spears, harpoons, darts ; and in its entrails, stretched thin and dried, he even finds a substitute for our window glass.

There is not a necessity of life which is not supplied in some way by this Protean animal.

Man has become here a mere parasite—eating, living, sleeping on this creature, regulating his movements by it; going where it goes, abandoning the places it abandons, and finally dying where it becomes extinct !

The Eskimos display a wonderful skill in fashioning the bones and skin of the seal for their various purposes. Their oars are tipped with bone, giving them an elegant and finished appearance. The edges and corners of their kayaks are also ornamented with a continuous border of bone, showing a neatness and skill not to be surpassed by the most practised joiner, and these canoes, which are often made entirely from different parts of the seal, are remarkable and beautiful specimens of nautical workmanship.

The kayak is used for hunting only. It is just large enough for one man, and so light that it requires long practice, something like that on the

tight-rope, to keep it from capsizing. This being
the case, it is necessary that all the arms and
implements used in hunting be firmly secured, to
prevent their being lost. This is done in the
most ingenious manner. The kayaker's spear
and dart are placed before him on the kayak,
fixed on little bone brackets, so that they cannot
be washed away by the waves, and yet in such a
manner that the hunter can seize them instantly.
His harpoon-line is coiled securely, but is nevertheless free to pay out when the spear is thrown.
A large bladder, likewise taken from the seal, and
used to enable him to float the body of his captured prey, is placed behind him, securely attached
to a bone hook.

The construction of the harpoon and dart is
most ingenious. The spear is thrown by means
of a short handle laid against the shaft about the
middle. This handle detaches itself from the
shaft, and remains in the hand; and the shaft,
after striking the animal, detaches itself in its
turn from the point, but remains hanging to it by
a thong.

This arrangement prevents the shaft from being
broken, or the barbed point from being twisted
out by the efforts of the animal to get away. To
the after-end of the shaft is fastened a small
bladder, which prevents it from sinking when the
mark is missed, and likewise retards the movements of the seal in the water, when struck.

It will be seen that with the spear, dart, handles, bladders, lines, and paddle, there are a good many things to look after; and as these things cannot be hastily thrown down on top of the kayak without almost instantly falling overboard, each instrument as it is successively used must be replaced in its proper position, which necessitates on the part of the kyaker a curious methodical, automatic motion, as though he were moved by clock-work.

He first poises himself carefully, to counteract the movement of throwing the spear, which would otherwise capsize the frail craft; then, with his paddle lying across the kayak before him and held in the left hand, he throws the spear with the right. The handle remains in the hand, and is then placed on its brackets; the shaft is drawn back, placed on another pair of brackets, the handle again picked up, placed on the shaft, and the line coiled up before the spear is ready to be hurled again.

All this is done with the right hand, with a quickness and dexterity that is surprising, while the left is used in holding the paddle and keeping the balance of the light, trembling craft.

All these movements have to be performed in the same methodical, automatic manner, no matter what the excitement and danger of the chase; otherwise the hunter would lose his weapons.

In former times, before their intercourse with Europeans, wood was in great demand among the Eskimos, as it is the only material of which they can make the shafts for their spears ; and their only supply was the pieces of drift-wood that now and then were found floating in the water. They never knew where this wood came from, how it grew, nor what it really was.

They have never seen a tree or a forest, and it would be difficult to make an Eskimo understand what sort of thing a tree really is. They thought the wood was sent them by the good people of the under-world up through the sea.

For curiously enough their ideas of Heaven, and the other place, are exactly the reverse of ours. Good people, they think, go to a warm and comfortable place in a lower world, while the bad go up and are doomed to wander about on the surface of the great glacier freezing and starving—in their climate a not unnatural way of conceiving a state of future punishments and rewards.

It will be understood of course that with regard to many of the Greenland Eskimos these remarks would only apply to the past, as they can now obtain wood, iron, and tissues in limited quantities from the Danes. But the people known as the Arctic Highlanders at Cape York, the inhabitants of the western side of Hudson Bay, Boothia, and the shores of the Great Fish River, live without a single one of the many things we think necessary to existence.

The Eskimos furnish an example of a race of men living under conditions corresponding exactly to those of that strange unknown glacial period during which Europe lay buried, for so many centuries, beneath a sea of ice. Scientific men say they may be classed with the races of the pre-historic age of ground stone tools, with the exceptional use of metals.

If this theory could be taken to mean that the Eskimos were separated from the rest of mankind during the pre-historic period, and that they have remained in the same condition in which they then were, the importance of the study of these people—their language, manners, customs, and ideas, could scarcely be over-estimated. We would have before us a living example of Man, during that dim, mysterious period which preceded the era of authentic record, the invention of letters, and the birth of history, of which we have, only dark and shadowy glimpses. We could study his spiritual tendencies and longings before any of the modern religions had produced their effect upon him; we could see what were his abstract ideas of justice before modern notions of right and wrong were established. We could measure his intellectual capacity; we could judge, perhaps, to what degree of development the human mind had attained at that time; and we should have, as it were, a picture of the civilization of that mysterious epoch—a living people who think, act, believe, and live as did the pre-historic man.

If this were true, and the theory could be

taken to mean so much; if we were to judge of the pre-historic man by the modern Eskimo, I must express it as my opinion, that the pre-historic man was not a bad sort of fellow at all, and that his civilized descendants have scarcely improved upon him. For the Eskimos in many things, as their domestic relations, their kindness to each other, the generous way in which those who have, share, in times of scarcity, with those who have not, their care for children, their respect, love, and tenderness for the aged and infirm, prove themselves to be far in advance of more cultivated peoples.

But the theory only means that the Eskimos are an example of a modern people living amid conditions that correspond to those amidst which the pre-historic inhabitants of Europe existed, and not that they were separated from the rest of mankind at that interesting period.

I have spoken of the superiority of the Eskimos in many respects, over more cultivated peoples. I know little about them from personal observation, and as I do not wish to be accused of exaggeration, I will give in evidence some statements of those who have had better opportunities of judging of their character than myself.

Dr. Simpson, who was surgeon to the ship of discovery PLOVER, and who passed two winters with the Eskimos at Point Barrow, North America, says,—

" Their conjugal and parental affections are strong ; the latter especially while the children are young. For the tender solicitude with which their own infancy and childhood have been tended, in the treatment of their aged and infirm parents they make a return which redounds to their credit ; for they not only give them food and clothing, sharing with them every comfort they possess, but on their longest and most fatiguing journeys make provision for their easy conveyance. In this way we witnessed among the people of fourteen summer tents, and as many boats, one crippled old man, a blind and helpless old woman, two grown-up women with sprained ankles, and one other invalid, besides children of various ages, carried by their respective families, who had done this for many successive summers. When a man dies, his next of kin supports his widow, and orphan children are provided for in the same way. Adoption is so frequent among them that it becomes almost impossible to trace relationship. The adopted child takes the place of the real one, and performs his duties towards his benefactors, as to his own parents. Having but little food adapted to supply the place of milk, it is not unusual to see a boy of four or five years take the breast, and the indulgence with which children are treated is attributable in some degree to the difficulties of rearing them. We have seen a child of four years demand a chew of tobacco from his father, and, not receiving it immediately, strike him a severe blow with a piece of wood, without giving offence. It is not improbable that such indulgence should have a permanent effect on the temper and character of the people, for though the children fight and bully each other in their play, among the grown-up men and women we have never seen anything approaching to a quarrel; and generally they are particularly careful not to say anything displeasing in each other's presence. If a man gets angry or out of temper, even, his nearest friends keep out of his way, trusting to his recovery in a short time.

A man seems to have unlimited authority in his own hut, but with few exceptions his rule is mild; and the domestic and social position of women is one of comfort and enjoyment. There is no affected dignity or importance in the men, and they do not make slaves and drudges of the women. On the contrary, they endure all the principal hardship and fatigue, in the coldest season of the year, only calling the women to assist when too wearied themselves to bring in the fruits of their industry and patience; while the women appear to think it a privation not to share the labours of the men."

Dr. Rink says,—

"The education of children was apparently managed without any corporal punishment; but threatening them with the vengeance of malevolent spirits was one of the means employed to keep unruly urchins in check.

"Widows, or unmarried women with children, rarely set up housekeeping by themselves, and were generally provided for by their housemates or kindred. If there was more than one son, a subsequent one sometimes, on acquiring a boat and tent, left home and established a separate family or household. The owner of a boat or tent was thus considered the chief or head of the family, and it was principally he who was called the *igtuat* or provider of the others.

"When a man died, his eldest son inherited the boat and tent, along with the duties incumbent on the provider. If no such grown-up son existed, the nearest relative took his place, and adopted the children of the deceased as his foster-children. But when these were grown up, and had themselves become providers, their widowed mother was at liberty to establish a separate household, without any further obligation to the foster-father. As regards inheritance in general, it must be remembered that among the Eskimos it represented a question of obligations and burdens rather than a personal gain.

"From their living together in small habitations *a friendly way of conversing* was necessary; and all high words or quarrelling are considered unlawful. The Eskimo language is, therefore, devoid of any real words for scolding. The general mode of uttering annoyance at an offence is by silence, whereas the slightest harshness in speaking even to younger or subordinate persons is considered an offence in so far that it may give rise to violent quarrels and ruptures."

This is evidence of writers who have lived a number of years among the Eskimos; and when we compare the way in which they treat their children, the aged, and the infirm, with the systems of baby-farming, workhouses, the labour of children in brickyards and factories, adopted in all civilized countries, I think I may safely say that in these respects at least the Eskimos are far in advance of cultivated peoples.

They seem to be a quiet, amiable, kindly, peaceful, and gentle race. Crime is scarcely known among them. Even before their conversion to Christianity by the Danes, they appear to have possessed the same genial and kindly characteristics, and to have been almost free from crime.

Dr. Rink says,—

" There was not even a Court of Justice among them, to secure the maintenance of the laws. With the exception of the part which the Angakoks, or magicians, and the relatives of an offending person sometimes took in inflicting punishment upon the delinquent, public opinion formed the tribunal, and the general punishment consisted in the offender being shamed in the eyes of the people.   The only regular courts were the public meetings, which at the same time snpplied the national sports and entèrtainments, and greatly contributed to strengthen and maintain the national life.   If a person had a complaint against another, he forthwith composed a song about it, to be sung at one of these meetings, and invited his opponent to meet him, announcing the time and place, when and where, he would sing against him.   These songs were called Nith songs, and were used for settling all kinds of quarrels, and punishing any sort of crime or breach of public order or custom, with the exception of those only to be expiated by death, in the shape of the blood revenge.   Generally, and always in cases of importance, both sides had assistants, who, having prepared themselves for the task, would act the parts of the principals if the latter happened to become exhausted.   The cheering or dissent of the assembly at once represented the judgment and the punishment."

They still have one of the prettiest customs I think I ever heard of among any people, it is the following :—When any one dies, leaving near reations, as brother or sister, father, mother, or even cousins, the next child born in the village is named after the departed one, and replaces to a certain extent the loss.   The infant becomes the pet of the bereaved family, who look upon it almost as their own, treat it in the most affectionate manner, and always extend to it through life the greatest kindness.

They have been converted to Christianity by the Danes, who established their authority throughout the whole of Greenland, about a century ago. Nearly all can read and write their own language. There is no country in the world in which the schools that have been established in every village are better attended; and there are very few of the Greenland Eskimos who cannot read and write.

The introduction of intoxicating liquors has been prevented, and those acts of violence and oppression which in every other country have destroyed and degraded primitive races, have been here altogether unknown. This may be said to be the only case in which white men have not perpetrated the foulest wrongs on the natives of the countries they have subjected, the only instance in which they have treated their weaker brothers with any degree of justice. To their honour be it said, the Danes have always endeavoured to elevate and educate the natives, and they have refused to profit by selling them things which they thought might prove prejudicial to their health and wellbeing.

This example of moderation, kindness, and justice, should entitle the Danes to more respect and consideration than if they could marshal a million of men on the field of battle.

Clements R. Markham has written a most interesting paper on the origin and migration of the Innuit, for the use of the Arctic expedition commanded by Captain Nares. In this paper, he maintains that the Eskimos came originally from Asia, that great cradle of the human race, and that it is among the Tuski tribes of northern Siberia that we must look for their origin. He believes that their separation from those tribes took place at a comparatively modern period—not earlier, perhaps, than the eleventh or twelfth century. This paper of Markham's is not easily accessible to the general public; and as it is written in a very condensed form, I find I can do no better than to make the following interesting extract from it :—

"Until within the last nine centuries the great continent of Greenland was, so far as our knowledge extends, untenanted by a single human being—the bears and reindeer held undisputed possession. There was a still more remote period, when fine forests of exogenous trees clothed the hill-sides of Disko, when groves waved, in a milder climate, over Banks Island and Melville Island, and when corals and sponges flourished in the now frozen waters of Barrow's Strait. Of this period we know nothing; but it is at least certain that when Erik the Red planted his little colony of hardy Norsemen at the mouth of one of the Greenland fiords, in the end of the tenth century, he apparently found the land far more habitable than it is to-day.

"For three centuries and a half the Norman colonies of Greenland continued to flourish; upwards of 300 small farms and villages were built along the shores of the fiords from the island of Disko to Cape Farewell. The ancient Icelandic and Danish accounts of these transactions are corroborated by the interesting remains which may be seen in the Scandinavian museum, at Copenhagen. During the whole of this period no indigenous race was seen in that land, and no one appeared to dispute the possession of Greenland with the Norman Colony. A curious account of a voyage is extant, during which the Normans reached a latitude north of Cape York; yet there is no mention of any signs of a strange race. The Normans continued to be the sole tenants of Greenland, at least until the middle of the fourteenth century. Our last historical glimpse of them shows them living in two districts, in villages along the shores, with small herds of cattle finding pasturage round their houses, with outlying colonies on the opposite shores of America, and occasional vessels trading with Iceland and Norway; but no grain would ripen in their fields. They seem to have been a wild, turbulent race of hardy pirates, and their history, short as it is, is filled with accounts of bloody feuds.

"All at once, in the middle of the fourteenth

century, a horde of men, short of stature, appeared on the extreme northern frontier of the Norman settlements of Greenland, at a place called Kindelfiord—the modern Omenak fiord—north of Disko. These men resembled exactly some men Thorwald the Viking had met with on the shores of Labrador, and whom he had contemptuously named Skroellings (chips or parings). Eighteen Norsemen were killed in an encounter with them; the news of the invasion travelled to the southern settlements, then called East Bygd; one Ivar Bardsen came to the rescue in 1349, and he found that all the Norsemen of the West Bygd had disappeared, and that the Skroellings were in possession. Here the record abruptly ceases, and we hear nothing more of Greenland until the time of the Elizabethan navigators, and nothing authentic of either Norsemen or Skroellings until the mission of Hans Egede, in the middle of the last century.

"When the curtain rises again, all traces of the Norsemen have disappeared save a few Runic inscriptions, extending as far north as the present settlement of Upernivik, some ruins, and the broken church bells of Gardar. The Skroellings, or Eskimos, are in sole possession from Kingitok to Cape Farewell. And the ancient Norse records are fully corroborated by the traditions of the Eskimos, in the statement that they originally came from the north.

"The interesting question now arises—whence

came these Greenland Eskimos, these Innuit, or men, as they call themselves ? We look at them and see at once that they have no, or only very remote, kinship with the red race of America ; but a glance suffices to convince us of their relationship with the Tuski or northern tribes of Siberia. It is in Asia, then, that we must seek their origin, that cradle of so many races, and the search for some clue is not altogether without result.

"During the centuries preceding the first reported appearance of the Skroellings in Greenland, and for some time previously, there was a great movement among the people of Central Asia. Tugrul Beg, Jingîz Khan, and other chiefs of less celebrity, led vast armies to the conquest of the whole earth, as they proudly boasted. The land of the Turk and the Mongol sent forth a mighty series of inundations, which flooded the rest of Asia for several centuries, and the effects of which were felt from the plains of Silesia to the shores of the Yellow Sea, and from the valley of the Ganges to the frozen tundra of Siberia. The pressure caused by these invading waves on the tribes of Northern Siberia drove them still farther to the North. But these regions were formerly inhabited by numerous tribes which were driven away still farther north, over the frozen sea. Wrangell has preserved traditions of their disappearance, and in them, I think, we may find a clue to the origin of the Greenland Eskimos. Their migrations did not probably take place at one time, but spread over a period of one or two centuries; and the age of Mongol invasion and conquest was doubtless the age of tribulation and flight for the tribes of Northern Siberia."

Mr. Markham finds the first traces of their migrations in ruined yourts on Banks Island; thence he follows them to Melville Island, where a piece of timber, standing upright on the summit of a low, flat-topped hill, was found; by Byam Martin Island, where were some ruined huts, to Bathurst Island, where were found seven huts and some circles of moss-covered stones; to Cornwallis Island, where were found more huts, a portion of the runner of a sledge, and some very perfect stone fox-traps. From there he traces them down Wellington Channel, along the east shore of which was found an Eskimo lamp lying on the beach near Cape Lady Franklin; to Griffith Island, where Mr. Markham himself found the sites of four summer huts, some bones of birds, and the runner of a sledge, and the piece of a whale's bone marked with cuts from some sharp instrument; to Prince of Wales Island, where was found an old Eskimo cache, containing bones of seals and bears; to North Somerset, where Allen Young found some circular walls of very ancient date, used for watching rein-deer; to North Devon, where Markham again found the remains of huts, and twelve tombs built of limestone slabs, containing skeletons; to the Cary Islands, where he found old ruined huts and a stone fox-trap, and so on to the coast of Greenland, where they would have arrived about the time of the invasions of the Skroellings reported by the Norsemen.

The region through which they passed, Mr. Markham thinks, would not afford the necessary conditions for permanent abodes of human beings. Open water during the winter in pools and lanes at least appears to be necessary for the existence of Man in any part of the Arctic regions, because seals are to be captured only where there is open water, and this essential is not to be found in the frozen sea through which we have traced them. These pilgrims were without bows and arrows, and had no means of catching large game on land. They would therefore travel gradually onward, looking for open water, where they could kill seals with bone spears and darts, until they came to the coast of Greenland, which was very well suited to be the home of these hardy Asiatic wanderers, and here at length they found a resting-place. "Its granite cliffs are more covered with vegetation than the bare limestone ridges to the westward. Its bergs and currents keep the water open during the winter, to which walrus, seals, and bears resort. Without bows and arrows, without canoes, and without wood, the Eskimos of Cape York can still secure abundance of food with their bone spears and darts."

In addition to the facts already stated, Mr. Markham evidently inclines to the opinion that the Eskimo is a Siberian language, and would class the languages of Greenland, Labrador, Iglulik, Boothia, Kotzebue Sound, and parts of Siberia as dialects of the same mother-tongue, and he gives a list of some of the most common words of the same meaning, in both languages, which certainly are strikingly similar. Dr. Rink, however, is of opinion that the Eskimo tongue is more nearly allied to the languages of America.

It is probable that the North American Eskimo and Siberian languages have a common origin, but, until all the languages spoken in Northern Siberia and North America, as well as that of the Innuit are better understood, the subject must remain in considerable obscurity.

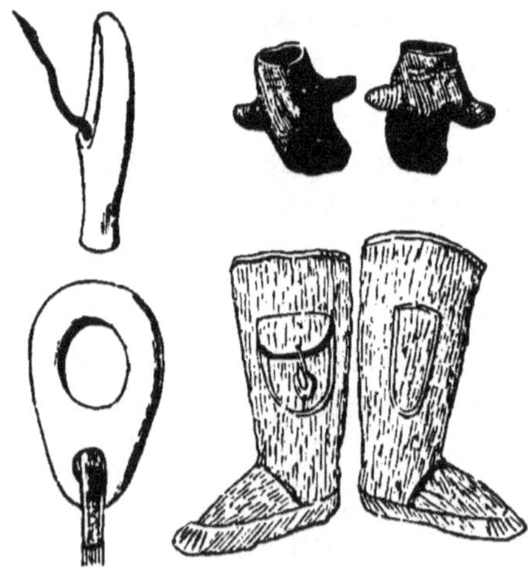

CHAPTER X.

ESKIMO LITERATURE.

THERE are few people who have read Mr. Ralston's charming books, "Russian Folk Lore," and "Songs of the Russian People," that will not turn with interest to a work of a similar kind —Dr. Rink's "Tales and Traditions of the Eskimo."

This book is a collection of tales, probably the most curious that have ever been published. They are entirely different from those stories which comprise the folk-lore of other peoples, and resemble them neither in construction, in incident, nor in the dominant idea which governs them.

As is well known, the folk-lore of all the nations of Europe and of Asia may be considered identical. All the well-known English and German tales, such as Cinderella and Bluebeard, are found to exist, with variations, not only in all the languages of Europe, but likewise in those of Asia and India. The stories of all these peoples seem to have had a common origin, in the far-away East, at a time perhaps long anterior to history; and this would account for their striking resemblance to each other in every country and language.

But here is a folk lore, a series of tales that, with the exception of three or four, perhaps, have not the slightest likeness to those stories which for ages have been the delight of the other races of mankind; here is a people who have no share, no part in this wealth, the common property of the rest of Mankind, but who have a rich mine of their own, infinitesimal in quantity as compared to the combined treasures of the rest of the world, but in some respects superior in quality.

The first remarkable characteristic of the Eskimo folk-lore, which distinguishes it from that of other peoples, is in the perfect picture it gives of Eskimo life. Their manners and customs,—their dress, their means of gaining a livelihood, their arms and implements and houses, their religious beliefs, their ideas of justice, of right and wrong, are all described with a minuteness that is astonishing. There is not a weapon nor an implement in use among them, nor a peculiarity of their way of life, that is not mentioned in these stories.

The kayak, or "hunting boat," the umiak, or "woman's boat," the harpoon, the dart, the hunting bladder, the summer tent, the winter habitation, the oil lamp, which furnishes at the same time heat and light, the funnel or chimney which carries off the smoke, the entrance to the houses, the ledge or platform whereon is placed the skins that constitute the bed, their manner of hunting the seal, even the habits of that animal itself, are all so accurately described that any one who had never even heard of the Eskimos could from these stories alone give a very good description of the people.

Manners and customs form so important a part of this folk-lore that the stories could not have been borrowed from any other people, unless from a people living amid exactly the same conditions. Nor could any other people adapt the tales to a different kind of existence, so essential a part of them are the conditions amid which their scenes are laid.

The story of "Jack and the Beanstalk" is of such a nature that it can be told and understood by any people, and actually is told with little variation in every known language.

But the story of the boy who used his sister and mother as a hunting bladder is essentially an Eskimo tale, and could only be understood by a people living amid like conditions.

Although magic, enchantment, the use of amulets, and various other supernatural agencies, play important parts in these tales, they are employed in the most direct and unconditional manner. They either confer great bodily strength, by means of which prodigies are performed, or else aid in the every-day affairs of life, as seal-hunting and kayaking.

A man may, by the use of the magic art, by intercourse with the mysterious and benevolent beings of the lower world, acquire great strength; or he may be enabled always to find the seals and to kill great numbers of them, where ordinary hunters cannot find a single one, or he may acquire the faculty of seeing things that are happening far away in distant places, and even transport himself long distances through the air.

But this power is always used in a direct and absolute manner. The Eskimo hero has no need of seven-leagued boots nor flying horses to make his journeys; nor does he require magic rings, handkerchiefs, or other enchanted objects to accomplish his wishes. The magic power rarely lies in any inanimate object, which might therefore pass from hand to hand, but in the man himself on whom the power has been conferred.

There appears to be none of those complicated conditions which ordinarily attend the use of magic, and necessitate so much care on the part of the magician to prevent this power escaping from him, and perhaps even turning against him. The might once obtained is generally absolute.

Even the power ascribed to amulets seems to proceed rather from the owner of the amulet than to be inherent in the amulet itself. This most useful article is only useful to its own master, and its power cannot be transferred to anybody else. It is something which seems to form as essential a part of him as his soul or will.

When a child is born a bone or part of some animal is given it for an amulet. This bone, at the bidding of its master, is capable of suddenly turning into the animal from which it has been taken, and this magic animal becomes a powerful auxiliary, and for its owner's enemies a terrible adversary.

It is a curious circumstance, showing how individual prowess is valued, that the power of magic is in most cases employed to obtain great bodily strength, by means of which prodigies are performed.

The hero fights and kills bears with his hands alone, without the aid of weapons; he picks up his enemies and flings them on the ground and crushes them, or tears them limb from limb, by sheer brute force. Tremendous strength of this kind is evidently prized more highly than mere skill in the use of weapons, and this characteristic would seem to point to the great antiquity of the tales.

Another peculiarity of these stories is the absence of all reference to kings and queens, princes and princesses, who play such important parts in the folk-lore of other peoples.

The Eskimos have neither kings nor queens, nor even chiefs, and there is nothing in the least approaching royal authority known among them. All their tales have a direct relation to the every-day affairs of life, as kayaking and seal-hunting, and their heroes are mere ordinary mortals.

In fact, their favourite hero—one who appears in a great number of the tales—is a poor orphan boy, who grows up and becomes a mighty hunter.

Several of the tales are evidently traditions of events that actually took place; as those referring to intercourse, encounters and fights with the "Inlanders," who are, Dr. Rink thinks, no other than the Indians of North America.

There are only three or four of the tales that bear the slightest resemblance to the well-known stories of other countries. It is worth remarking that one of these is the famous Bluebeard.

But the grim old hero has here turned cannibal, and not only kills, but eats his wives, by way of showing, probably, how much he loves them. The incident of the secret chamber has therefore disappeared; the Eskimo Bluebeard had no occasion to keep a secret room, as he stowed his dead wives away in a far safer place!

There are likewise two or three variants of the well-known story about the man who discovers a number of pretty girls bathing, and steals the clothes of one of them, thus making her a prisoner, while her companions turn into seals or birds and fly away. As in our version he induces her to marry him, and she, after living with her husband a number of years, suddenly disappears, and is never heard of again.

There are also two or three relating to the union of earthly maidens with mysterious supernatural beings of the underground world, which remind one somewhat of the Biblical tradition of the loves of angels for the daughters of men.

There is one, however, of a mythological nature, relating to the origin of the sun and moon, on which it would be interesting to have the opinion of Gubernatis, as it is utterly unintelligible to the ordinary reader.

Although Dr. Rink dwells principally on the historical and ethnological significance of these tales, they possess for the ordinary reader an interest of a far higher kind.

It is the field they offer for psychological study of the Eskimo mind. There is a fascination in observing and analyzing the literary methods and effects that are employed in these tales, in endeavouring to seize and follow the thought which animates them, in determining the qualities and characteristics that have made them popular, and which on the principle of the survival of the fittest have made them live; thus to construct, bit by bit, objectively as it were, the mind of this strange people who live amid such extraordinary con ditions, so long separated from the rest of mankind.

There is little brilliancy of imagination and not much ingenuity of invention displayed in the stories. These people are too closely absorbed in gaining a livelihood to find leisure for flights of fancy; the struggle for existence is too implacable and inexorable to allow time for indulgence of the imagination. Even Love, the universal theme, is here scarcely mentioned; the fire which in warmer climes glows with such fervent heat here waxes dim, and is scarcely taken into account at all.

But there is displayed a rugged power in the presentation of facts, in the recital of events, which is striking. The grotesque, the hideous and frightful are depicted in crude but effective colours, and there is a fearful realism in many of the descriptions that makes one shudder.

But it is not only in the portrayal of material facts that this power is displayed. In many of the tales an idea is presented with a unity and force that places them in point of merit far above the stories of any other people.

There is among them a tale of vengeance that ought to satisfy the most vindictive nature. It is of a poor, sickly orphan boy, left to the care of people who, instead of treating him kindly, half starve, beat, and maltreat him in the most cruel manner. They are in the habit of picking him up

by the nostrils and tossing him about, and—here
the grotesque comes curiously in—the result is,
that only his nostrils grow, while the rest of his
body remains stationary. He becomes ugly and
repulsive, which only causes him to be the more
persecuted. His tormentors, by way of amusement, are in the habit of covering him with filth,
and out of mere gaiety and lightness of heart,
they often fill his clothing with snow, and then
keep him out in the cold for hours at a time.

Finally, a benevolent and supernatural being of
the mountain takes pity on the poor boy, and by
wrestling with him every day for a long time
teaches him how to grow strong.

He begins to increase in size and vigour, and
as he grows up becomes a very giant in strength,
without his tormentors ever suspecting the trans-
formation.

One day, however, three bears appear on an
iceberg near the village. There is nobody among
the hunters courageous enough to attack them,
and great is the surprise of everybody upon
seeing Kagsaksuk, the despised orphan boy, advancing towards the bears without even a
weapon.

They think at first that he is crazy ; but what
is their astonishment and terror upon seeing him
ascend the iceberg, seize each bear successively
by the fore-paws and beat it to death against
the ice !

The last one he flings among his former persecutors, and kills two or three of them. He then descends from the iceberg, and inquires whether anybody wishes to lift him up by the nostrils! But they all tremble at the mere suggestion, and invite him into the house, give him the place of honour, and offer him food.

The cowardice and pusillanimity of the people who are capable of ill-treating an orphan child are then depicted in the most striking manner.

He asks for a drink of water, and it is brought to him by the daughter of one of his persecutors, who had herself been particularly forward in tormenting him. He takes her in his arms as if to kiss her, and squeezes her till the blood gushes from her mouth, then hands her to the father with the remark, "I think she is burst." To which the father replies, "Never mind, she was good for nothing but fetching water." He next kills a young man in the same way, but the father only said, "It is no matter, he was no hunter." He kills several more by crushing them to death, or tearing them limb from limb, but the others only applaud, until it comes their turn. Finally, he destroys his persecutors to the last one, and then becomes a mighty hunter, and the provider of all the widows and orphans, and of all those who ever showed him any kindness when he was a weak and sickly child.

With regard to the severity of the punishment

in this case, as compared to the offence, it may be remarked that the one unpardonable sin in the eyes of the Eskimo appears to be the ill-treatment of orphan and sickly children. Although there are other tales in which the idea of revenge occurs, it is only referred to incidentally and without sympathy, while in this case all the details of the vengeance, as tearing the offenders limb from limb, and crushing them to death, are dwelt upon with evident approval and relish.

The idea of revenge does not occur often in these tales. On the contrary, there are several in which the favourite hero, an orphan boy, although not very well treated in his youth by his house-mates, grows up, becomes a great hunter, and returns good for evil, by providing, in times of scarcity, for the whole village, including the people he had least reason to love.

The orphan Iliarsorkik after having been alternately adopted and turned out by several people, is finally taken in by a poor widow. He too becomes a great hunter, repays his foster mother by the greatest devotion, and finally one terrible winter when the blow-holes of the seals are frozen over, when all the hunters return home bootless, and the people are on the very verge of starvation, he, alone, by his great skill, is able to find and kill game, and he becomes the provider of the whole village.

Once when far out on the ice he is beset by a

fog, and endeavours to find his way home by the wind. But the wind changes, and he is led by this strange guide to another village, where the people are starving. He becomes their provider likewise, and the good deed performed by the poor widow in taking care of the orphan, is thus paid back, to the whole world, a thousand-fold.

The ability to provide for a great number of people would seem to be the greatest glory to which an Eskimo can aspire.

When he becomes thoroughly civilized, this barbaric idea will of course be duly eradicated, and his ambition will then be to slaughter the greatest number.

To merely terrify an orphan child seems to be considered a grave misdemeanor. One story turns altogether on the following incident.

A poor orphan boy who had no friends was at work one day trying to make a kayak, with no instruments but sharp stones and shells. A wicked man put on a bear-skin, stole up behind, and frightened the boy nearly to death, with the result that he was very much tormented and ridiculed by everybody. But when the people afterwards came and saw the instruments the poor boy was working with, " they were greatly moved at the sight."

The boy grew up, and as usual became a successful hunter, and an *angakok*, or magician, as well. It then occurred to him to be revenged.

This he did by putting on a walrus skin, and playing at walrus with the man who had played at bear with him. He went into the water where his former tormentor would be sure to see him, and thus tempted him to throw his harpoon. This he seized and carried off, by diving under the water, to the great mystification of the hunter.

Finally he exposed the trick, and made his old enemy the laughing-stock of the village.

The idea of returning good for evil often occurs in the folk-lore.

There is one in which an old man is severely beaten, and finally driven out of the village, because he will not give his daughter in marriage to a man she does not love.

He goes off to another place, builds a house, hunts seals, and lives all alone with his child.

Upon awaking one morning just before daylight, he observes a man slipping through the doorway. He questions his daughter, and finds to his great joy and satisfaction that she is secretly married to one of the mysterious beings of the mountain.

His supernatural son-in-law now becomes provider, and supplies seals in abundance. The old man does not have to go kayaking any more, but can take his ease all day long in his house.

While living thus in the greatest abundance he hears that his old neighbours are in the severest need, and he instantly loads a boat with provisions, which he takes to them as a present. Then, after giving them a great feast, he taunts them mildly with their former behaviour, vaunts the prowess of his son-in-law, becomes reconciled with them, and promises that he will always supply them in time of need.

Of all the forms of an avenging Nemesis, I think the most frightful and ghastly ever conceived is that of the Eskimos. It is characteristic too that it should only appear as the avenger of child-murder. Examples of the avenging power of this Nemesis occur in two of these stories, and I do not think that even Bluebeard himself could read them without a shudder.

In one of these, the daughter of a magician gets married secretly against her father's wishes. As soon as he finds it out, he packs up everything in his *umiak*, or boat, and with his whole family determines to move to another place, taking with him his disobedient daughter. When he is starting the husband comes and claims her; but the father refuses to give her up, and takes her away.

He camps after two or three days on an island, and here the daughter secretly gives birth to a child, which she destroys. Finally, a long time after they have arrived at their future home, the father decides to give her in marriage to another man.

She consents, lives happily with her new husband, and gives birth to several fine children.

But each when it comes to a certain age, on a certain day and hour, suddenly utters a shriek, the blood gushes from its head, and it dies.

Finally, the magician determines to try a conjuration, to learn the meaning of this terrible visitation, and he then discovers it to be the ghost of the babe murdered years before, that is thus avenging itself on its younger brothers and sisters!

This spectre is called an *anghiak*, and it often takes a bodily form.

In another story there are a number of brothers who refuse to allow their only sister to marry, because there is no other woman in the family, and they want her to stay at home and keep house for them. She gets secretly married to her lover. But after a time the brothers discover what she has done, and so torment and persecute her that at last she brings forth a still-born child.

The corpse of this child, like the Russian Vampire, becomes animated with a demoniac kind of life and intelligence. It gets up from its grave and wanders forth in the daytime invisible, and takes to persecuting the brothers as the cause of its death.

With the skull of a dog for a boat, it follows them out to sea when they go kayaking, and one by one capsizes and drowns them.

At night the ghastly thing returns to its mother's couch, creeps under the coverlets, and sucks her breasts.

Finally, when it has avenged itself on its uncles by drowning them to the last one, it goes forth on the world a terrible scourge—a kind of destroying angel. It has become such a horrible thing to look upon, so ghastly an apparition, that everybody who sees it is frightened to death! All the inhabitants of one whole village are destroyed to the last man by merely looking upon it!

At last, a priest-magician makes a conjuration to find out what is the meaning of this scourge, and he discovers it to be the *anghiak* of the murdered child. He utters an incantation to destroy it, and the frightful ghost returns to the dustheap beside its mother's house, buries itself there, and dies!

But the idea of retributive punishment does not seem to be a necessary one to the Eskimo mind. There are several stories in which the conception of poetical justice, as we understand it, is altogether absent.

Among the Eskimos, if a man commits a crime, there is no regular tribunal before which he can be taken but that of public opinion, no legal punishment to which he can be subjected but the hatred and contempt of his fellows. The result is, that certain crimes, and even murder, may go unpunished, unless avenged in the shape of the blood revenge, by a relative of the murdered person.

As might be expected, this state of things is

reproduced in the folk-lore, and there are several tales in which the interest hangs upon the fact that murder has not been punished.

The Eskimo mind does not perceive the necessity of that kind of justice which demands an eye for an eye, and a tooth for a tooth. But he has replaced it by a far higher and grander conception. It is that of REMORSE !

Several of these tales turn upon this idea alone, and they have touches of pathos that are not surpassed by anything in our own literature.

There is one relating the dissensions among a family of brothers. The eldest of the family was a famous hunter, and in times of scarcity he and his brothers used to supply the whole village with food by their skill and prowess. But their wives, in distributing the provisions, offended two old men, who the first time they found everybody out of the house worked a charm in its walls.

The result is, that the eldest brother quarrels with his wife and beats her. At this the youngest son begins to cry, whereupon the child's uncle interferes between man and wife, and a struggle ensues between the two brothers. The other brother interferes to separate them, and a free fight, in which several of the neighbours join, is the consequence.

Then the eldest brother takes all his things, moves to another place, and builds himself a house. But from this time war is declared between the brothers, and they mutually conspire how they can kill each other.

The younger brother at last, by the help of a number of conspirators, succeeds in capturing the elder, and kills him by piercing him many times with his spear. But he no sooner sees his brother lying dead at his feet than he thinks of all the kindness he has received at that brother's hands, and he repents bitterly.

He weeps and says, " Alas! we have killed him who did well towards us. In the short, dark days when we were almost starving, when the sea was covered with ice, and the land with snow, he did not mind toiling for us. He has saved our lives many a time, and we have killed him. I am sorry, indeed; now kill me also."

But they refuse to kill him, and he lives on many years, always tortured by the pangs of remorse.

It will be seen that the Eskimo poet has conceived the true idea of remorse. It is not a mere feeling of regret at having done wrong, of having violated a law, but that pang we feel at having inflicted an irreparable injury on a being who loved us. It is a far higher and more pathetic conception of the idea than that contained in the story of Cain. For Cain flees before the wrath of an avenging God, and we see only his terror at having brought condign punishment on himself, but no feeling of sorrow for his murdered brother.

In the Eskimo tale, on the contrary, it is remorse for the murder of the brother who had loved and cared for him, unmixed with the baser sentiment of fear.

It will be observed that the brothers in the preceding story are unconsciously driven to quarrel with each other by some mysterious occult power set in motion by an enemy. They are forced to commit crimes for which they are not responsible; they are made to suffer for no fault of their own; they are playthings in the hands of some fearful diabolical power that amuses itself by torturing and crushing them. The story closes with a reference to the fact that the charm worked in the walls by the two old wizards was thus fulfilled, and it is strange that the old Greek idea of the helplessness of man under the blind, stupid, cruel, relentless decrees of fate should thus appear among a people so utterly different from the Greeks in every respect.

There is another story about two friends, who, almost inseparable for a number of years, finally quarrel; they become partly reconciled, and visit each other, but one of them is very vindictive, and still harbours ideas of revenge.

At last he tries to poison his friend by offering him meat, one side of which he has rubbed against a corpse. But the other is warned by a friendly spirit to turn the meat over, and eat only from the under side. This he does, and escapes uninjured.

He now determines to be revenged, and in his turn offers his friend food that has been poisoned in the same way. The latter has no familiar spirit to warn him, and unaware that his own plan has been unmasked, he eats without suspicion and returns home.

A few days afterwards the other begins to repent of what he has done, and goes to see his friend. He approaches the house, but nobody is to be seen about. As it turns out, the housemates and companions of the poisoned man have all fled in terror. He enters the house, and beholds his friend lying on his back, his head hanging over the edge of the couch, and his eyes staring wildly. The other goes up and asks how he does, but gets no answer. A moment afterwards the sick man suddenly springs to his feet, and shrieks " Because thou hast feasted me basely, I will now devour thee," and then rushes at his visitor.

He is a raving madman !

The other flees in terror, is pursued by the madman to his kayak, and barely has time to escape.

He returns again and again to the house of the madman, and is always received in the same manner. His housemates try to dissuade him from going, but he only replies, " I must go, I cannot stay away," and it seems as though he were continually drawn there by some invisible power which he is unable to resist. He rarely eats now, and still more rarely speaks. He is thinking of

the old days when they were children and play-
mates together; of the love they had for each
other; of their life-long friendship; of the dark
crime he has committed; and while thus under-
going the pangs of remorse, he is obliged to
witness the fearful sufferings of the madman,
without being able to relieve them. The latter
always springs at him with the same reproachful
words, "Because thou hast feasted me basely, I
will devour thee too."

No more terrible punishment can be imagined.

This continues for a long time; the same visit
repeated, day after day; the same desperate
struggle, always with the same result. But the
madman is steadily growing weaker and weaker.
One day he is found lying on the floor, his eyes
far protruding from their sockets staring wildly,
and "his nose as thin as a knife-blade." The
same oft-repeated scene takes place; but when
the friend returns next day, the madman is gone.
The visitor follows his tracks to a cave far up in
the mountain, and there he finds him, sitting bent
up in the cave, and looking out with staring,
bloodshot eyes.

The friend speaks, but receives no answer.
Then he goes up and touches him, but the madman never moves. He is dead.

Then the other closes up the mouth of the cave
with stones and earth, and goes forth into the
world a lonely, friendless, despairing man.

Such an ending contains the Eskimo idea of poetic justice; the only punishment, the only artistic climax required by the Eskimo mind.

It should be remembered that these translations give us probably but a very imperfect idea of the story as told by the composer or poet.

They have come down to us shorn of all their original beauty of language. We have them in the merest outline, and none of them exceeds in length more than four or five pages of this book. In some, the dominant idea is barely preserved; in others it is evidently quite lost, and the story remains utterly pointless. This is not the fault of Dr. Rink, who has done his work in the most thorough and conscientious manner, but of circumstances over which he had no control.

The greater number of the tales were sent to him in manuscript from different parts of Greenland. They were written down by nearly illiterate Eskimos, who could barely read and write; persons for whom writing would be a great labour, and the filling of three or four pages of foolscap, a colossal undertaking. It is not probable that under such circumstances they would give more than the barest outline of the story; and in truth this is all they have done.

These stories were evidently poems, and they were related or sung by professional story-tellers, or minstrels, who would preserve the original poem in its purity, with all its beauty, life, colour and dramatic effect. But the very men who from their command of verbal language would become the most popular story-tellers are the ones who would probably find the greatest difficulty in putting on paper a story partly recited, partly acted, partly sung, with all the aids of intonation and gesticulation; and, as might have been expected, they have given us the merest skeleton outlines. These have been translated into Danish, and from Danish into English.

Suppose the plays of Shakspeare to have been transmitted to us in the same way—written down from memory by almost unlettered rustics, then translated through two foreign and utterly dissimilar languages, and they would appear in as poor a garb as these tales. But the grandeur of conception would remain wrapped up in homely words and phrases, like a beautiful woman clothed in rags, or a statue of Phryne, over which somebody should have thrown a beggar's cloak. So it is with these stories. Once you can seize the idea that is vainly struggling for utterance in the simple, homely, ill-chosen words, you are astonished at its originality and beauty.

I do not think there is a grander conception of remorse found in any literature than that contained in the story of the Blind Boy.

It readily falls into the dramatic form, and although very short it contains the material for a five-act tragedy; homely as is the language in which it is given, it is equal in sombre power of conception to Manfred, while it has none of the morbidness of Byron's masterpiece. Although it is probably founded on some event in real life, it would almost seem as though the Eskimo poet had constructed the story solely to develope the Eskimo conception of remorse. It is as follows :—

There was once a woman who had a son and a daughter. As the son grew up he became a hunter, and one day he killed a thong seal, from the skin of which he proposed to cut some thongs. But the mother wanted the skin for some other purpose, and she and the boy quarrelled about it.

Then she went and pronounced a charm on the seal-skin, and when he went to cut it up the end of a thong flew up, struck his eyes and made him blind.

The winter came on, they were destitute of seal meat, and had to live entirely on mussels, for the blind hunter could go hunting no more.

But one day a bear appeared at the window, and began to eat away the window pane, which was made of skin. The mother and daughter fled to the other side of the house, but the stripling asked for his bow. His sister gave it to him; he bent it, asked her to take aim for him, and then he shot and killed the animal. The mother said, "Thou hast missed." But the sister whispered, "Thou hast killed the bear."

They had now plenty of meat, but the mother

refused to give the boy any, pretending that as he had not killed the bear there was none, and only gave him mussels. But the sister gave him his share of the bear-meat in secret.

Finally, in the spring, a flock of wild geese restored the boy's sight, and he resumed his hunting occupations.

He with his sister used to go out on the edge of the ice where the seals and white whales (a kind of dolphin) were seen, and he would kill them with his harpoon. He had no hunting bladder, but he used to tie the harpoon line round his sister's waist instead, and when the animal was struck, they would drag it up on the ice by means of the line.

One day he asked his sister, " Dost thou like our mother ? "

She made no answer, but upon his repeating the question she replied,—

" I am fonder of thee than of her."

" Then to-morrow," he replied, " she shall serve us for a bladder."

The next day he accordingly proposes to his mother that she should help in the hunt, and to this she consents without the slightest suspicion. He ties the line round her waist as he had done to his sister, but she now begins to grow frightened at " the look that is in his eyes," and when she sees him preparing to throw the harpoon, she cries,—

"My son, choose a small whale, choose a small one."

Just then a large white whale rises to the surface of the water at the edge of the ice near his feet. He throws his harpoon into the animal, and then lets go the line.

The whale instantly begins to drag his mother towards the edge of the ice, she struggling with all her might to get free, and crying out for a knife to cut the line.

But the son only reproaches her with her cruelty in having made him blind, and says, "This is my revenge."

Then she cries out, "Oh my ullo! my ullo! it was I that suckled thee, it was I that suckled thee." And this she continues crying until the whale drags her into the water. She floats for a few moments on the surface, still crying, "Oh my son, it was I that suckled thee, it was I that suckled thee;" then disappears for ever.

The brother and sister gaze a few minutes at the spot where she went down, and then, terror-stricken, turn and flee.

But the cry of their mother continues ringing in their ears, and follows them wherever they go.

They finally fly from the village to the interior of the country, far away from any human kind, with this voice still pursuing them—still ringing in their ears, "It was I that suckled thee, it was I that suckled thee !" like the refrain of " Macbeth shall slee p no more," in Shakspeare's sublime tragedy.

They disappear, and nobody who knew them ever sees or hears of them again.

But they are not dead.

Their death would not carry out the Eskimo idea, and the poet has added one more act to the tragedy in which there is a grandeur of conception not unworthy of Shakspeare himself.

The event recorded in this act takes place a long time afterwards ; nobody knows how long. It may be a hundred years, for all, even the children who knew the matricides, have grown old and died. The tradition of the crime is almost forgotten.

The scene is laid in the interior of the house of the *angakok*, or priest-magician. It is night—a winter night in the arctic, with an arctic moon throwing its glamour over the plains and mountains of ice and snow. Inside the house the priest magician is performing a conjuration, and the people are gathered around, silent and trembling, listening to his muttered incantations.

Suddenly they hear a cry outside, and the *angakok*, says " Something evil is approaching."

They go to the door and look out. There they behold a gigantic hunter a little distance away, standing in the moonlight. His hair is white as the snow on which he stands, and it hangs down over his shoulders in long silvery locks.

But his face is black as night.

They watch him for a moment, and he gazes at them with burning, fiery eyes.

Then the *angakok* comes forward and asks the stranger who he is, and what he wants.

The other replies,—

" Do you not know me ? "

They answer in the negative.

Then he asks,—

" Do you remember the son who used his mother for a hunting bladder ? "

A very old woman then remembers hearing her mother talk about the crime when she was a very little child.

The hunter replies,—

" I am that man, and I still live."

Then he tells them something of the life of himself and his sister have lived since that time ; says they are still suffering all the tortures of remorse as on the day of their flight; that he has been driven by some mysterious power to come and denounce himself to the people that the crime may not be forgotten, and —fearful retribution—during all this life of three generations, day and night, the voice of their murdered mother has been always ringing in their ears,—

" Oh, my son, it was I that suckled thee, it was I that suckled thee ! "

Then he disappears, and is never heard of more.

CHAPTER XI.

ESKIMO JOE.

WHEN Captain Allen Young decided to undertake an Arctic voyage, one of the first men he engaged to go along with him was Joseph Eberbing, better known to the world as "Eskimo Joe." Joe arrived in due time, and shipped in the PANDORA as able seaman, hunter, and interpreter; but his accomplishments in the latter capacity proved to be somewhat limited; for although to all appearance a master of the Eskimo tongue, and speaking its various

JOE IN FLEET STREET.

dialects more or less fluently, he knows scarcely any English. This somewhat impairs his usefulness as interpreter, as it is almost as hard to understand his interpretation as it is the original expression in the mouth of a wild Eskimo.

On the outward voyage I was rash enough to undertake to learn the Eskimo language, with Joe for a teacher, an enterprise which I may as well confess resulted in an ignominious failure. It proved to be the most heart-breaking work I ever undertook; partly because the structure of the language is so utterly different from that of any other, and I had been unable to obtain a copy of either of the three or four grammars that have been written on it, but principally because Joe's vocabulary is very limited and meagre, and his ideas of the meaning and uses of the English verb are of the most vague and indefinite description.

But if I did not learn much of the Eskimo language, I learnt a good deal about Joe himself, and he proved to be by far the most attractive study of the two. For Joe is one of the most interesting and pleasing characters I ever met. It took me some time to discover that there was any more in him than appears at first sight, for he is naturally of a retiring disposition, which, with the fact that he speaks little English, and knows that he is liable to be misunderstood and even laughed at, makes him reticent and reserved.

There is, besides, a quiet dignity and gravity about him which effectually repels anything like idle curiosity. He resents the idea of being regarded in the light of the mere show, which people are only too apt to behold in a poor Eskimo. It was only after a long series of exasperating lessons in his native tongue, which usually ended in a talk about Captain Hall and the Polaris Expedition, that I won his confidence.

The first thing Joe did when he came to London, although he had absolutely no clothes except what he wore on his back, was to buy an umbrella, in which investment he spent, I think, his last penny. It is true that in the climate of London an umbrella is not the least useful thing one could have, but I do not think Joe was moved by any considerations of weather or fear of rain in making this acquisition. I am inclined to the opinion that he bought it because he looks upon an umbrella as the highest expression of civilization, and, as such, a right and proper thing for every man to have. For Joe professes a great admiration for civilization, and everything pertaining thereto. He would walk about the streets of London with the umbrella in his hand, viewing everything with an admiring though critical eye, and a grave, complacent air that was very pleasant to behold.

"London—big place," he would say, "pretty good noise—plenty buggy—hansom—go fast— two wheels—hurt him head—not hear speak pretty good—streets stony—pretty crooked—not find him right road hotel—not pretty easy— plenty men want speak me—not know him."

By which I understood him to say that— "London is a very large and beautiful city, but that the noise, however, is deafening and terrible, owing to those strange-looking vehicles the hansom cabs, of which there are an infinite number, and that, mounted on two wheels, go dashing over the stone-paved streets with such velocity that the uproar actually hurts your head, and at times prevents your hearing yourself speak. The streets, too, are very intricate and complicated, so much so, that it is almost impossible to find one's way about, and very difficult to find one's hotel. There are a great many people who want to speak to me, but as I see they are prompted by mere idle curiosity, I repel their advances, and decline to enter into any conversation further than is absolutely required by the laws of politeness."

He was not in very good health when in London, just before starting. His face was thin and hollow, and he had a disagreeable cough, which was probably caused partly by the warmth of the summer, but principally, I am afraid, by an inordinate use of tobacco, of which he is as great a smoker as General Grant. "By'n bye git him little seal-meat, then all right," he remarked, in reference to this cough; and his predictions were quickly fulfilled. We had no sooner got amongst the ice, and killed a seal, than he began to grow fat, his cheeks began to puff out, and his whole expression to change. Whether it was the seal-meat, or the cold, bracing, icy air, and healthy active life, or all those things together, I am unable to say, but certain it is that Joe was another man from that time forth.

It was pleasant, on a bright sunny day, when the ship was gliding almost silently along over the smooth, still water, and slipping now and then noiselessly past some huge iceberg, to get Joe to talk about Captain Hall and the POLARIS Expedition. If it were his watch, and there was nothing to do, I would generally find him leaning against the rail, or a boat, smoking his pipe, and watching the sea. His face always wore a sedate, grave expression, which was, however, tempered by a gentle, good-natured look, that made it a very pleasant face to see, in spite of its Mongolian features.

" Joe," I would say, perhaps, " how would you like to stay out here all winter ? "

" Don' know," he would reply; " long time— stay all winter—think better go home—like see Hannah."

" You are lonesome without Hannah, are you ? " I ask.

" Yes—little."

" You wouldn't like to winter, then, would you ? "

" Oh, yes, if Cap'n Young winter I like winter too. But think better winter New York."

" You wintered a good many times with Captain Hall ? "

"Yes; five, six, seven winters Cap'n Hall."

"How did you like Captain Hall?"

"Like him vely much—vely much; he vely good man—good to me; vely good to me. No other friend like Cap'n Hall."

Then, after a pause, looking away out to sea,—

"Dead now."

"Do you think, Joe," I ask after a moment, "if Captain Hall had lived, that he would have gone very much farther north?"

"Yes, think he do it—he want go furder—North Pole—you know—nobody on ship un'erstan' Cap'n Hall vely well—he think—read good deal. Nobody know him pretty good; vely good heart—give everything go North Pole. Want to go good deal—nobody un'erstan' him."

"Joe, what was the reason you did not all go on to the North Pole after Captain Hall died?"

"No cap'n; nobody cap'n. Cap'n Budding, he cap'n. Captain Tyson, he cap'n. Doctor, he cap'n too. Mr. Chester, cap'n. Mr. Myers, cap'n; me cap'n; everybody cap'n—no good."

"Why didn't Captain Buddington go?".

"Guess he got about enough—not want go no furder—maybe couldn't—don' know.

"What kind of man is Captain Buddington?"

"Vely good man—like him vely much—like Mrs. Budding' too—good friend Hannah—come to see her—help her—tell her what to do."

I asked him one day about that unfortunate

affair Captain Hall had one day with the four sailors of a whaling ship, whom he employed to go with him in an attempt to reach King William's Land. As is well known, these men mutinied, and Hall shot one of them.

"You heal (hear) about that too?" he asked, when I mentioned it to him.

"Yes," I replied, "a little, not much; how was it?"

"Want to take him boat—Cap'n Hall want boat heself—speak him not take boat—men not mind—all go down—see boat—one man get in—Cap'n Hall shoot him."

"What did the others do then?"

"Run back house—get guns, shoot Cap'n Hall —no gun there" (with a chuckle)—"I take him— hide him—no can't find him gun."

"Then what did they do?"

"Everybody shake hands."

"What did they do that for?"

"Vely good friends. Do what Cap'n Hall speak him. Say Cap'n Hall, you good man—we wrong—not take him boat no more—all right."

"What did they say to you?"

"Me all right too—good friend—Hannah all right—everybody all right—shake him hand."

"Did the man who was shot die quick?"

"Die after while—pretty soon—same day."

"Did he say anything after he was shot?"

"I never heal (hear) him say nothing—pretty

bad—plenty hurt him—not can speak—think he not know much—everybody very sorry—die after while—bury him."

. I asked him once if they had seen any Eskimos on King William's Land. He said they had, and that they were at first disposed to be hostile.

"Men all come out meet us—no women—no children—bad sign—march like soldier—one after other—ten, fifteen—all carry spear—some, knife tied stick—don know where he learn him—never see Eskimo march that way."

"What did they say?"

"Say want to fight."

"What did you say then?"

"We speak him—not want to fight—not come fight—come find white man lost—Franklin."

"What did they do then?"

"Throw down spears—hold up hands—say all right—we not fight—friends—then women, children all come out see us—speak, go in house—give us plenty seal meat."

To my questions about what the Eskimos would probably do with Franklin's papers, if they found any, he said,—

"Think give him children play with him—after while tear him up—burn him."

The most interesting talks I had with him were, however, about the winter on the ice with Tyson's party. He speaks very kindly of everybody in this party, but his feelings seem to be rather a

compound of pity and forgiveness than of friendship, and the truth is that Joe had a good deal to
pity as well as to forgive in their behaviour towards
him.   I have just been reading over again the old
accounts of that wonderful winter on the ice, as
given in the papers by Captain Tyson and his
comrades; and I must say that I could scarcely
repress my indignation when I saw that the name
of Joe is not even mentioned.   They tell us how,
when they found there was no hope of reaching
land, they built snow-houses, in which they lived
all the winter; how they hunted; how they suffered
from the cold; how they shot seals and bears and
birds, with which they eked out their store of
ship's provisions; how, when they were once out
of food of all kinds, they managed to kill a great
Ugjuk seal; how another time, when they had not
tasted anything for thirty-six hours, they killed a
bear, which was sent in their way, and which supplied them with food for a few days more; and we
melt with pity and admiration at the recital of
such steady, undaunted courage and fortitude.

A long time afterwards it turns out that it was
Joe who built them their snow-houses; that it
was Joe who hunted for them through the long
terrible winter; that it was Joe who killed so
many seals; that, in fact, nobody else but Joe
and Hans killed a single seal; that it was he who
killed the big Ugjuk when they were at the point
of starvation; that it was Joe who killed the bear,

without which they must all have died; that it was in fact Joe, and Joe alone, who saved the lives of the whole party.

And yet there is not a word of Joe in all the first accounts of the disaster. He is incidentally referred to as one of the "natives," and we are left to infer that they, with their children, were dreadfully in the way. It is true that a long time afterwards, when the journals of some of these men were published, journals written at the time when the danger was still before them; when Joe was feeding them from day to day like children; when he gave them every moment a fresh display of skill and hardihood, cool courage, and simple devotion to duty; when the impulse was still warm in them, we find an acknowledgment of their debt to Joe, in words that overflow with gratitude, and bear an impress of sincerity and truth.

Herron says in his journal, "Joe is very much to be praised, also his wife Hannah. We may thank them and God for our lives, and for the good health we are in. We could never have got through thus far without them. If we ever get out of this difficulty, they can never be too much paid." Tyson also renders Joe a tardy kind of justice in his journal, but, even here, the passages referring to the Eskimos are written in a carping tone. These "natives," he says, were employed as hunters for the expedition, and paid for that purpose, and therefore they were doing nothing more than their duty." But when the danger was over, when these men were safe aboard a good strong ship, and there was no more need of a seal-hunter, they appear to have forgotten Joe. These noble white men evidently did not think it worth while to speak of so poor a creature as an Eskimo—a kind of negro—who had saved their lives.

It must not be supposed, however, that Joe looks upon them as ungrateful. I sounded him on that point, but he said,—

"They all vely good men—like me good deal—meet him—say Joe—how you do—you save our life—come take a drink—give cigar sometimes too." And in this he seemed to think that they were very generous.

"Did they ever try to go out and kill seals?" I asked him.

"Kill him seal. No! never go out house—try keep warm—afraid go out—pretty cold—vely weak "—(with a great deal of contempt)—"not know how kill him seal—nothing but starve."

It seems that they not only never went out to look for seal themselves, but that when Joe would bring in one, they would often take it and divide it up in their own way, giving him just as much as they thought he ought to have. Hans used to object to this, and more than once threatened to run away and leave them to shift for themselves;

but Joe, whom he obeyed in everything, made him stay. Hans, besides, had little success as a hunter, and fully nine-tenths of the seals brought in, were killed by Joe. When Joe killed the big Ugjuk seal, they took it into their heads that he was trying to cheat them out of the liver, because he told them it was not good to eat. The liver of the Ugjuk seal, like that of the bear is poisonous, while of other seals it is a great delicacy. They therefore determined to eat the liver. Joe's account of the result was very amusing.

"After while, all sick—skin all come off face, look very bad—one man black—nigger-man"—(there was a negro in Tyson's party)—"after while little skin come off here—little there—then he spotted—by'n by skin all come off—then he white man—he! he! he! he! he!" And his sharp black eyes twinkled, his face expanded, and his sides shook with half-suppressed laughter, as the picture of the negro turning into a white man, by eating Ugjuk liver recurred to him.

Tyson says in his book that Joe and Hans were afraid of being killed and eaten by the men, and that he himself suspected some of them of this design. Indeed, Herron says in his journal, "I hope we won't be reduced to cannibalism; but if the Lord wills it, we must try and submit."

This pious expression of submission to the

possible necessity of eating the man who was
providing for them is highly edifying.

When I asked Joe about this, he only laughed.

" Kill me ! no danger, kill me—not get any
more seal—know better—try kill me—take
Hannah—run away—build house—kill him plenty
seal for me and Hannah and little Ponney. Poor
little Ponney dead now "—and he looked very
sad.

Little Ponney, Joe's child, died some time after
their return to America.

" Captain Tyson seemed to think they were
going to eat you and Hans, and the women and
children," I said.

" Maybe Captain Tyson think so—I not think
so—I not afraid o' that, couldn't do it."

" But, Joe," I said, " why didn't you take
Hannah and little Ponney, and go away off on the
ice somewhere, build a house, and catch seals for
yourself? Three or four seals would have been
enough for you all winter. You must have killed
sixty or seventy."

" All die."

" All who would die ? "

" Captain Tyson and everybody."

" But they sometimes wouldn't give you some
of the seals you had killed ? "

" No, that not so—always give me little—sometimes not much—Hans he not like that."

" But why didn't you run away, Joe ? "

"Cap'n Hall not like that—say—Joe, you come with me—you kill him plenty seal for expedition—I come to hunt him seal, reindeer, bear."

"But Captain Hall was dead!"

"Yes; dead now. Cap'n Hall good man; *good* man. If Cap'n Hall alive, *he* not run away. I not run away neither."

I took his hand, and shook it involuntarily, saying, however,—

"In your place I would have run away, Joe."

"What for run away? If men all die, what I speak him Sec'ry Robeson when get home America? Before start—Sec'ry Robeson—he say—Joe, you hunt him plenty seal—kill him plenty bear, reindeer—by'm by—I come back—men all dead—Sec'ry Robeson speak him—He say, Joe, you bad man—you no do right—Sec'ry Robeson good man—vely good man—then I feel pretty bad—I no like that—no good."

It will be seen that Joe has very good old-fashioned ideas on the subjects of honesty and duty, even though he does not speak English with all the correctness and fluency which could be desired. I have endeavoured to give his own words as nearly as possible, because Joe's talk is a part of himself, and once you get accustomed to it, there is a certain charm in his rugged inter-jectional English.

Usually, when a savage is brought within the

influences of civilization, he becomes degraded and depraved, and soon unites in himself all the vices of a civilized and of a barbarous state, with the virtues of neither. This has not been the case with Joe ; he appears to have dropped all his savage vices, if he ever had any, and to have acquired only the virtues of civilization, thus solving in his own person a problem which usually takes three or four generations to work out.

He had been with Hall for several years, and Hall, who was one of those rugged, honest, devout, sincere men, an old-fashioned believer in right and wrong, seems to have implanted his principles in Joe. Joe appears to try, even now, to be like " Cap'n Hall," and always to do as he thinks Hall would have done. I believe it was in trying to imitate him, in holding up Hall as a model for himself, that this poor uneducated Eskimo learned how to become a hero—a hero, too, of the grand and noble type. There is not in the whole history of Arctic Exploration, and it is full of acts of courage, of fortitude, noble devotion, anything that surpasses the heroism of this simple Eskimo.

I defy anybody to read the evidence contained in the report of the Secretary of the United States Navy, Captain Tyson's journal, and the journals of the other men, without feeling a generous glow of admiration for the sturdy, uncomplaining fortitude, the cheerful hopefulness in the midst of despair, when the lives of the whole party depended alone upon his unaided exertions; for the cool courage and steady hand, when he knew that if he missed his shot, the whole party, his wife and child included, must perish; for the quiet, unconscious heroism displayed by Joe throughout.

Day after day, if the word "day" can be used in connexion with what for a great part of the time was total darkness, during the long cold winter, with the thermometer fifty degrees below zero, Joe went out to hunt. He would remain for hours in the darkness, and driving snow-storms, waiting beside some hole in the ice for the appearance of a seal. No number of failures seemed to discourage, no length of waiting to weary him. Storm and darkness, wind or bitter cold, it mattered not. He would return nine times out of ten with nothing, perhaps, but he would start out again and again; he would watch for hours, and even days, beside a seal-hole, until, at last, his patience would be rewarded by the appearance of the long-expected seal, when they were on the very verge of starvation.

Herron's journal is full of such entries as these:—

"*Wednesday, March 5th.*—Joe went out in the last blow; it seems he cannot stay in; he is a

first-rate fellow; we would have been dead men
long since, had it not been for him.

" *November 6th.*—Joe caught a seal, which has
been a godsend; we are having a feast to-night;
three-fourths of a pound of food being our allowance.

" 21*st.*—The natives caught two seals.

" 22*nd.*—Joe caught one seal; another good
supper we had.

" *Dec.* 20*th.*—Joe found a crack yesterday, and
three seals; too dark to shoot.

" 29*th.*—Joe shot a seal, which is a godsend, as
we are pretty weak; we have had a good supper,
thank God.

" *Jan.* 26*th.*—Joe caught a seal in a blow-hole
to-day; this will get up our strength, as we barely
live on the scoush.

" *Feb.* 20*th.*—We must soon get a good lead of
water running in shore, and so escape, or kill
seals; else our time in this world will be short.

" 21*st.*—Joe shot a seal.

" *April* 22*nd.*—Mr. Myer is starving; he cannot
last long in this state; chewed on a piece of
skin this morning that was tanned and saved for
clothing.

" Joe ventured off on the ice the fourth time,
and, after looking a good while from a piece
of iceberg, saw a bear coming slowly towards
us. He ran back for his gun. We all lay
down and remained perfectly still, Joe and Hans

going out some distance to meet the bear. Getting behind a hummock, they waited for him. Along came Bruin, thinking he was coming to a meal, instead of furnishing one himself. Clack, bang, went two rifles, and down went Bruin, to save a starving lot of men. The Lord be praised ! this is His heavenly work. We cannot catch a seal for the pash-ice, and we are in bad sealing ground. He therefore sends a bear along where bears are seldom seen, and we certainly never expected to find one. The poor bear was hungry himself; there was nothing in his stomach. Joe, poor fellow, was looking very much down on our account. Everything looks bright again now."

March 2nd.—Captain Tyson writes :—" Joe has shot a monster oogjook, a large kind of seal, the largest I have ever seen. It took all hands to drag him to the huts. Peter fairly danced and sang for joy. No one who has not been in a similar position to ours can tell the feeling of relief which his capture produced. How we rejoiced over the death of this oogjook it would be impossible to describe. It was indeed a great deliverance to those who had been reduced to one meal of a few ounces a day. Hannah had but two small pieces of blubber left, enough for the lamp for two days; the men had but little, and Hans had only enough for one day. And now, just on the verge of absolute destitution, comes along this monstrous oogjook, the only one of the seal species seen to-day, and the fellow, I have no doubt weighs six or seven hundred pounds. Truly, we are rich indeed. Praise the Lord for His mercies. A few dovekies were also shot, but the oogjook is the joy of our eyes. Our glorious oogjook proved on measurement seven feet nine inches in length from head to tail, excluding the latter; adding the hind flipper, he measured fully nine feet. What a godsend!

"17*th.*—Soon after sunrise I espied a large oogjook. Joe was at a distance, and not having had as much practice as he, and fearing I might not kill it with my inferior rifle, I beckoned Joe to come along with his Springfield. In the meantime, to keep the creature from slipping away, I commenced whistling. I whistled until Joe crept along to within shooting distance, and killed the oogjook. He has killed three seals to-day, but one sank and was lost.

"*Jan.* 16*th.*—Found the natives had shot a seal. It seems as though God lets one get to the verge of despair, and then sends some mitigating circumstance to relieve the gloom. I ordered the seal to be taken into Joe's hut to be divided; as he did the most towards getting the food, I thought this was right. One of the men, however, took it upon himself to take it into their hut. They have divided the seal to suit themselves, and I hope they are now satisfied; but it does seem hard on the natives who have hunted day after day in cold and storm, while these men lay idle on their backs, or sat playing cards in their huts, built by these same natives whom they thus wrong. A native will sometimes remain watching a seal-hole thirty-six or forty-eight hours before getting a chance to stroke, and if the first stroke is not accurate, the game is gone for ever.

" 19*th*.—Joe and Hans hunting, but it was blowing heavy and very cold. Joe says he tried to shoot, but that he shook so with the cold that he could not hold his gun steady, and that his fingers were so numbed that he could not feel the trigger, and so the seal escaped.

" 22*nd*.—Joe is not well, I hope he will not get down sick, for we depend greatly upon him. Though such a little fellow, he is a mighty hunter in his way.

" 29*th*.—The Esquimaux off as usual on the hunt. They do not stop for fog, cold, or wind. Were it not for little Joe, Esquimaux though he be, many, if not all of this party must have perished before now. He has built our snow-huts, and hunted constantly for us, and the seals he has captured have furnished us not only with the fresh meat so essential to our position, but without the oil from the blubber we could neither have warmed our food, nor had any means of melting ice for drink. We survive through God's mercy and Joe's ability as a hunter.

" *Feb.* 1*st*.—Little Puney, Joe and Hannah's

child, a little girl, is sitting wrapped up in a musk-ox skin; every few minutes she says to her mother, 'I am so hungry!' The children often cry with hunger; it makes my heart ache, but they are obliged to bear it with the rest.

"*7th.*—We have had some little trouble over the seal this evening. Hans, if he gets a seal, which is seldom, for he has shot but few, wishes to appropriate it all to his own family's use. He is a very thoughtless Esquimaux, or selfish; he is not a successful hunter, like Joe, nor has he Joe's sense. He does not know how to build a hut for himself, or, at any rate, he did not do it; Joe built it for him. He threatened this evening, not to hunt any more. He was hired, and will be paid if we ever get home, for the very purpose of hunting for the expedition; it is no favour on his part."

The thoughtlessness and selfishness of Hans consisted in wishing to give the game he had captured, to his starving wife and children.

"*19th.*—Saw only one seal to-day, Joe shot him. This seal the men took possession of, and divided as they pleased. Joe was very angry, which was no wonder. Joe and Hans are exposed many hours every day to the wind and cold, and it comes very hard that these idle men should take the seals from them."

Be it remembered that Joe was in no wise bound to stay with these men. He could at any moment—when they were huddled together in the house he had built for them, trying to keep a little warmth in their starved bodies, and afraid to stir out of doors—have picked up his few effects, and, with Hannah and the child, gone off fifteen or twenty miles on the ice, and there have built a snow-house for himself. Here he would not have been obliged to share the hard-earned spoils of his spear and gun with others; to take the food out of the mouths of his wife and child to give to a lot of men who, according to their own accounts, were ungrateful, and often unjust towards him, and who evidently looked upon him as a poor creature of an inferior race.

But, "Cap'n Hall not run away; I not run away neither."

And yet when these men were finally rescued, they did not, in the accounts they gave the papers, say a word about Joe, nor even mention his name.

When, on the publication of these journals, a long time afterwards, the truth did appear, it did not come out in such a way as to attract public attention. Joe speaks little English; his old friend, Captain Hall, was dead; and there was nobody to look after him.

Joe told me he has not received all his pay for the time he was engaged in the POLARIS expedition. I do not know how this is, as he speaks English so badly that it is impossible to get a clear idea of the contract he made, how much he was to get, nor what he actually did receive. But I think that either some collection agent got part of this money, or else that Hall had promised him a good deal more than his regular pay from the Government, a promise which of course he would have fulfilled, had he ever returned. As it is, Joe is cast loose on the world, with no means of gaining a livelihood, except by going with Arctic ships, and that he cannot always do. He is too light and small to do heavy work, and he has no trade; his only dependence now is Hannah, who is obliged to sew for a living.

If Secretary Robeson had systematically organized this POLARIS expedition with the intention of making it a failure, the arrangements, I think, could scarcely have been more perfect. In the first place he gave two foreign scientific gentlemen to Hall, to take charge of the scientific department, who, for the reason that they were highly educated in the best Universities of Europe, could not understand the rough-and-ready merits of Hall, and had in fact a good deal of contempt for him. The result was that they soon quarrelled, and that one of them at least mutinied before they had been long at sea. I use the word "mutinied" advisedly, for in a man-of-war he would have been put in irons. Hall was no seaman nor navigator, and could not of course handle a ship; but to make up for this, they gave him an old whaling captain, who was utterly unfit for the position,[1] who cared no more to reach the North Pole than to reach the moon, and who looked upon the whole business as the most extravagant nonsense; and yet this man, owing to Hall's ignorance of seamanship, was really commander of the expedition. As if this were not enough, they gave him a mongrel crew of Germans, Danes, Russians, English, and Americans, and then bundled them all off together to the North Pole. In this American expedition there were only four or five Americans, all told, and there were but two or three English. Thus many of the crew were unable to understand each other. Captain Tyson complains in his journal that the men were always talking German, and that he could not understand a word they said. An expedition organized in such a manner could only result in failure.

But there was one man who made amends for all these mistakes; one man whose heroism redeemed the faults of all the others, whose courage saved the expedition from ending in a terrible and frightful, as well as disgraceful, disaster. He was an Eskimo, a being of an inferior race, who spoke English badly. Secretary Robeson therefore discharged him when his services were no longer needed, without reward, without a shake of the hand, or word of thanks.

[1] See Appendix.

JOE ON HIS NATIVE HEATH.

[Page 160.

CHAPTER XII.

LEAVING THE WAIGAT.

WHAT a miserable, dirty, disreputable-looking ship
the PANDORA was next morning after coaling! A
dull, damp, heavy fog, that made the coal bluffs of
Kudliset loom up high and indistinct on the starboard beam, that seemed to hang about the shrouds
and rigging in festoons, and trickle down the ropes
in little streams and drop on the decks in puddles,
where it turned to ink in the coal-dust, which now
covered the ship like a thick coat of dirty, black
paint. Her decks, when she left Portsmouth,
bad as we then thought them, were clean and
respectable and orderly when compared to their
present condition. Coal everywhere, from the
jibboom to the taffrail; everything was covered
with it; you could not touch a rope without
having it trickle through your fingers in a thick,
dirty ooze, nor lay your hand on anything without
getting it painted black. It seemed to travel and
climb, too, for it went below and invaded the
wardroom and cabins, turning everything a dirty
black, and I found it on the shrouds at the main-

M

top. The PANDORA, in short, was reeking with coal, saturated with coal, drunk with coal; she had greedily gorged herself until she rolled and staggered deep down in the water, when we commenced getting her under way, and groaning as though protesting against being disturbed until she had digested her gluttonous meal.

The dogs ran about with drooping tails, and hair streaming with dirty, inky water, seeking in vain a place to lie down in; and even "Mr. Hogan," the pig, had changed his coat of white for one of sooty black, as though he had been disguising himself with a view of escaping to avoid attendance on a Christmas dinner to which he had long since been invited. In a short time each of us was transformed into a kind of cross between a coal-heaver and a chimney-sweep, and we went about glaring at each other like negro minstrels, with distended eyeballs that seemed to have suddenly turned all white.

But this was a state of things we had expected, and which we knew had to be endured until our deck-load of coal should be consumed, and we therefore made the best of it.

We got out of Waigat Strait during the day, and following the coast of Greenland, were soon favoured by light breezes blowing from the south, south-west, and south-east—almost the first fair winds we had had since leaving England.

We got into Upernivik on the morning of the

13th, but did not drop anchor, as Captain Young only proposed to stop long enough to leave letters and buy, if possible, a couple of dogs. The Governor soon came off in his boat, kindly bringing with him his meteorological journal, by which we were enabled to see what had been the direction of the winds during the last three months—an important factor always to be taken into consideration in ice navigation.

It is upon winds more than anything else that navigators depend for breaking up the ice and opening the way to the higher latitudes within the Arctic circle. If strong northern winds prevail during the early part of the summer, then the ice which is breaking up will be driven south through Hudson Bay and Davis Strait into the broad Atlantic, and the northern waters will be found in August and September quite clear. If, on the contrary, the winds blow mostly from the south, the ice will move out very slowly, or perhaps not at all, and the northern seas will remain closed until the rapidly returning winter locks them up again for another year.

We found, upon looking over the Governor's journal, that northern winds had been blowing steadily from the 22nd of April until the 1st of June, and that during the months of June and July they had for the most part prevailed, with only an occasional breeze from the south, which had, however, never lasted long. The probabilities then were that the ice would have been all driven south from Melville Bay and the north part of Hudson Bay, and that this would be a favourable season for Arctic navigation.

The Governor informed us that the English expedition had sailed from here on .the 22nd of July, having only stopped one day to get a number of dogs.

It was blowing and raining hard all the time we were here, giving promise of a south-west gale; and Captain Young, anxious to get out to sea again declined the Governor's repeated invitations to go ashore. We therefore, after getting two more dogs, which were sent off to us, put to sea, having stopped only two hours; and all we saw of Upernivik was in passing glimpses through the driving rain.

Three or four little houses, perched on a round knoll, behind which rise some mountains that appeared at that time to be covered with a thin carpet of grass or moss, make up the village ; and it is situated on one of a number of little islands which hem it in on all sides, and make its access somewhat difficult without a pilot. It is a dangerous harbour with a north-west gale blowing, as it is not sufficiently protected on that side; and the American man-of-war, the JUNIATA, when feeling her way in, had to drop anchor in eighty-five fathoms of water, to avoid running ashore! Whether she ever got it up again is not stated.

Upernivik was the last Danish station at which we expected to touch, and we had now seen our last of civilization until we should return. We still hoped to have one more chance of sending letters by some whaler we might meet in Lancaster Sound, but this hope was a faint one, as the whaling ships usually leave there about the 1st of August, and we were now at the 13th.

We stood out to sea far enough to be well clear of the land and then continued our course to the north under steam and sail, with foggy, cloudy weather and light variable winds, mostly from the south. The next morning the fog and mist cleared away, it turned out a beautiful day, and we found we were just off the great glacier which at this part of the coast, latitude 74°, comes down to the sea.

It is a great inclined plane, seventy or eighty miles long, and extends back to the interior in a smooth, icy slope that rises by a gentle incline as it recedes, until it mingles high up in the sky, two or three hundred miles inland. It was of a bright, pale, transparent yellow, like silver slightly washed with gold, and it was impressively grand and beautiful as it lay shining in the morning sunlight, a world of luminous ice. We were forty miles out to sea, and its foot, which presents a perpendicular wall of ice rising between one and two hundred feet above the water, was below the horizon, but we were all the better enabled to form an idea of the grandeur of the great glacier of Greenland; for, immense as was the mountain of ico that we now beheld, we knew it was nothing but a small corner of the great lone, silent, dreary world beyond!

CHAPTER XIII.

A BOOTLESS SEARCH.

AND now we enter Melville Bay, in the north-east corner of Baffin's Bay, a sea much dreaded of whalers, and a place of anxious apprehension for Arctic explorers; for it is the place on the great highway to the north which offers the greatest difficulties and dangers to navigation.

Baffin's Bay itself never gets quite clear of ice, as it is continually filled by that which comes down from Smith Sound, Jones Sound, Lancaster Sound, Barrow Strait, and Pond's Bay. All this ice moving down the middle of the great sea of Baffin keeps it filled up, leaving, however, a passage along the eastern and western shore, which in July is barely practicable for ships, and which in August and September often gradually widens from 100 to 200 miles, as the last of the ice moves slowly down the middle. But, again, it sometimes happens that Melville Bay never gets free, and it is often only toward the end of August that ships can get through.

The Fox was caught here about the middle of August, was carried down Baffin's Bay and Davis Strait, only finally getting free the following spring, having thus lost a year without accomplishing anything toward the task she had undertaken. The ice in Melville Bay is, therefore, so uncertain that it is a place of ill repute, and navigators always enter it with anxious forebodings, and the utmost caution.

Strange to tell, we had as yet seen comparatively little ice. With the exception of a few giant icebergs here and there, some aground, some drifting, and which rarely form any impediment to navigation, we had seen absolutely no ice since leaving Waigat Strait. It was in about this latitude that the Fox was so unfortunately beset, and yet here, where then was a vast sea full of floating ice, there was scarcely a speck to be seen. As Captain Young had predicted, the winds blowing continually from the north had already cleared out Melville Bay, and now we had only to sail forward on a sea as smooth as glass, over which the ship glided along as gently as though she had been on some little river. The days of the 15th and 16th were beautiful in the extreme, and I thought there could be nothing more delightful than navigating these still northern waters in such weather.

Up to this time we had had very little sport in the way of shooting, as we had seen no seals since we left the Spitzbergen ice, near Cape Farewell, and in truth they are rarely seen far away from the ice. Here, however, one evening Joe came running aft, with a pleased, excited face, to get his rifle, saying there was a bear swimming near the ship. Everybody made a rush for the guns, and in a moment a lively fire was opened on Bruin, who, however, swam off under this shower of bullets unharmed. In the meantime the Captain and Mr. Lillingston had lowered a boat and started after him.

It proved to be a close race, for the bear swam with a speed I had little suspected, looking around at his pursuers now and then and redoubling his exertions when he saw they were gaining upon him. I pitied the poor brute with all my heart, for he had not, of course, the ghost of a chance, and he swam hard for his life. Soon the boat had approached within ten feet of him. Then there were two reports, and he suddenly stopped swimming and lay lifeless on the water, shot through the head. It was certainly not very good sport, as the poor brute could in the water neither get away nor fight; but the truth is we were out of seal, and we needed him as a change from salt meat.

This bear betokened the presence of ice, for ice-bears, as these animals are sometimes called, never go very far away from it; and, sure enough, about ten o'clock at night, when the sun was still an hour and a half above the horizon, we suddenly came upon the ice. It was, however, not very formidable, as it was only in thin, loose floes, that offered little resistance to the sharp prow of the PANDORA. As often happens, however, when getting among the ice, we were soon enveloped in a thick fog, which prevented our making much progress as long as it lasted, and we did little during the night. The thermometer went down five degrees—from 37 deg. to 32 deg., the freezing-point,—in less than an hour.

When the fog cleared away, which it did very early in the morning, we found we were off Cape York, the north-west extremity of Melville Bay, with a stream of ice before us that looked suspiciously like a pack. We soon made out from the masthead, however, that it was only a tongue or point that extended a few miles south from Cape York, and which, in truth, usually keeps its hold on the land until very late in the summer.

Standing south along its edge for half an hour, we found, not a lead, but a place where it seemed less compact; and, as we could see the open water shining beyond at the distance of three or four miles, Captain Young pushed into it without hesitation, and the PANDORA was soon engaged in crushing her way through the loose, rotten floes that obstructed, but were powerless to completely bar the way.

It was very pleasant to climb to the foretop with the sharp, bracing sunny air blowing in one's face, and look down over the forechains and watch the ship's head as she threaded her way industriously through the floating ice field—now pushing laboriously through the soft " pash " ice, that seemed to hang on her and clog her with its dead, passive, stubborn resistance ; then knowingly making for a short lead of open water, that sometimes offered a narrow but unobstructed passage ; now darting suddenly to the right, to turn some heavy floe that doggedly barred the way ; again veering to the left, to get into a little open lake that invitingly offered itself ; and sometimes, when it was impossible to avoid the ice, dashing bravely at it, full speed, like a knight in armour, her long, sharp jib-boom seeming to pierce it like a lance and overthrow it, as it broke up and tumbled aside in great massive pieces—pushing, twisting, butting, squeezing, elbowing, wriggling herself through like a live and reasonable being.

The fat burgomaster gulls or " mollymawks " of the sailors came sailing around, beneath, in great airy circles, as you sat on your lofty perch, and down deep in the clear cold water the eye could follow the little auks that always dived at the approach of the ship, and watch them as they flew down deep beneath the surface with lowered head and outstretched neck, as easily as though they were gliding through the upper air.   Is not this

better than even a life of luxurious ease in the
dusty, sweltering cities of civilization ?

In an hour we were clear of the ice and out in
the open water beyond, the " North Water " of
Baffin's Bay. From here our course lay a little
south of west, to Lancaster Sound, which forms the
only practicable entrance to that labyrinth of
straits, sounds, bays, inlets, and islands on the
north coast of the American continent.

But instead of taking this direction the PAN-
DORA's head still pointed toward the north, and
all that day and the next, until six in the evening,
she kept steadily ploughing the waters northward against a strong head wind and sea, on the
track followed by all the exploring expeditions in
search of the Pole. This was the route followed
by Kane, by Hayes, by Hall, and last by the
English expedition of the present year.

On the evening of the 19th of August we were
at the Cary Islands, in latitude 76 deg., 100 miles
north of Cape York, and 100 south of Littleton
Island, where that part of the POLARIS' crew under
Captain Buddington passed their second winter.
We had come thus far out of our course to get
news of the ALERT and DISCOVERY.

Captain Nares had left a letter at Disko for
Captain Young, stating that he intended to touch
at the Cary Islands and leave there despatches
for the Admiralty, and this was the reason we had
come so far out of our course.

The north-west island of the group was the one he had fixed upon, and to this one we accordingly steered, in the teeth of a strong breeze from the north, which made it a somewhat difficult job to approach. At length the ship was hove to off the south side of the island, which rose in a high, irregular mass of stones and rock, bare and desolate, to the height of 700 feet above the water.

Although we were two or three miles out to sea, we could perceive on the top a cairn, that we immediately took to be the one left by Captain Nares, of which we were in search. A boat was lowered, and Captain Young, leaving Lieutenant Pirie in command of the ship, put off with Lieutenants Lillingston, Beynen, myself, and four or five sailors, taking two casks full of letters for the ALERT and DISCOVERY that we had brought from England, and which we proposed to leave here, as arranged with Captain Nares. Hoisting a sail, our sharp, light little shell of a whaleboat shot through the water like an arrow, and we were soon in a little bay, on a rocky beach, where we had some difficulty in landing.

We found ourselves at the mouth of a kind of valley covered many feet deep with large boulders and stones, worn round and smooth by grinding against each other as they are gradually forced down into the sea. Beneath could be heard the rushing of a little river formed by melting snow, and on either hand rose a mountain of broken stones and rock, heaped up in a steep, ragged slope, as though the island were one monstrous cairn built by a giant.

This ascent to the top proved to be a somewhat long and difficult one. It was easy to break one's legs scrambling over the round, smooth boulders that covered the little valley, and easier still to break your neck climbing up the steep mountain side on a ladder made of loose, sharp, broken, jagged stones, that threatened at every moment to start down in an avalanche and carry you with them to the bottom.

We at last succeeded in reaching the top, when we found not one, but two cairns within a few yards of each other. But, strangely enough, neither of these cairns proved to be the one we were in search of, although this was the exact spot Captain Nares had indicated. We searched the ground thoroughly, not only twenty feet magnetic north from each, as had been agreed upon, but in every direction, without discerning a trace of the expedition.

This was a grievous disappointment. We had lost two days, a fair wind, and several tons of coal to reach here, and had found nothing. Had we profited by the wind against which we had been steaming for the last two days, we might have been almost through Lancaster Sound by this time, if not stopped by the ice, to say nothing of the useless expenditure of coal, to us the most precious of minerals.

We concluded that Captain Nares had not been able to land when passing here, owing either to fog or ice, or perhaps a gale, and we reluctantly gave up the search. The two cairns proved to have been built by a whaler who had been here in 1867, as we learned from a paper he had left in a bottle hid away in the cairn.

He had also left a half-pint of rum, which, having undergone eight successive freezings and thawings, had become as rich and mild as some fine old Rhine wine. And we drank the whaling captain's health.

On the extreme north-west point of the island we descried another cairn down close to the water's edge, about three miles distant, and Mr. Beynen volunteered to go and examine it also. It took him quite two hours to go and return, while in the meantime the wind on the top of the mountain was blowing a hurricane from the north, which chilled us to the marrow of our bones.

We built up a wing to one of the cairns, to break the force of the blast, and crouched behind it. While waiting, Captain Young wrote a letter to be left here for Captain Nares in case he should send a boat down this far next summer, informing him where he would find the two casks of letters.

The view from the top of this island was very grand. Far below us we could see the PANDORA, looking as small as a child's toy-boat, in the great dark ocean of water that rose to the horizon far beyond; to the north the coast of Greenland, stretching away for miles and miles until it was lost in a line of purple haze that mingled with sea and sky, almost at Littleton Island, at the entrance of Smith Sound. And as far as we could see there was not a speck of ice; that far, at least, the way to the Pole was as clear of ice as the Mediterranean.

The ALERT and DISCOVERY must have passed up here nearly three weeks previously, but could hardly have got much farther than Littleton Island at this time.

Smith Sound is rarely open before the latter part of August; but as it was thought that Captain Nares intended to put the DISCOVERY into winter quarters, somewhere near Littleton Island, he would, of course, endeavour to reach there as early as possible. But it is not probable that he would start up Smith Sound much before the 1st of September. It has been the mistake of all the Arctic navigators who have attempted to reach the Pole by this route that they have started too early in the season. Where Kane and Hayes found in Smith Sound an impenetrable barrier of ice drifting south, Hall found two weeks later open water, and the probability is that, had he been ten days later, he would have found Robeson Channel as clear as Smith Sound. The disadvantage of starting too early is that the ice will be met drifting down before the northerly winds that usually prevail here, and the navigator is obliged to either put about and run before it, thus losing all the ground he has gained, or to take shelter in some little harbour along the coast. If he adopts the first course he has gained nothing by his early start, and besides has incurred the danger of getting beset in his moving pack and held until the season is past. If he adopts the second course he will be almost immediately frozen in by the ice which, even in August, often commences forming in sheltered bays and inlets, where it is undisturbed by the wind, when the channel, a short distance from the land is quite clear and open.

It would appear from the evidence of the officers of the POLARIS that not only Robeson Channel, but the water to the north into which it gives entrance, was open until late in the winter; and it is pretty certain that had the POLARIS been a few days later she would not have encountered the barrier which stopped her on the 31st of August. It would even appear, according to the evidence of Chester, Tyson, and Meyers, that on the 4th of September, when the POLARIS went into winter quarters, Robeson Channel was nearly clear of ice, and would have allowed the passing of the ship into the open water beyond had Captain Buddington been disposed to attempt it.

The English expedition will reap all the benefit

of Hall's experience, and as the season, owing to the long succession of northern winds which have blown during the whole summer, appears to be even a more favourable one than Hall had, there is little doubt that Captain Nares will take his ship to as high a latitude as it will ever be possible for a ship to reach.

At length Lieutenant Beynen returned, his search having proved a bootless one, and we prepared to descend to our boat, glad to escape the biting wind and the dreary desolation of the lonely, barren, shivering isle.

What a weird, barren, desolate, stony place it was! The peak on which we stood was 700 feet above the water, and we could see nearly all over the island, which was, perhaps, three or four miles in diameter, and resembled a huge heap of stones covered here and there with snow. The only sign of vegetation was two or three specimens of the little yellow flower we had seen at Disko. There was no sign of life to be seen, nor beast, nor bird, nor insect; silent and lonely and desolate it stood there in the cold, unnatural light of the midnight sun like some old battered, weather-beaten, crumbling but gigantic monument, mourning for a lost and vanished world.

The Cary Islands was the highest latitude we reached, seventy-six degrees, and this was the only time we saw the midnight sun. His lower limb barely touched the horizon, and then instantly commenced mounting again, rolling in a wide, low curve along the surface of the sea. The next evening we were so far south again that he set twenty minutes before twelve, and we saw him no more at midnight.

We left the two barrels of letters on a little knoll overlooking the bay where we landed, on the south side of the island, built a cairn to mark the spot, which could be easily seen from the sea, and put off to the ship with a breeze that turned into a gale as soon as we got out of the lee of the island.

CHAPTER XIV.

A PET BEAR.

RUNNING south all next day before a rattling
northern breeze, we arrived at the entrance of
Lancaster Sound on the morning of the 20th, and
soon were in sight of ice.

Here we had another bear hunt. Forty miles
away from any land we found an old she bear and
two cubs swimming about as leisurely as though
water was their natural element. A boat was
instantly lowered, and an exciting chase took place.
A fresh breeze was blowing at the time, which
caused a rough, chopping sea, and the bears struck
out to windward, as though they instinctively
knew this would put the boat at a disadvantage.

They appear to be very intelligent and affectionate animals. The old bear swam a short
distance ahead of the young ones, but kept
continually turning about, as if to encourage
them and urge them on. It was pitiful to see
the poor beasts swimming thus for life, without
a hope of escape, the more so as they appeared

to be quite aware of their danger, and made the
most desperate efforts
to get away. It was all
in vain. What chance
had they against four
stout pair of arms pull-
ing a light shell of a
boat that, under the
rapid stroke of the oars,
shot over the water like
an arrow? In ten mi-
nutes the boat had got
up within three or four
yards of them; there
were two shots, and
the old bear and one
of the cubs stopped
swimming, and lay life-

less on the water. Captain Young had shot one
and Lieutenant Pirie the other.

But they determined to capture the third, and
with much difficulty and not a little danger, Pirie
succeeded at last in throwing a running noose
over his head.

He resisted with all his might, setting up a
fierce howl, and trying to capsize the boat, which
he would very soon have succeeded in doing had
he but been able to get one paw over her thwarts.
Finding the boat was too swift for him, he tried to
hold back. He swam, and struggled, and dived,

and tore, and bit at the rope, and half drowned himself, howling savagely all the time. They at last brought him alongside, and fastened him up to the nettings, giving him line to swim about, while the bodies of the other two were dragged up over the side.

He watched the operation with strange, wild, intelligent eyes, as though wondering what his mother meant by going in so quietly, and, curiously enough, began trying to get in too. He was only a baby bear after all, and thought that if his mother went in it must be all right. ,

He did not resist when hauled over in his turn, but scrambled up willingly, snapping viciously at everybody, however, when he got a chance, evidently much frightened nevertheless. He was chained up to the side, but kept up a terrible howling until the body of the other cub, still warm, was thrown to him. He instantly sprang upon it, and began rooting and smelling at it, pushing it with his nose, uttering all the while a plaintive moan, and occasionally biting it gently as though trying to awaken it.

Then he lay down beside it, with his head on the body, and watched us with his sharp, inquiring, intelligent eyes, in an imploring way, as though asking us what we meant by treating him in that cruel manner. He howled hideously when the body was taken away from him, but consoled himself with the skin of the old one, which was thrown to him, and upon which he lay down and slept.

Poor little fellow! He was as frightened as a child by the terrible and powerful beings around him, and found a dreary kind of company in the skin of his dead mother.

We pushed forward steadily during the 20th and 21st, seeing only a little ice, and that was along the northern shore of Lancaster Sound, which we were now traversing. On the evening of the 21st, when off Cape Warrender, we were enveloped in a heavy cloud of fog, which came rolling off the land, and soon after we came into loose drift-ice. We could not see what might be before us, and we were obliged to heave-to and wait. As this fog and drift-ice probably betokened a pack, we kept off during the night, and worked slowly down toward the south coast.

When the fog cleared away next morning we found ourselves on the edge of an extensive pack, which seemed to cover the whole sound, and beyond which no water could be seen. So we stood again for the north shore, pushing through the loose ice here and there, but keeping outside the pack until two in the afternoon, when we were close enough to the land to see there was no more hope of a lead here than there was on the south side, and we therefore hove to again.

So much ice in Lancaster Sound in August is very unusual, and we were greatly disappointed at finding our way blocked, the more as it was already getting late in the season, and we had not yet arrived at the critical part of our voyage. However, there was nothing to do but wait patiently for a change.

An Arctic navigator can commit no greater mistake than to plunge into a pack beyond which he can see no open water. For the slightest movement of the ice is sufficient to make either advance or retreat impossible, so that after having made only three or four miles he may find himself beset for the winter, with open water in sight, which he would be able to reach had he not allowed his ship to get beset. The best plan is to wait, and the lightest wind will sometimes cause wonderful changes in the ice in a few hours.

We had proof of this upon the present occasion. The ship had been allowed to drift against a floe, to which she was moored, but we had not been here more than two hours when the ice began to move, and, before we knew it, we were almost caught by the loose floes which came drifting down upon us, threatening to jam us against the pack. It required some sharp dodging to get out of this trap, but we effected our escape with as little delay as possible, and again proceeded along the edge of the ice toward the southern shore.

A light southerly breeze had sprung up, and it was this which had put the ice in motion, driving it toward the northern shore. We were delighted with the view of open water here on the southern side of the sound, and, putting on sail and steam, began to force our way through. It was close, hard work, which tried the ship to the utmost; but towards evening we got fairly into open water, and then had the pack on our starboard beam. We were then fairly past the barrier, which but a few hours before had appeared impenetrable, having been delayed here just twenty-four hours.

Lancaster Sound was discovered by Baffin in 1616, and entered by Sir John Ross in 1818, and pronounced by him to be a bay, although he had scarcely entered it. It was afterward navigated by Parry, in 1824, who proved it to be a sound that connected with a strait, which he called Barrow, that in its turn conducted into a channel, which he named after Wellington, and another broad ice-bound sea, afterwards named Melville Sound. Lancaster Sound has of late years become a fishing-ground for the Dundee whalers, who generally come here in July, and sometimes push as far west as Regent Inlet. They leave about the 1st of August with the whales, and we met none of them; nor did we even see a single right whale, although there were many white ones and any number of finbacks.

CHAPTER XV.

REEFING TOPSAILS.

It is seven o'clock in the evening; we have just had tea, and we are all, except the skipper, sitting around the table smoking, while engaged in an angry discussion on the relative merits of French and English cookery, which has become for us a subject of absorbing interest. Suddenly we hear the voice of the captain overhead :—

"All hands on deck—shorten sail."

Pipes, cigars, and cigarettes are thrown aside, and we rush up the companion ladder. A snow storm ! A splendid one, that darkens the sky and brings on the night an hour before its time. The breeze has freshened until it promises a gale, and it becomes necessary to make all snug for the night.

"To'-gallant halliards let go."

Down drop the top-gallant yards, and the top-gallant sails begin to jerk and flap, as though determined to tear themselves into shreds and ribbons.

"Let go your sheets—haul up your clew-lines."

And we haul away with a will, while the snow whirls about over the deck in eddies, and flies through the rigging in great, soft white flakes like feathers. The lower corners of the sails climb up to the middle of the yards, where they meet.

"Buntlines."

We drop the clew-lines—seize the buntlines and pull away, looking aloft to watch the sails; and the soft white flakes beat gently in our eyes as though trying to blind us with kisses, and then melt and run down our cheeks in tears of chagrin at the failure. Now the sails are looped up in festoons, ready to be furled down snug to the yard.

"Hands aloft to furl to'-gallant sails,—let go the top-sail halliards—man the reef tackle;"— and the deck rattles to the trampling of many feet, as we rush about from rope to rope; the top-sail yards in their turn slip down the mast, and the top-sails suddenly begin to make tremendous leaps and jerks, in a mad effort to get away. They rattle and roar and flap against the mast, like two gigantic birds caught in a net, with a booming noise like thunder; while the snow whirls and dances about them, as if for very joy at the capture, and revels in the confusion and up-roar.

"Haul away on the reef tackle."

The captain's voice is scarcely heard in the noise; it seems to come from somewhere far away in the storm, like a vagrant voice wandering about without an owner. "He-oh-heave-oh—he-oh-heave-oh." Will we ever be able to haul the sails up close while they plunge and struggle in that fearful way?

"All hands aloft—close reef."

In a moment the shrouds are alive with sailors running up like so many squirrels; a moment later they are strung along the yards, and I see the active young "Tromp" at the weather earring, far out over the water. They lie down across the yard and hug them close, pulling at the refractory sail. How it leaps and tears and struggles! what a terrible deafening roar it makes! It is the dashing of breakers on a rocky shore, the booming of heavy guns, the sharp ear-splitting thunder-clap, the crashing rush of a hurricane through an oak forest, all mingled in a confused din and uproar that is awful. The top-sail has rebelled, and refuses to be enslaved any longer. It jerks at the yard with such tremendous force, that it would seem yard and mast must be carried away with nearly the whole of our crew, who are swinging aloft there in that perilous situation. Gradually, however, they reduce the monster to submission; slowly they haul it up and bind it down. But it is half an hour before they have finally secured it.

Then the order comes, "Haul out the sheets;" the sails are again spread, reduced to half their size, and the PANDORA is then snug for the night, under close-reefed top-sails.

It has taken us an hour to do this, and we are all aglow with the exercise, as well as the snow that beats in our faces, and we think there is no finer work in the world than reefing top-sails in a snow-storm.

The ship has already turned white; the snow is an inch thick on the deck, the rigging and cordage is festooned with it and the vessel looks like a moving forest of pine-trees in winter. All is still now that rebellious sails have been reduced to submission, and made to do their work, and the ship glides silently through the whitish obscurity, which is rendered strangely spectral by the thickly falling feathery snow.

The man at wheel is wrapped up until he looks as though he had been stuffed for roasting, and he has a very warm and comfortable appearance, with the binnacle light shining in his face. Here and there may be seen two or three more gleams of light that come up through the deck, and shining on the snow turn it into stripes of gold.

Below there is a bright coal fire in a miniature grate, throwing its ruddy glow over our miniature mess-room. All hands are sitting around the table smoking; the table itself is ornamented with divers glasses and bottles; there is a steaming flavour of punch, and the same animated discussion on the respective merits of French and

English cookery, which, I am sorry to say, has degenerated into a mere enumeration on the part of the disputants of all the good things they have ever eaten, or expect to eat, when they return to the far-off South. Such is one of many pleasant memories I retain of life in the Arctic.

On the morning of the 24th, when about opposite Regent Inlet, we were again enveloped in a dense fog, which settled down over us like a huge wet blanket, and clung to us for two days, almost stopping our progress. We groped our way cautiously through Barrow Strait like a blind man, for we were now so near the magnetic pole that the compass was utterly useless.

Of all the perils that beset the seaman in the Arctic there are none so great as that of a fog, because a fog seems to include every danger. It hides alike sun, moon, stars, and coast-lines. The sailor can see nothing. He may be within fifty yards of a rocky coast, going straight towards it, without knowing anything of his danger. He may run directly into a line of reefs, or strike a rock, or go ashore without a moment's warning. No matter therefore what his hurry, how necessary it may be to get forward, how pressed he is for time, he is obliged to heave to and wait—wait when he knows that every hour lost may cost him months. No human power can remove or destroy a fog, or produce the slightest effect upon it. Slight and insignificant as it may appear considered as a barrier, it holds him in toils from which there is no escape. He is entangled in an impalpable net that he cannot even touch; that mighty steam giant his ship, with its ribs of iron, its sinews of steel, is caught as in a spider's web, and is as helpless as a fly. It may hold him for hours or for days; he never knows how long he is to be imprisoned, and when he will be set free.

At length, about five o'clock in the evening, the fog suddenly opened, and showed us, at the distance of half a mile, a tremendous wall of rock several hundred feet high, which, in the slowly-lifting mist, seemed to rise into the clouds. When the fog quite cleared away we found we were on the north side of Barrow Strait, just at the entrance of Radstock Bay and in sight of Beechey island, which point we were trying to reach.

We had actually groped our way through nearly the whole length of Barrow Strait, without compass or sun, for two days, and then found ourselves almost at the very point we were in search of. If luck, it was very good luck, but there must have been some good management on the part of our captain and navigating officer.

CHAPTER XVI.

OUR DUMB COMPANIONS.

I HAVE said little as yet about the dumb companions of our cruise. It is a curious fact that people on a long voyage of this kind form a peculiar friendship with whatever animals may

MR. HOGAN.

be on board, and take an interest in them which they would scarcely credit themselves with when on shore.

Cut off from the outside world, your attention is concentrated upon the few square yards to which you are confined; you look at everything as with a microscope, and you are astonished to see that this little world is so full of interest. So it was on the PANDORA that the dogs, the pig, the cats, and the bear became subjects of conversation and interest, quite as absorbing as the opera, theatre, and politics would be on shore.

I am afraid I shall have to upset some good old traditions about Arctic dogs. Most writers describe them as irreclaimably savage brutes, little better than wolves, always ready, should the occasion offer, to sup on their masters, and only kept down by a constant application of the lash.

Any dog will become savage and ferocious if cruelly beaten and brutally treated by his master. Not dogs only, but men have been known to eat human flesh when driven thereto by the terrible pangs of hunger. We had ample proof that these ill-famed Arctic dogs, with kind treatment, are the most affectionate and grateful animals in the world. One of our dogs—a young one—frightened at being dragged in over the ship's side, bit Mr. Pirie's hand through in the most savage manner, mangling it so that he was unable to use it for several days.

Most people would of course have beaten the brute half to death, "to teach him better," and, in return, he would have repeated the bite upon the first opportunity. But Pirie only swore a little, and would not allow the dog to be touched. "I would bite too," he said, "if I were to be dragged about in that manner by a lot of people I did not know;" and he set about trying to conciliate the dog. In two days this same savage little brute, as soon as Pirie came on deck of a morning, would jump on him, fawn upon him, and lick his hand—the same hand he had bitten—in the most affectionate manner.

When the dogs first came on board they were, of course, very much frightened, and they cowered away in a corner, growling and trembling, whenever anybody approached them ; but they soon came round under kind treatment. In three days they had grown extremely fond of us, and would come running up of a morning when we came on deck, wagging their tails, leaping upon us, and putting up their heads to be caressed.

It was touching to see how quickly this universal canine instinct of love for the human race was developed in these poor brutes, that had never received a kind word, nor a caress, nor anything, indeed, but kicks and blows, from human kind. It was all the more strange as they were always fed by Joe, and it was rarely that any of us gave them anything to eat.

They repaid us well for our care, for they were a source of infinite amusement. The first four we got at Yuryarasusuk. One of these was an old fellow; the other three were young. They were all a dark brown colour, with short, sharp ears, like those of a fox, a heavy fur coat, and the old one, especially, had a magnificent, thick, heavy collar, and a long, bushy tail, which gave him a very majestic and dignified appearance. This, together with the fact that his sway was undisputed by the other dogs, suggested " King " as a name for him—a name which he soon learned to answer.

Two of the young ones were so much alike that we could not at first tell them apart, until at last somebody observed a funny peculiarity with regard to them. This was that one curled his tail up over his back to the right, the other to the left, a difference which enabled us to distinguish them. They were therefore called " Port " and " Starboard " respectively.

These three—" King," " Port," and " Starboard "—were very good friends, and evidently belonged to the same family; but the fourth appeared to be a stranger, and positively refused to associate with the others. For a time he kept all alone by himself, snarling, showing his teeth, and growling whenever one of the others approached.

We at first thought he did this because he was a misanthropic, ill-natured brute, who took sceptical views of life, and scouted all ideas of fun and good fellowship; that he was a sad dog, in short, and we therefore called him "Snarley." It turned out, however, that he was no more ill-natured than the others, but that the two young ones, whenever they got a good chance, were in the habit of "double-banking" on him and thrashing him. He had therefore good reason to be of a misanthropic and suspicious turn of mind; but after Port and Starboard had been soundly beaten for their disgraceful conduct, they all became better friends, and finally Snarley was admitted into the general mess.

At Upernivik we had bought two more dogs. They, however, formed a separate and distinct camp, and never mingled with those from Yuyarsusuk.

One of these was a most disreputable, dirty, villainous-looking dog, and was named "Dublin," for what reason I could never make out, and he turned out to be a very low character indeed. He was always thieving and getting into trouble, and was evidently regarded with much contempt by the Yuyarsusuk dogs. But he nevertheless managed, with his comrade, to hold his own in the face of superior numbers, for he proved to be a most desperate and reckless character in a fight. His pluck made him a great favourite with the men, one of whom took him under his especial protection ; and when this man came to take his turn at the wheel, Dublin always came aft—he and his companions generally kept forward of the mainmast—and, despite the growls of the others, who looked upon him as an intruder, sat down gravely beside his protector, and remained there until the end of the watch.

The cleverest of them all was the one we had called Starboard, who proved to be a dog of infinite jest and most excellent fancy, and afforded us a great deal of amusement.

He was the most intelligent and affectionate dog, where human kind were concerned, I think I ever saw, but he nevertheless had some grave defects of character. He was of a very jealous disposition, and when he saw anybody patting one of the other dogs, he would always come up, and, while wagging his tail and pretending to smile in the most unconscious and innocent manner, would quietly crowd the other dog aside—elbow him out of the way in short, and thus get all the petting to himself. Naturally the other dogs used to resent this conduct, and it often ended in a pitched battle between the legs of the person whose favours were thus disputed.

Starboard did not possess that open frankness and boldness of character one would naturally have expected in an Arctic dog that had never been brought within the debasing influences of civilization. He seemed, on the contrary, to have a liking for crooked ways, and was rather inclined to compass his ends by guile and chicanery than by open, honest combat. This disposition often degenerated into a low cunning that would not have been unworthy of an English fox.

One day the whole ship's company were witness to the means he employed to steal a bone which Joe had given to one of the other dogs. This dog was rather small and somewhat timid, unless Dublin—her natural protector—were there to take her part; but Starboard knew that if he tried to take the bone by force, Joe would interfere in an unpleasant manner with a whip. So he went to her with a smiling face and a wagging tail, and, leaning against her, began to push her aside in the most friendly way possible. She, not quite understanding this manœuvre, let go the bone, and commenced to growl in a very threatening manner. This is what Starboard had expected apparently, for he instantly lay down on the treasure, and looked around in an unconscious and abstracted manner, as though nothing were farther from his thoughts than the bone. The other dog sniffed around a little, evidently not understanding the trick, and then walked away, growling in high dudgeon. Starboard then discovered, to his great astonishment, that he was lying on a bone, and proceeded to pick it with a hypocritical assumption of unconsciousness that must have been extremely offensive to Snarley, who had been an interested spectator of the proceeding, and who expressed his contempt for such tricks by a growl.

Starboard had besides a low turn for practical jokes, and was of a treacherous disposition where other dogs were concerned. I have often seen him, when they were all playing together in the most pleasant and friendly way, give Snarley a sly nip when they were all in a heap, so that it was impossible for the latter to tell who did it. But Snarley was of a suspicious temper, and had besides an ill-concealed dislike for Port, whom he invariably accused of these underhand attacks. The result would be a set-to between Port and Snarley, while Starboard would look on with an excited though critical air, throwing in a bark now and then by way of encouragement, until the old King would come along and thrash both of the combatants soundly.

Starboard was not, however, altogether devoid of courage when he considered there was a sufficient cause for a display of it.

One day the King had been punishing him rather severely for some breach of canine etiquette probably, and Starboard was lying on his back, doing his best to propitiate and conciliate the old fellow, who was standing over him and growling in a threatening manner.

Snarley was watching the scene with evident satisfaction, and he could not help expressing his approbation by a low growl. Starboard, still lying on his back, looked around and beheld Snarley showing his teeth.

A look of defiance passed over his face, which was quite as expressive as that of a man. He seemed to say, " I'm obliged to knuckle down to the old man, you know, but I'll stand none of *your* nonsense!" and as soon as the King let him up, he went at Snarley, and they had a regular mill, until the King interfered and separated them.

But there was one subject upon which all the dogs showed a remarkable unanimity of sentiment, and that was the suitability of " Mr. Hogan" as an article of food.

Mr. Hogan, it will be remembered, had taken passage with us, at Ivigtut, upon an agreement tacitly consented to on his part, somewhat hastily perhaps, that he would furnish us with favourable winds during the rest of the voyage. I do not think he fulfilled his engagement with that strictness which had been expected of him, but he nevertheless soon succeeded in making himself a universal favourite by his cleverness and gaiety.

Mr. Hogan, therefore, with his little sharp, black eyes, his impertinent manners and funny, intelligent looks,—pigs, it is well known, are among the most intelligent of all animals,—became a great favourite; and a very pleasant time he had, running loose about the deck, rooting among the coals, sleeping in the sun, as free and independent as though he had been on ice, until we reached Yuyarsusuk.

There we took on the dogs, and although they had never seen a pig before, they no sooner laid eyes upon him than they instantly, with a unanimity that was astonishing, understood that he was intended for the table, and made a most desperate onslaught upon him, with the intention of putting him to immediate use. A terrible conflict ensued, during which the deck of the PANDORA, what with the savage barking of the dogs, the high, piercing treble of Mr. Hogan, and the angry shouts and oaths of the friends who had interposed to save him, became a very pandemonium.

From that moment Mr. Hogan bade farewell to freedom and independence, to the easy, happy existence he had hitherto led. His life became one of constant fears and alarms, of dangers and hair-breadth escapes, of fearfully unequal combats, of cautious sallies out, and hurried skurryings into his barrel, of frantic gnashings of teeth and snorts of rage and defiance, in answer to the hungry, disappointed barks of his enemies.

He could scarcely slip out to take a quiet root in the coal, or a meditative turn about the capstan, or an inquiring excursion among the slop-buckets, but one of his terrible enemies would pounce upon him with the leap of a tiger, and he would rarely escape without painful loss. First his tail went piece by piece, then bits of his hams, and finally his ears began to grow shorter instead of longer, until they were as short, sharp, and vigilant as those of his enemies.

His nights were as wakeful and full of terrors as though he had committed murder; he could never go to sleep with the assurance that he would not find himself in the stomach of one or all of his enemies before morning. They organized night attacks upon him; and more than once we were awakened by the demoniac uproar of the conflict.

The sunshine in which he was wont to bask so luxuriously became a trap, the coal-heap a snare, and his barrel a prison, out of which he emerged at rare intervals. He seemed to be trying to accustom himself to being salted down, and confined his thoughts to eating, sleeping, and growing fat.

In this he succeeded so well that although he might have been put into a cigar-box when he came on board, he weighed a hundred and fifty pounds at the date of a big dinner, at which he had somewhat unwillingly consented to be present.

CHAPTER XVII.

BEECHEY ISLAND.

A BOLD, high promontory, rising several hundred feet above the surf that dashes against its base, streaked with alternate layers of brown and black, like a wall of massive masonry; a little bay running in behind this promontory, along whose shore may be seen, first—a large boat dragged high up on the beach, with a tall mast standing up in her; farther along two more boats, likewise hauled up on the shore; then a house, with masses of boxes and barrels scattered around in heaps, and a flagstaff in front.

It is midnight; and the steep, high walls of rock that shut in the little bay on all sides, are bleak and bare and dark, except where lighted up here and there with streaks of snow; and they rise up against the bright northern sky still aflame with the departing glory of the Arctic sun, in masses of rugged, sullen grandeur.

But there are no lights shining from the windows of this house, no children about the door,

no figures on the beach to wave us a welcome, no
fishermen moving about among the boats, no nets
strewed along the shore, no flag on the flagstaff;
there are no dwellers in this dwelling, no inhabitants in this habitation. The place is sad, silent,
and lonely as a graveyard. And it may well
appear lonely, for no human form has crossed the
threshold of this house, no human foot trod the
beach, no human voice disturbed the long, dreary
silence for twenty years.

It may well appear silent and mournful, for it is
Beechey Island, where was picked up, after years
of search, the lost trail of Sir John Franklin,
where were found the first tokens of the passage
of the lost expedition. Ominous and sinister
tokens they were, that seemed to point, but too
surely, the way the expedition had gone; for they
were graves—the graves of three men the expedition
lost when wintering here.

It was here Sir John passed his first winter
after leaving England. This was evident from
many things that were found—such as boards,
the remains of a house, fireplaces built of stones,
and a blacksmith's forge. Last but not least
was a huge cairn, built of empty meat tins,
most of which had contained rotten meat, furnished by a man now known among Arctic navigators and explorers as "Goldner the Infamous."

But not a line of writing was found, nor any
indication of the movements of the expedition,

nor what had been accomplished, nor what plans were made for the next season, nor which direction they were going, except the ominous indications furnished by the head-boards of the graves.

As long as the search for Sir John Franklin was kept up Beechey Island was made a starting-point, and place of meeting for the different ships that were sent out, and at one time no less than ten ships of different expeditions were lying in the little bay.

At length, when the search was finally abandoned by Sir Edward Belcher in 1854, he landed all the stores which he did not need, and which would have been useless out of the Arctic, and left them for the use of future expeditions. He left likewise two large lifeboats, an India-rubber boat, a light wooden boat, together with carpenters' and blacksmiths' tools, and a great number of other useful things. He built the house called "Northumberland House," and, upon leaving, stowed away part of the provisions in it to protect them from the bears. The yacht MARY had been previously left by Sir John Ross in 1851.

Sir Leopold McClintock visited it again in the Fox in 1857, since which time it has remained undisturbed by any human visitant, waiting through the silent, dreary years for the arrival of the next ship. That ship came at last, and she was the PANDORA.

Captain Young's object in coming here was to examine the state of the stores, in order to know whether we could depend upon finding provisions here, in case we should be obliged to abandon our ship in Peel Sound, McClintock Channel, or Franklin Strait.

Upon going ashore a scene of devastation and ruin met our gaze, which we were little prepared to see. "Northumberland House" had been broken into, and half the stores apparently destroyed. The ground outside was strewn with tins of preserved meat and vegetables, forty-pound tins of pemmican, great rolls of heavy blue cloth, hundreds of pairs of woollen mittens and socks, rolls of soft white flannels, bales of blankets, bales of clothing, hanks of woollen yarn—all scattered over the ground in the most admired disorder.

The fine, warm blue cloth, the flannels and blankets and clothing, were for the most part torn into shreds and strings; the meat and pemmican tins, where not torn open, were pierced with holes; the little wooden boat was split and broken into fragments, while scarcely anything was left of the India-rubber boat. The house itself, which was built of boards, was considerably damaged.

The marauders had apparently broken in at the window on the south side, which had probably not been nailed up, and, to enlarge the opening, had torn away half the boards on this side. The snow

NORTHUMBERLAND HOUSE.

[Page 206.

had got in during the winter and partly melted during the summer, frozen and thawed again during succeeding winters and summers, so that now, everything to a depth of three feet from the ground was imbedded in a solid mass of ice. In short, the ruin and destruction were so great that the place resembled the scene of a first-class railway accident more than anything else I could think of.

But who were the marauders that had so wantonly destroyed everything? Who were these thieves that steal for fun—these burglars that leave their booty behind them—housebreakers that not only break houses but everything else they can lay their hands upon, instead of carrying their spoil to the nearest pawnbroker?

Evidently the Polar bears. The marks of their claws were everywhere and on everything. They had even gnawed into two or three barrels of salt beef, which they had quite emptied, and it was their claws that had punched holes in the heavy pemmican tins. Polar bears seem to be possessed of the very genius of destruction.

Nothing that they can destroy, injure, mutilate, bite, scratch, deface, claw, or throw down escapes them; and they do it apparently without any other object than destruction for its own sake. They seem to have gone systematically to work, and to have left nothing untouched or uninjured that was not absolutely too strong, and it

only remained for them to apply the torch, as
men would have done, to complete the work of
ruin.

A great part of the provisions, however, as flour,
beef, sugar, preserved milk, some of the tinned
meat, was put up in solid, heavy iron-hooped
barrels, which they had found too strong for their
claws, and which were consequently uninjured.

Captain Young made a survey of everything, in
order to report to the Admiralty on the condition
of the stores. The yacht MARY proved upon inspection to be in good condition, and, with a few
slight repairs, would be quite seaworthy. Her
sails were stowed away beneath deck, quite dry
and well preserved, and she was provided with
oakum, caulking and carpenters' tools, which,
although rusted somewhat, were nevertheless
capable of being used. The two lifeboats were
not in such good condition, but might still be
made seaworthy with a little work. The flour,
sugar, and salt meat in barrels were uninjured,
as was a considerable quantity of the tinned
beef and mutton that the bears had not been
able to get at. Many of the cases of pemmican
had holes punched in them, and were consequently spoiled; but even many of those that
the bears had apparently been throwing at each
other had escaped injury, and there were probably
a couple of hundred that had not been disturbed.

We found several barrels full of boots and shoes,

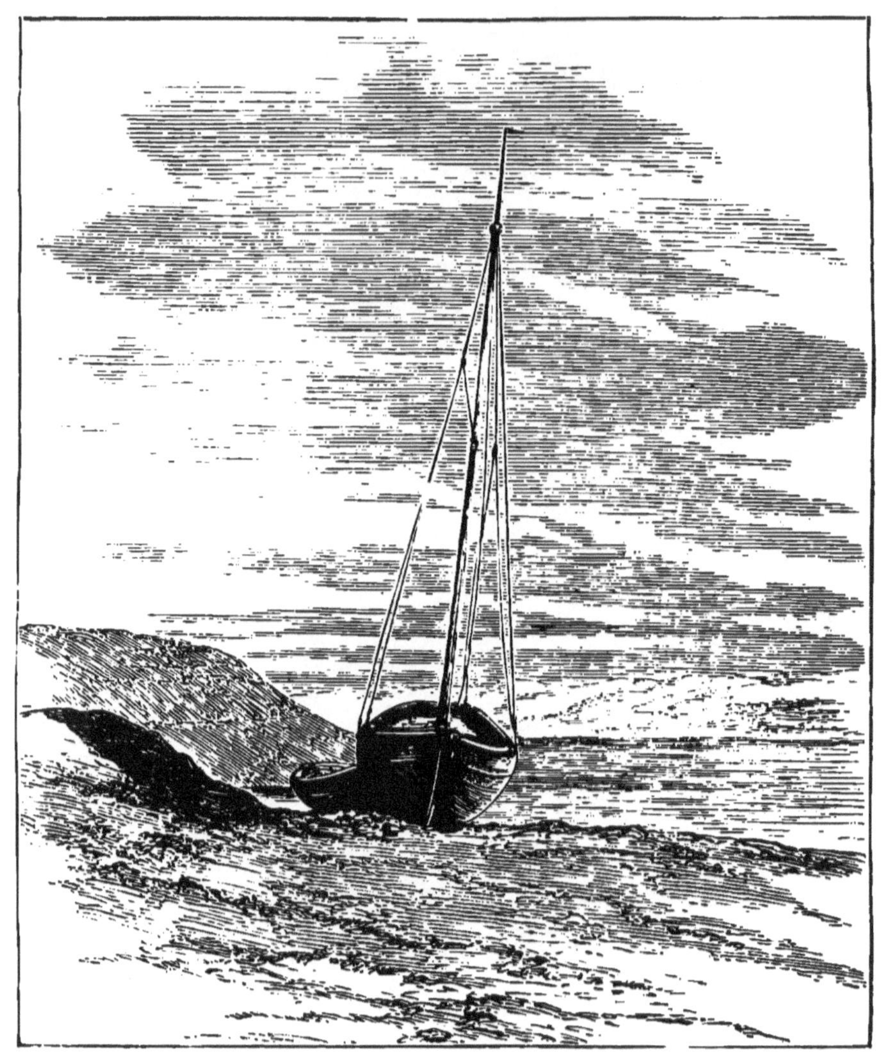

THE YACHT MARY.

[Page 200.

most of which were in excellent preservation. Part of them were made of felt, with cork soles an inch thick, and others of beautifully prepared seal-skin as soft as kid, with ordinary sole leather soles, and with the exception of one or two barrels that had probably let in the rain, they were, after twenty years lying here, quite as good as new. They all bore the mark of " Jeffs, Oxford-street," and certainly did the maker credit. There were also a barrel or two of leather shoes of an old fashion, with square toes and low quarters, many of which were so small they must have been intended for girls. The milk we found to be well preserved, although it had lost much of its virtue, whether through the fault of its original preparation or the great number of the freezings and thawings it had undergone, we could not tell.

Captain Young made a complete survey of the stores, taking a few of them he thought we might need, headed up all the barrels, nailed up the boxes, and repaired the house, which was sadly going to rack and ruin. Among our men was one, " Old Florence," who had not only been here in the Fox, but also in the NORTH STAR, and had helped to build the house. He was then a young man, but he is now old, weather-beaten, grizzled and worn, and a fine example of the old-fashioned sea-dog.

Near the house is the monument of Lieutenant Bellot, the young French naval officer, who lost his life in the search for Sir John Franklin when serving with the expedition of Belcher; and lying at its foot on a stone platform, was a marble slab, the tombstone of Sir John Franklin, set up by Sir Leopold McClintock when here in command of the Fox. Both monuments were sent out by Lady Franklin.

Up nearly at the head of the bay, about three miles from Northumberland House, are the graves of three of the crew of the EREBUS and TERROR, Franklin's ships, and two of the NORTH STAR's crew. They stand in a row, and are marked by simple head-boards of oak about two inches thick, on which the names are cut, with the name of the ship, age, and date of their death. In addition there are engraved on two of them the following lines of Holy Writ :—

"Choose ye this day whom ye will serve."
"Thus saith the Lord, Consider your ways."

Such texts are not ordinarily chosen for inscriptions on grave-stones, and they seem to hide some mysterious meaning as sinister as that of the graves themselves.

This Arctic graveyard is situated on a gravelly slope, which rises up from the little bay toward the foot of a high bluff, that frowns down upon it as though resenting the intrusion of human dead in this lonely world. Sad enough looked the poor head-boards as the low-sinking sun threw its yellow rays athwart them, casting long shadows over the shingly slope; silent, sad, and mournful as everything else in this dreary Arctic world.

CHAPTER XVIII.

A CAPSTAN SONG.

" Up Anchor ! "

The order comes from Captain Young on the bridge. Lieutenant Pirie has taken the wheel, Lieut. Lillingston is on the top-gallant forecastle to superintend the operation, and every other man on the ship runs forward to the capstan. The dogs, catching the excitement, fly about among our legs and trip us up, barking and yelping boisterously, and " Mr. Hogan " lifts up his bristles, and dashes into his barrel with a snort, where he bids defiance to his enemies by champing his teeth with a vicious smack.

In go the capstan-bars, and around we start with a run. Everybody on board our ship is expected to put his hand to the work. There is no question of precedence, nobody stands on his rank when there is work to be done. Making sail, shortening sail, taking in reefs, shaking out reefs, hauling at the ropes, heaving around the capstan, officers and men, from the captain to the cook, all work alike. Sometimes in a freshening breeze, the captain himself takes the wheel, while every other hand on board is working hard reefing a refractory topsail; and when the order comes "up anchor," there is not an idle man on the ship.

Round and round we go, easily and rapidly at first, as we are only taking in the slack cable, of which there are some thirty fathoms out. Old Randerson, one of the petty officers, an old whaler, sets up a capstan song, with a refrain at the end of every line, in which we all join. It is a kind of old-fashioned, monotonous chant, but as it swells up on the air, borne on twenty strong, deep, male voices, it is full of a wild, sweet melody that might make Wagner tear his hair in despair.

> "Oh, Shanadoa, I longs to hear you.
> *Chorus*—Ha! ha! the rolling water.
> Oh, Shanadoa, I longs to hear you.
> *Chorus*—Ho! ho! the cold, pale water."

Now we have taken in the slack of the cable, and the ship has moved up until she is directly over the anchor, which lies asleep at the bottom of the sea, a hundred and fifty feet below. Here comes the tug, for it lies with its hooks and claws buried in the mud, like a monster devil-fish, and refuses to let go.

> " Oh, Shanadoa, I've seen your daughter.
> *Chorus*—Ha! ha! the rolling water.
> 　　Oh, Shanadoa, I've seen your daughter.
> *Chorus*—Ho! ho! the cold, pale water."

How the monster sticks to his slimy couch, and hooks his claws around it, and clings to it, as though he would never let go!   How hard it is to tear him away from his ocean love!

> " Oh, Shanadoa, I loves your daughter.
> *Chorus*—Ha! ha! the rolling water.
> 　　Oh, Shanadoa, I loves your daughter.
> *Chorus*—Ho! ho! the cold, pale water."

We set our shoulders against the bars, and heave with might and main, keeping time to the measure of the song.

> " When I return I'll wed your daughter.
> *Chorus*—Ha! ha! we are bound away.
> 　　When I return I'll wed your daughter.
> *Chorus*—Ho! ho! the rolling water."

What a strange picture it would make if we could only see it from the bottom of the sea! The ship riding a hundred and fifty feet high on the top of the clear water, so transparent that it seems only a denser atmosphere, down through which drops this heavy, black, iron cable, looking, with its great articulated links, like the backbone of some leviathan, with this devil-fish at the end of it.

The vessel tugs and jerks at it wildly as she rolls and rocks with the swell in her frantic efforts to break away, like a captive balloon.

> "For seven long years I woo'd your daughter.
> *Chorus*—Ha! ha! old Shanadoa.
> For seven long years I woo'd your daughter.
> *Chorus*—Ho! ho! the rolling water."

One more heave and the monster begins to turn over in his bed, his claws are getting tired, and he relaxes his hold.

> "Oh, Shanadoa, where is your daughter?
> *Chorus*—Ha! ha! the rolling water.
> Oh, Shanadoa, where is your daughter?
> *Chorus*—Oh! oh! the cold, pale water."

Sluggishly he gets up out of his slimy couch, and slowly he begins to crawl up the iron chain to the dizzy height above, like a huge black spider climbing his own thread.

> "Oh, Shanadoa, beneath the water.
> *Chorus*—Ha! ha! the rolling water.
> Oh, Shanadoa, beneath the water.
> *Chorus*—Oh! oh! the cold, pale water."

Up, up he mounts, moaning as if from pain, growling low, and threatening vengeance on his tormentors; and the ship, finding herself free, suddenly starts off, as though trying to escape from the hideous-looking monster that is climbing steadily up to her throat.

> " Oh, Shanadoa, there lies your daughter.
> *Chorus*—Ha ! ha ! the rolling water.
> Oh, Shanadoa, there lies your daughter.
> *Chorus*—Oh ! oh ! the cold, pale water."

The silent, sullen cliffs seem touched by the music, and, half awakening from their mournful sleep, repeat it softly in a dreamy refrain, as though it were the echo of their own great sorrow. The melody has touched a sensitive cord hid away deep in their great, stony, frozen hearts, and it responds like the string of a violin when its corresponding note is struck. They murmur the refrain softly to each other as though it were part of a dream ; the rocks are connected by some strange, subtle sympathy like the strings of a harp, and the wild, tender melody vibrates around the bay, while the echo comes back to us across the water broken up into discordant, sobbing notes, like a funeral wail.

And now we begin to see the shore move around us in a circle—the steep, bare cliff, seamed and scarred with many a hack, and capped with a thin layer of snow, like a hoary-headed old giant; Northumberland House, with the boats and the flagstaff, all so sad and silent and lonely in the yellow evening sunshine ; then the yacht MARY, with her black hull, like a widow in mourning, waiting for the captain who shall sail in her no more—all circle around in sorrowful procession, until we have before us the cold, icy glimmer of the sea.

And so we look our last on Beechey Island.

CHAPTER XIX.

UNKNOWN WATERS.

WE are steering for Peel Strait, and the ship's head is towards the north. To the north? How can that be? Peel Strait is due south from Beechey Island, and Beechey Island is directly astern, therefore Peel Strait must be directly ahead.

Yet the north end of the needle points exactly in the same direction as our jib-boom,—that is, to the south!

What strange revolution is this? Is the world turned upside down, or has some Arctic sprite, to bewilder us, reversed the card on the needle, making the north south, and the east west? This cannot be, for the north end of a long, fine needle, suspended without the card, points likewise to the south. We know it is the south, unless—fearful supposition!—the earth has begun rolling the other way, and the sun is going backward to set in the east.

No; it is the compass itself which is reversed, and which now points to the south instead of the

north. We are here north of the magnetic pole,
and this accounts for the strange revolution of
the needle ; but it moves feebly now, and is not to
be trusted. Of the five or six compasses we have
on board, no two point in the same direction by
twenty-five or thirty degrees. Our guides henceforth must be the sun and stars.

We were now entering upon unknown and unexplored waters. No ship, as far as has been
ascertained, ever penetrated into Peel Strait.
McClintock attempted it in the Fox, but was
stopped almost at its very entrance by ice, which
rendered any further advance impossible. As his
object was to reach King William's Island, he was
obliged to turn back and make an attempt by way
of Regent's Inlet and Bellot's Straits.

It is generally supposed that Franklin's ships,
the ill-fated Erebus and Terror, passed down Peel
Strait to reach the point where they were finally
beset, never to escape again. This, however, is
by no means certain. It is possible that after
reaching their highest latitude in Wellington
Channel, instead of going back to Peel Strait, they
turned due south through McClintock Channel,
hoping to find open water in Victoria Strait. This
is the more probable as Peel Strait was then
supposed to be an inlet, as King William's Island
was believed to be a peninsula.

Notwithstanding the chances against getting
down through Peel Strait, Captain Young had

decided to make the attempt. He thought that if successful in reaching as far as Bellot's Strait, he would have a better chance of getting through the pack which he feared he would find there. McClintock actually succeeded in getting through Bellot's Strait, but his further progress was stopped by a pack just outside of its western entrance, a pack which he never succeeded in getting through. By going down Peel Strait and approaching this pack from a side on which he would have more sea room, Captain Young hoped to discover some part through which he could force his way.

All our hopes were therefore fixed upon getting down Peel Strait. Should we find it sufficiently clear of ice to allow us to push through? or should we, like other ships, be arrested at its very entrance? In the latter case our only plan was to turn back, go down Regent Inlet, and Bellot's Strait, as the Fox had done, with the hope that the pack which stopped her might be broken up. As to the route by way of Wellington Channel and Melville Sound, it may be as well to state that Arctic navigators have long since abandoned all hopes of ever penetrating far in that direction. These waters have never yet been found open, unless indeed, Franklin found them so. Neither in summer nor winter have they ever been known to put off their icy armour.

We soon had reason to believe that our worst fears were to be realized. By nine o'clock in the evening of August 27th, twenty-four hours after leaving Beechey Island, we were at the entrance of Peel Strait, and lying up against a pack which —joined to the coast of North Somerset on the south and stretching away to the north-west as far as the eye could reach—seemed to effectually bar our further progress. We made fast to a floe, and Captain Young decided to wait.

The adoption of this plan may prove somewhat disappointing to the reader. It is expected of an Arctic ship, I believe, that she should dash into a pack, and crush her way through it, like a reaping-machine through a field of wheat. But such a feat cannot, in fact, be accomplished. It is only upon very rare occasions that a ship can work for even a short distance through a close, heavy pack. The power upon which Arctic navigators depend to open a way through such an obstacle is neither that of steam nor gunpowder, nor any other force within the control of man. It is the power of the wind.

Very few people, probably, have anything like a correct conception of the sort of thing an ice-pack really is. It is not a smooth, level sheet of ice, over which you might skate; but a broken, uneven plain, covered with little hummocks, peaks and ridges, formed by huge pieces of ice, that have been rolled upon the surface by the grinding of immense ice-fields against each other. It will be easily understood that such a plain, with all these irregularities and projections acting as so many sails, offers an immense surface to the action of the wind.   In truth, the slightest breeze sets the whole pack moving with a might that is irresistible.   The best plan, therefore, for the navigator is to wait and count upon the assistance of this powerful auxiliary.   An hour sometimes will suffice to open a passage that weeks of blasting and sawing would not have made; or even completely to break up and disperse a pack that seemed as solidly fixed as the rock itself.

Captain Young maintains that the greatest requisite in ice navigation is patience—patience to wait for a change which is almost sure to come sooner or later—patience not to push blindly into a pack in the hope of getting through somehow, as well as not to turn back and abandon the attempt too soon.

This is what he decided to do in the present case, and the PANDORA was put alongside the ice, and made fast for the night.

No change had occurred next morning, and as

we were short of water we proceeded to take in a
supply, a kind of work which proved to be as
pleasant as play; for it gave us an opportunity of
stretching our limbs and running about over the
ice. Mr. De Wilde busied himself making sketches
and photographs of the ice, the ship, and the
coast of North Somerset. The coast extended
along the sky in a low, black line on our left, as
far as Limestone Island, which appeared as a round,
dark mount far away to the south. The doctor
went shooting gulls, and Joe took his rifle and went
to look for seals; the rest of us amused ourselves,
after we had done watering ship, by playing on
the ice with the dogs.

About noon a light breeze sprang up from the
south, and almost immediately the ice began to
move. In an hour or so, an opening commenced
to show itself not far from the shore, and into
this Captain Young decided to push, although no
open water was visible beyond the pack, which
extended to the horizon. But he perceived to the
south, hanging over Peel Strait, what is termed
a " water sky," giving indications of open water
below the horizon, and it was this sign which
induced him to risk his ship in the pack. We
worked through the loose ice which filled up the
lead with much difficulty, and by six o'clock in the
evening we were off Limestone Island, in a wide
lane of open water. But although this lane,
which was two or three miles wide, ran south

along the coast of North Somerset, as far as we could see, the pack still continued stretching away to the horizon. Evidently we were by no means past it.

Captain Young decided to land on Limestone Island, and to search for a cairn, which it was supposed some former navigator had left there.

He found no signs of a cairn; but he remarked many traces of the Eskimos, in circles of moss-covered stones, evidently of a very ancient date. He returned to the ship, and decided to steer through the narrow channel between Limestone Island and the coast, the passage of which was accomplished without accident.

LIMESTONE ISLAND.

[Page 224.

CHAPTER XX.

THE LAND OF DESOLATION.

THE weather had, in the meantime, changed. A cold, drizzling rain set in, accompanied by the inevitable fog, and gave promise of a bad night. The wind began to blow in gusty blasts, that swept the rain over the decks in rushing, splashing showers. On the starboard beam an occasional gleam of white told where the pack we had not yet passed was lying in wait for us. On the left, the coast of North Somerset rose up, dark and frowning, like a heavy black cloud, scarcely distinguishable against the lowering sky.

What a wild, desolate place is this Arctic world! On the charts it looks like any other part of the globe. Land and water, islands and peninsulas, straits and bays, inlets, continents, such as you see on the charts of the equatorial zone. But what land! and what water! and how different from the smiling, bounteous world of the tropics!

The islands of North Somerset and the Prince of Wales Land, between which we are sailing, are mere heaps of stones and boulders. For hundreds of miles in every direction it is the same. The whole north coast of America, from Behring's Straits to Hudson's Bay, with the great Archipelago north of it, is nothing but stone and rock and ice, not only without a tree or shrub, or blade of grass, but without even a handful of earth to hide its savage nakedness. The water is ice, the land is rock; the sea a frozen corpse, the earth a bare, grinning skeleton, that meets you everywhere, that seizes you in its bony clasp, and will not let you go; the skeleton of a dead world.

There is something unaccountably oppressive in this Arctic universe. The immensity of these regions, their dreariness, their silent immobility that appears like the stillness of the grave, have a strangely depressing effect. They weigh upon the mind, and bear it down like some fearful incubus, like that half-waking, half-dreaming, indistinct consciousness of weight upon the chest felt in the oppression of nightmare.

I believe that to this depression of spirits is to be attributed—almost as much as to the lack of proper food—the prevalence of scurvy in Arctic ships. The effects of it were plain and unmistakeable on those of our men who were most impressionable and superstitious. They grew despondent and low-spirited, and went about their work in a half-hearted way, as though afraid to touch anything. Our petty officers grew over-cautious and timid. One of them, a most exemplary man in England, suddenly took to drink; and another went to bed, and remained there until we were far on our way home. Both these men, and others I could have pointed out, would inevitably have died had we wintered in the Arctic; while all of us, even the strongest and most buoyant, were affected by this mysterious influence.

Nature never smiles here. In sunshine or shadow, in light or shade, she is always gloomy and taciturn. When the sun comes out bright and warm, as it does sometimes, tingeing the bare, bleak rocks with a melancholy yellow, she is silent, sad, and mournful; when the grey leaden clouds are drawn over the sky like a dripping canopy, she is silent, sombre, threatening; always gloomy, stern, inexorable, implacable.

She shows here no rich carpet of grass and flowers to delight and refresh our eyes; no fields of waving grain; no grand old forest with its ocean of green foliage; no rustle of leaves whispering their mysterious secrets; no chant of birds nor hum of insects; no murmur of life and love and joy. Her voices are hushed, her smile is gone, her face is cold.

We are used to a smiling, bounteous Earth, clothed in verdure and flowers, that opens her arms to us, that warms us on her breast, that gives us life and light, and warmth and plenty.

Here we are like children looking on the pale, cold face of a dead mother; we are struck with terror. There is something fearful in the rigid features that were so full of expression, in the closed eyes that beam no more; in the still hands that move not—a strange, dreadful mystery which appals. This is the first impression.

It is succeeded by something far more fearful and terrible—a feeling I have tried to seize and analyze without success. It is as though you gradually began to perceive a sinister meaning—a darker signification in this lonely, silent world. You begin to feel that it is endowed with a sullen kind of life—a sombre intelligence that you vainly try to comprehend. You feel that something terrible has happened here, or is going to happen.

We have hitherto been accustomed to look upon the world as made for our particular convenience and use. The Earth brings forth its fruits for us and teems with plenty; the flowers bloom for us; the sun rises and sets for us; it rains, because rain is necessary to our well-being. The moon revolves around the Earth only because we need a moon; the stars adorn the sky for us to look at; the Earth, the World, the Universe, in short, is made for us and our wants. But here is a world uninhabited and uninhabitable by man—a world that can never have been made for him; that has been created without the slightest regard for his wants or necessities—a world that will not afford him sustenance for a day. Nature, wrapped in her own silent, desolate, mysterious sorrow, ignores his existence; she is indifferent whether he lives or dies; she will let him perish without offering him a berry or a root.

This is a new idea that presents itself to his mind, that forces itself upon him; a fearful, inexorable fact which shatters all his preconceived ideas, his habits, his education, his methods of thought, and flings them to the winds.

The result is stupefaction; a vague, oppressive feeling of blank terror. You begin to feel that instead of the world being created for you, you are only an accidental atom, an insect upon it, and that it is a wonder you have not perished long ago. You begin to divine around you gigantic forces, blind, savage, brutal, cruel, relentless, that may crush you as you crush the worm beneath your feet, without seeing you or even knowing of your existence.

It is then that the conviction of its utter nothingness forces itself upon the mind with overwhelming force. The strongest and most powerful organizations shrink and tremble before it; the weak and despondent wither and die.

CHAPTER XXI.

A NIGHT IN PEEL STRAIT.

THE night comes on apace. The clouds gather thick and black overhead, and the darkness rises up out of the earth like a sable spectre; the wind drives the rain about in furious torrents that sweep over the rocks with a continuous swash. The darkness, lined with the inevitable fog, gradually grows black and impenetrable, and the bleak, bare, savage world sullenly sinks into the gulf of night without fire, or light, or life.

But no! we are mistaken. There is a light, a single solitary spark that gleams through the darkness like a Will o' the Wisp; and see! there is the dusky shadow of a ship flitting through the gloom, like a twilight ghost.

This great, lone, silent universe is then not quite deserted. Where there is light there is life, and that dusky shadow is a real ship, feeling her way along the forbidding coast, groping through the darkness like a blind man.

Who is she? How has she found her way here?

What is she doing in this dreary world, where no ships are ever seen, where there are no eyes to see them, flitting like a shadow through the night and storm.

She is scarcely visible from her own deck. The light we saw is from the binnacle, and it casts a yellow flare on the black face of night like a splash of gold. In it is seen the face of the man at the wheel, gazing steadily and earnestly towards the head of the ship. His body is invisible, only his face is seen; and it floats there in that splash of light, like a grizzled, bronzed, nautical cherub. Everything else is in darkness: the sails rise up like ghostly shadows to an immense height, and blend with the gloom; the rain dashes over the deck in plashing waterfalls that wash everything with a rushing, sleepy murmur.

Leaning against the port nettings is a dark figure, gazing steadily into the night, with the fixity of a statue. It is Captain Young. He has been there for two hours, and he will be there two hours longer, peering into the darkness, watching for the first shadowy outline of the land, the first white gleam of breakers to warn him of the too near approach of danger. The wind whirls around him in fitful gusts, the rain dashes over him in torrents, but he never moves. The safety of his ship, the lives of his crew depend upon his keenness of eye, his soundness of judgment, his promptness of decision, and he is for the moment as insensible to the storm as the statue he resembles.

There is no other sign of life; all below is dark and still. The wind soughs overhead as it meets the sails, with that deep eternal sigh heard in a forest of pines; the rain patters on the deck with a low, continuous plash. But for the flare that lights up the anxious face of the man at the wheel, and the bottom of the mizzen trysail above his head, it might well be a shadow ship. It is a wild and fearful night, a night to make the hardiest seaman tremble.

There are few people who have any idea of the dangers that beset a ship, even under ordinary circumstances; who have any conception of the common, every-day perils of navigation; for they are dangers that are only understood and appreciated by seamen. This is, perhaps, just as well; for if the thousands of people who now cross the ocean, and commit themselves to the mercy of the sea with such lightness of heart, understood to what dangers they are exposed, three-fourths of them would stay at home.

To any one who has ever taken the trouble to reflect upon the matter, a ship is a marvel, a kind of continuous miracle. Of all the conquests of mind in the never-ending combat with matter, in that unceasing struggle with the blind, reckless forces of Nature, there is none so great, so wonderful as a ship. Its very existence is a victory over the most powerful forces on the globe, a subjugation, control, utilization of those forces which are its greatest enemies, and without which—a strange contradiction—it could not be. Its greatest foes are those very elements that make it possible. But it is a conquest only maintained by almost superhuman effort of science, vigilance, and skill.

We severely censure officers who lose their ships, and we talk lightly about neglect and imprudence, carelessness, blunders, incapacity, as though a ship could not possibly be lost, unless her officers were guilty of the most idiotic incapacity, or the most reprehensible neglect of duty. We do not know anything of the skill, coolness, judgment, prompt decision, unremitting vigilance required to handle a ship—a kind of vigilance which demands a continued power of concentrated attention—almost beyond the capacity of the human mind.

We think it requires days and weeks of negligence to result in the loss of a ship. We do not know that a single moment, a second of distraction on the part of the captain, or the officer of the watch, is sufficient sometimes to lose a vessel; that the slightest accident to the machinery, the smallest mistake in the reckoning, a wrong turn by the man at the wheel, which is often made by the oldest sailors, may, in a moment, send ship. and crew to the bottom.

The wonder is not that accidents do sometimes happen, but that they do not always happen. The wonder is not that ships are sometimes lost, but that they are not always lost as soon as they go to sea. The captain, on whose skill and presence of mind the safety of a ship depends, is up and down all night; he often does not undress to sleep for a week at a time, and the sleep he does get is broken by fits and starts. He may be said to carry his ship about on his back. It is a crushing burthen that he can never lay down even for a moment. Sleeping or waking, it is always upon him, always with him, always pressing him down, until it becomes a dull, heavy stupefying pain.

But if such are the perils of ordinary navigation, in known and explored waters, what were the dangers that beset us this night in Peel Strait?

A ship lost on the wide waste of the ocean, has in the sun, moon, and stars, hundreds of beacons to guide her. She has in the sextant a strange artificial sight which enables her to tell her exact position, to know where she is, no matter how long she has been lost, how far she has sped without her reckoning; in her chart, a guide which indicates her course from day to day, which points out coast-lines, capes, promontories, bays, inlets, shoals, rocks, and sand-banks, to the minutest detail; which, in shallow waters like those of the English channel, tells the depth of every square rood, and the kind of bottom that will be found there; in her sounding-line she has a sense of touch, by which when blinded by fog and darkness, her other senses fail her, she may feel her way along the bottom like a blind man with a stick; in her compass, a mysterious instinct, far more wonderful than that which enables birds of passage to travel half around the globe, and find their way home again. The approaches to dangerous coasts are shown by buoys, signals, and lighthouses; everything that human skill and science can do has been done to arm her for the great struggle with the ocean. And yet how often does the fight prove an unequal one? How many good ships go down, notwithstanding all these aids!

But all the dangers peculiar to the ocean seem to have gathered around us this night in Peel Strait, where we are deprived of all the safeguards provided by the skill and science of man. Had we been out in the broad Atlantic, we could wait for daylight, or until stars, moon, or sun should re-appear, as there would be no danger of running ashore. Here, with a rocky coast on one side, and the ice-pack on the other, we can afford to make no mistakes. We are like a blind man groping on the edge of a precipice, with the difference that the blind man at least can feel his way, while we cannot.

For us there is no transition between absolute safety and absolute destruction. We know we are safe as long only as the ship does not strike, but she may strike at any moment. Enveloped in fog and night, we have no kindly light of moon or stars to guide us; there is no friendly lighthouse on this wild, desolate coast, to warn us off; no buoys nor signals to show us the way; we have no pilot in these unsounded, unexplored waters, to point out shoals and reefs, and sunken rocks.

But we have one thing left to guide us— the compass, that unfailing friend of the mariner. We have it, at least, to tell us where the coast is. Its silent finger still points to where the danger lies!

No! Even that fails us here. The needle which in other parts of the world points so steadily, which, when everything else deserts the seaman, remains true, has here grown uncertain and wavering. In this night of tempest and darkness, in these wild, desolate regions, even the mysterious spirit that rules the magnet is bewildered and confused; it can tell us nothing. It wavers and trembles, and hesitates, like a guide who has lost his way.

But see! yes, there is one direction in which it points when set free on a universal pivot, with startled, trembling, excited finger. It is downward, straight down! What fearful thing is this?

Go where you will on the surface of the earth—South America, the heart of Africa, the islands of the South Pacific, the wilds of Australia, the wide, dreary plains of Central Asia, the close, dark, thick-set jungles of far-off India—everywhere you find this ghostly finger pointing silently, sternly, persistently here to this wild region like the finger of Fate. Now that we have obeyed its mysterious bidding, now that we have followed its strange guidance here, it points downwards, down to the bottom of the sea!

What is the mysterious treasure hidden here in the earth, that this spirit-finger has been pointing at for centuries, without being understood of man? What the dark and fearful secret it would disclose? What ghostly crime would it reveal?

Whatever it be, we can follow it no farther; it is no longer a guide for us; we must trust to something else. But what? The wind? Yes; the wind, the variable wind, that scarcely remains the same for an hour at a time. We are steering by a weather-cock; but it is the only thing left to guide us, and we must follow it or let the ship drift.

It was blowing on shore when last we saw the land, and we, consequently, keep the ship's head to it, and thus we know, as long as it does not change, on which side we have the coast. But suppose it veers slowly round, and blows off shore? In that case we follow it insensibly, unconsciously, until our head is landwards, and then we go ashore on the rocky coast. There is no help for it.

We cannot even drop anchor, and thus stop the ship until the fog clears away, or until daylight comes. The water is too deep, and there is no other way of stopping her. She will move in some direction, whether we will or no. We can only do our best, and trust to Providence that the wind may hold from the same direction.

Gradually the day breaks, and leaves hanging about us the grey curtain of fog which lined the night. A fog is worse than darkness alone, if the sky be not overcast. So long as the stars can be seen the sailor has a guide; but a fog hides alike the sun, stars, and land. Nothing can be seen, and the mariner is helpless. He can only wait for it to clear away. Daylight, therefore, brings little change in our position.

So we wait anxiously through the long, cold hours of the morning. The wind begins to fall light, and the danger therefore grows less, so long as it blows steadily from the same quarter. At length, towards ten o'clock, the sun gets the better of the mist, and breaks through now and then, showing us a pale, watery image. Then the fog lifts in heavy masses, like a curtain, and suddenly reveals close on our port-beam, the barren, rocky coast. In the space of half an hour a wonderful change is wrought. The sun shines out bright and warm, and we seem to have emerged into another world. For the moment the danger is past.

CHAPTER XXII.

NOTHING can be more sudden than the transitions from danger to safety which often take place here in the Arctic. With daylight, a clear atmosphere, and a light breeze, our position had completely altered from what it was a few hours before; and until another fog should come on, accompanied by a storm, we were quite safe. We found besides that one source of danger was removed, for the ice which had so hemmed us in the night before had quite disappeared. We had now plenty of sea-room, or what appeared so to us, at least after our cramped position of the night before. The ordinary navigator, unaccustomed to these waters, would still have thought himself in a most perilous situation, in case of a gale and fog, shut in between these two coasts.

The day turned out a beautiful one, and the contrast with the gloom of the previous night was striking. As the sun rose higher it grew warmer; the thermometer went up from twenty-seven to thirty-five—a temperature which to us appeared sultry—and but for the barren, forbidding coast, we might easily have imagined ourselves on some sunny inland lake of the far-off tropics. We were in a sea free of ice, for there was not a particle to be seen far or near; the cold, sharp sting to which we had been accustomed for days, had left the air, and the land was bare of snow, except where we caught glimpses of the highlands of the interior, on which here and there white patches might be perceived. We seemed to have got into another climate and another world. The strangest of all was the disappearance of the ice. We had partly worked past it during the night, but the storm also had probably driven it in the opposite direction, or towards Barrow Strait.

We were now far past the point at which the Fox had been turned back, and began to congratulate ourselves on our prospects of success. Contrary to what had generally been supposed, Peel Strait was clear of ice; and there now was every probability that we would find it open as far as Bellot Strait.

The wind now fell very light, and veered round to the south-east, a change which, had it occurred while the fog lasted, would probably have put us ashore on the rocks.

We continue our course under steam and sail, and all day long we glide down the silent, barren

R

coast, getting farther and farther south, nearer and nearer King William's Land, the goal of all our hopes.

The view from aloft is superb. I pass half the day on the topsail-yard, watching Peel Strait unroll itself beneath me, like a ribbon from a great reel, and gazing down into the clear, blue water, which is so transparent that it appears like another sky. The air is soft and mild as that of a May morning. Looking down from my lofty perch I see the deck of the vessel, a huge, long, narrow plank, that seems to swing beneath me like the car of a balloon; below which, far, far down, white, fleecy clouds are flitting across that lower liquid sky, scarcely more unreal than the clouds above. It is like being up in a monster balloon, floating between two skies, out of sight of earth.

The dogs are curled up down there on deck, asleep in the sun; the men have gone below to dinner, and there is no one to be seen but the look-out and the man at the wheel. The stillness is so complete that I can hear the ticking of the clock in the after-companion-way, a strangely unnatural sound; and up from the galley stove comes a steaming odour of plum-pudding, and the smell of frying bear meat.

Lifting my eyes, I behold to the east the shore of North Somerset, a mass of granite boulders, worn round and smooth, and heaped up in wild confusion, behind which the low mountains of the interior, capped here and there with snow; to the south, the glassy strait reflecting the rays of the sun in a long flash of dazzling light that blinds the eyes; to the west, the distant coast of the Prince of Wales' Land, high and mountainous, enveloped in a cloud of purple mist that hangs over it, a drapery of luminous gauze, sad, silent, but beautiful as a dream, in the golden light of the Arctic afternoon.

A good look-out was kept toward the shore, with a powerful astronomical telescope, to discover, if possible, signs of animal life, musk-ox or reindeer, as well as for cairns, the tokens of the passage of men.

But nothing of the kind could be detected. From time to time we could distinguish heaps of stones that looked like cairns, but these upon closer inspection always proved to be huge granite boulders, with which the coast and especially the ridges were strewn.

Towards evening we began to approach the farthest point reached by Ross and McClintock when coming down the coast on foot from the north, in 1849. They were wintering at Port Leopold, on the north-east shore of North Somerset, and this journey was made in the winter, in the hopes of finding some traces of the Franklin expedition, of which they were in search. They built a cairn, and left a record at the point where they had been obliged to turn back for want of provisions; and for this cairn we now kept a sharp look-out.

At length, about six in the evening, we descried the object of our search. The ship was hove to, half a mile from shore, and Captain Young, Lieutenants Pirie, Beynen, and myself got into a boat and rowed off. We found a little piece of ice fast to the rocks, and upon this we effected a landing without any difficulty, and then hurried up to the cairn, which was situated about 300 yards inland, at a point about ninety feet above the level of the water. We had soon all gathered around it. It was a heap of stones about five feet high; and after a moment's search we found the tin tube stuck in a chink between the stones, where it had been placed by Captain Ross twenty-eight years before.

I think there is nothing impresses one more forcibly with the utter loneliness of these regions than the finding of such a document. A scrap of paper placed here in a prominent position on purpose to be seen and found, yet which has remained all these years just as it was loosely placed on this heap of stones, by a hand long since turned to dust. Captain Young opened the tube, which was sealed up with red lead, and found a quarter of a sheet of blue foolscap, on which was written the record which I give below :—

The Record.

" *June 7th*, 1849.—The cylinder which contains this paper was left here by a party detached from her Majesty's ships ENTERPRISE and INVESTIGATOR, under the command of Captain Sir James C. Ross, Royal Navy, in search of the expedition of Sir John Franklin, and to inform any of his party that may find it that those ships, having wintered at Port Leopold, have formed a depôt of provisions for the use of Sir John Franklin's party sufficient for six months. The party are now about to return to the ships, which as early as possible in the spring will push forward to Melville Island, and search the north coast of Barrow Strait, and, failing to meet the party they are seeking, will touch at Port Leopold on their way back and then return to England before the winter shall set in.

Jas. C. Ross, Captain."

As a curious example of the discipline maintained by Ross on this expedition, I may remark that Sir Leopold McClintock never saw this record nor knew what it contained, although he was with Ross at the time it was written and placed here. And this, although they had been travelling together for weeks. I make the following extract from Captain Young's journal in reference to this record :—

"This simple paper, given as the record of a mere visit to the spot, really shows what a remarkable journey Ross and McClintock made when they travelled on foot from Port Leopold around this unknown coast in the days when sledge travelling was in its infancy.

"It also shows how strange are the chances of Arctic navigation, for Ross was in the exact track of the EREBUS and TERROR, and but one season in arrear of Franklin's party having abandoned their ships, and Ross's impression must have been strongly against the probability of Franklin having passed down the straits; otherwise he would have expressed his intention to follow this route with his ships the ensuing summer rather than the north shore of Barrow Strait.

"It was in 1859, in the month of June, that, having completed the journey round the south-west coast of Prince of Wales' Land, I again started from the Fox, and reached Brown's farthest on the north-west side of these straits; thence, in crossing over to this eastern shore, I met with so much water on the ice that I was prevented from reaching Ross's cairn, passing about four miles southward of it. I returned to the ship with the greatest difficulty, having found the ice between this point and Bellot Straits flooded with water to such an extent that we were travelling knee-deep in it and almost floating the sledge itself. I thus missed seeing this cairn, but I can claim to have discovered, under McClintock's command, the land on both sides of these straits southward of Brown's farthest on the western shore; and southward of the point or cape about eight miles south of this cairn, to which point Ross walked, having left his party to build the cairn during his absence. Having left a copy of Ross's Record, with another of my own, I took away the original paper, and after carefully closing the cylinder, deposited it in its former place, and then we returned to our ship."

Strange indeed are the chances, the fatality rather, of Arctic navigation! Ross was here within 200 miles of the spot where only the year before the crews of the EREBUS and TERROR had abandoned their ships. Even then there may have been some of the survivors dragging out a miserable existence on King William's Island, whom he might have reached, had he but known or suspected they were there.

How strange that this letter, written to Sir John Franklin, for it is really intended for him, should have been received by Captain Young twenty-eight years afterwards!

These few hurried lines, written in the cold, with benumbed fingers, carry us back to the time when the excitement about Sir John was just beginning; an excitement which moved the world to enthusiasm and pity, which led to sending out ship after ship in search of the lost expedition, and to the most superhuman efforts to save it; all, alas! without avail. The hands which should have opened this letter were even then cold and stark, wrapped in their winding-sheet of snow. And the eyes which should have read it, closed for ever. Many of those who took so lively an interest in unveiling the mystery of the lost expedition, have gone to solve that mystery in a more direct and surer way, each upon his own account, and at his own expense.

Lieutenants Pirie and Beynen took observations for the dip of the needle, which they found to be 89°, one degree from the perpendicular. We then descended to the beach, scrambling with difficulty over the round, smooth boulders, got into our boat, and rowed back to the ship.

CHAPTER XXIII.

SUSPENSE.

THAT night we were again beset by the fog; but the wind was very light, we had more sea-room, and the danger was therefore small compared to that of the previous night. When I went on deck next morning I was astonished to see the man at the wheel with his back turned towards the ship's head, looking astern instead of forward. In lieu of sun or compass, he was steering by the land, which was visible in that direction through a rift in the fog. Towards ten o'clock the fog cleared away, and we were favoured with another bright, clear day.

As an example of the difficulty of finding one's way in this part of the world in cloudy or thick weather, Ross relates that during one whole day he was beating up against a fair wind; or, in other words, working with much difficulty in exactly the opposite direction to his course.

We were now rapidly approaching Bellot's

Straits, and our eyes were anxiously turned southward.

What should we find there? the ice-pack which had stopped the Fox, or open water that would allow us to reach King William's Land? that wild, bleak, desolate island whose narrow shores contain the awful mystery that still hangs over the fate of Sir John Franklin.

If we should find no ice in Franklin Channel, or not sufficient to bar the way; if we should be able to reach the lone, sad isle in time for a summer search, what might we not find there in the way of relics!—books, papers, and journals, the log-books of the EREBUS and TERROR, and perhaps the grave and the skeleton of Sir John himself!

Besides, if we should get so far, there was good reason to hope that we would be able to go farther; that we would find open water all the way along the coast of North America to Behring's Straits, and thus make the North-west Passage.

That which has been the dream of navigators for centuries seemed to us a reality almost within our grasp. It was only fifty miles to Bellot's Straits, one hundred and seventy to King William's Island—a day's run—and there was no appearance of ice as yet. Twenty-four hours would decide the matter.

How excited we were that day! We discussed the probabilities in the most hopeful manner, all except the captain, who remained silent and taciturn. We said, " If everything goes well, we will be this time to-morrow in sight of King William's Island." If anybody had suggested that everything might not go well, we would have regarded him as a croaker, and have put him down.

We watched the silent coast with questioning eyes, as we glided by, for any indication of what we should find farther south; but it lay sullenly asleep in the warm sunshine, indifferent to our hopes and fears, and gave no sign.

Down the strait we fly under steam, for the wind has quite died out; rapidly we glide past little points, bays, and inlets, while the opposite coast looms up high and distinct on the western side, and the broad sheet of water stretches away before us to the south, like a grand and magnificent river, until it meets the sky. There is not a breath of wind, nor the sign of a current or tide, to raise a ripple on its glassy surface, and it lies there calm, placid, beautiful, clothed in the warm, trembling sunlight as with a quivering luminous veil. The dark hull of the PANDORA, throwing out a widening circle of rippling wavelets, looks like a monstrous black spider crawling over this silvery web, making it tremble and vibrate to its very edge.

And still no ice! What does it mean? This bright sunny weather, this iceless sea, this silence, this death-like stillness! There is something almost awful in it. It looks as though the Spirit of the place had laid a trap for us, and were only waiting for us to fall into it. Was it not down over these same waters that the doomed EREBUS and TERROR sailed on their last fatal voyage? Did not the sun shine as brightly on them as it now does upon us? Was not the water as calm, the sky as blue, the air as soft and warm? Were not their hopes as high as ours? And were they not caught in the fatal snare at last? Is it not possible that we may be entrapped in the same way? Apparently our captain thinks it very possible, for he casts many an anxious glance behind as well as before. Indeed, who can tell whether the pack we passed with so much difficulty at the entrance to Peel Strait may not drift down after us, fill up the narrow channel behind, and render retreat impossible?

For all we know to the contrary, the way back may be already closed. And then, if Franklin Channel should be full of ice, and impassable, our only hope of escape would be through Bellot's Straits into Regent Inlet. Our hopes, as we approach the critical point, begin to be troubled by many misgivings. We therefore look anxiously forward to reaching Bellot's Straits, not only as the critical point where the Fox was stopped, but as a means of changing, if necessary, our base of operations. The danger of waiting in Regent's Inlet would be far less than in Peel Strait, because there is less probability of the outlet being closed. If we can reach Bellot's Strait, therefore, we may wait several days for the ice to break up, should we find Franklin Channel blocked.

Onward to Bellot's Straits. It is only thirty miles now, and three hours more will decide it. We go below to dinner at one o'clock, as usual, and lively are the discussions which ensue. It is almost certain now that we will reach the Straits of poor Bellot; we suppose we will get that far as a matter of course; we ought to be there by five o'clock. But will we find the pack or open water? that is the great question. We have for dinner to-day pea-soup, fried seal-steak, and plum-pudding. We are dining unusually well, and feel gay, though excited and anxious.

We expect to be in San Francisco in six weeks, and we talk of what we will probably eat in the best restaurant the first time we go ashore there.

We chaff "Tromp" on the probability of his never seeing Darwa again, if we come out on the other side of America, and the young hypocrite pretends to be sorry. The skipper is, however, gloomy and taciturn, and does not take any part in our gay, light-hearted conversation; it turns out that before coming below he had observed certain ominous signs which had escaped our inexperienced eyes.

How uncertain are the chances of Arctic navigation! When we go on deck after dinner, a dark mound is rising far out of the water, away on the southern horizon, which is soon made out to be La Roquette Island, and behind and beyond it, stretching along the sky, a whitish glare, which we all recognize, too surely, as the dreaded "ice-blink."

As we advance white specks begin to appear on the horizon, that gleam like calcium lights in the bright sunshine. The thermometer begins to go down, keeping pace with our hopes, and we would be aware of the presence of ice without seeing it, by the raw cold that begins to creep through the air and chill us like a damp sheet.

Still there is hope. The ice we see may not be the pack, but only loose floes, through which we can force our way, as far perhaps as Bellot's Straits, from which we are now only twenty miles distant.

Rapidly the island of Roquette rises out of the water as though coming up from a prolonged plunge, and rapidly the white specks thicken behind it, until they present an unbroken, serried line, extending from shore to shore—the soldiers of the Ice Queen arrayed in her own white uniform, drawn up in battle array to oppose our further advance.

All hands are on deck; some on the top-gallant forecastle, some on the nettings, some up on the shrouds, anxiously and curiously watching this unexpected apparition. At four o'clock we are off

La Roquette Island, between it and the coast of
North Somerset; we stop steaming, and the PAN-
DORA drifts slowly up towards the ice, against
which she lazily flings herself at full length, as
though determined to take a rest after her long
run.

Several of us have already scrambled up to the
foretop, where old Toms, the gunner, is on the

look-out, and we ask him about the prospect.   He
shakes his head, and says, " It looks bad, but I
hopes we will get through it yet."   Old Toms is
always hopeful, but the prospect is not.

Just away to the south-east we can see a tremendous wall of rock, the continuation of the coast
of North Somerset, through which a deep gap is
cloven whose high perpendicular walls form a
mighty gateway.   This is the entrance to Bellot's

Straits, now only ten miles distant. But alas! these ten miles are ten miles of solid pack ice, through which no ship can penetrate. From Bellot's Straits across to the western coast it is the same, a solid plain of ice, extending from shore to shore.

We climb to the topsail yard, then to the dizzy fore-crosstrees, hoping to catch a glimpse of open water. It is without avail. Vainly we search with eager eyes for some dark streak along the distant horizon line that would tell us of water; vainly we sweep the plain with our glasses; the dull white floor reaches without a break to the yellow golden sky.

Although we were not yet sure of it, we had come to the end of our voyage. We waited here for three days, but we never succeeded in making another foot.

I am afraid people in general have a very imperfect conception of the conditions of ice navigation, and very exaggerated notions of the possibility of driving a ship through a pack. We read so much of sawing the ice, of blasting it with gunpowder, of turning the ship into a battering-ram and charging it, coming down on it with a run and a jump and crushing it, that we begin to think a ship can bore its way through any pack, however formidable. This is a very false notion. The truth is that only under exceptional and comparatively rare circumstances can any of these means be used. When the ice is thin, for in-

stance, say not more than a foot thick, when it
is important to put the ship in a safe position, or
to get her out of danger, and the distance to be
made is very short, say one or two miles, either, or
all of these means may be employed with advantage. But no navigator would think of entering
a solid and extensive pack, even one foot thick,
with the idea of boring his way through any
distance. His progress would in the first place
be very slow; two or three miles a day would be
good work. The pack would in the meantime
close behind, and he would be locked in, or
" beset."

While here he would probably have the chagrin
of seeing the ice open somewhere and leave
a passage which he would be unable to reach;
or the pack might commence moving off in exactly the opposite direction from that which he
wished to go, carrying him in its firm grasp twenty
miles to his one. The wind is the great engineer
on whom the navigator must depend for opening
routes through the ice; an engineer who in an
hour will do more than man, with all his puny
appliances, can accomplish in weeks.

In our case the ice was from five to thirty feet
thick, a mass of heavy floes jammed together and
piled upon each other in jagged heaps; in sharp
serrated ridges like a saw; in rugged, craggy hil-
locks and hummocks, that bristled with spiky
edges, angular cones and peaks, all welded to-

gether by freezing, and as solid as granite. No appliances ever invented by man would take a ship through such a pack. Our only hope now was the wind, which might yet kindly open us a passage, and allow us to get through to Bellot's Straits at least.

In the meantime we could only lay the ship to, and wait for a change. The captain went to his room, and turned in, to get if possible a few hours' repose. Lieutenants Lillingston, Beynen, and myself got into the dingey, and rowed off in quest of seals. The doctor took his gun and proceeded to shoot and skin gulls for specimens. Mr. De Wilde got out on the ice to do some sketching, and the crew smoked their pipes, and discussed the prospects.

We got several shots at seals that came popping their pudding heads up out of the water to peer at us in their curious, inquisitive way. But they were timid and distrustful; our boat was very crank, which made it difficult to shoot, and we did not succeed in killing a single one. This was another disappointment, as we had eaten our last piece of seal-steak that day, and would now have to fall back on our salt beef and pork, a not very agreeable prospect.

Salt beef and pork are undoubtedly very estimable things in their way, and they even have a certain commercial value, but they are not good to eat.

After wasting several cartridges with no effect. but that of making the seals duck with a suddenness that was surprising, only to reappear at a safer distance, we returned to the ship. We found the Doctor had been more successful than ourselves. He had bagged any number of birds, which he proceeded to dissect with as much apparent interest as if they had died under his treatment. Pirie was hard at work correcting the chart of the west coast of North Somerset; De Wilde was retouching some of the sketches by the light of the setting sun; Joe was leaning over the nettings, watching the ice, and complacently smoking his pipe; and Captain Young was still asleep.

The sun set at last, after skimming along the horizon an immense distance, as though looking for a good place to go down, then suddenly made a plunge and disappeared. Night came on and brought with it a fog, heavy, damp, and dismal, that made us glad to go below, where there was a bright coal-fire burning in the grate. There was nothing to do but wait. So we drank our tea, smoked our pipes or cigars, listened to the ice grinding against the ship's sides, and, as usual, dropped into a most violent discussion, this time on the general principles which ought to govern the tenure of land.

I have observed that people under such circumstances usually choose for conversation subjects that could not have by any possibility the most remote interest, the most distant connexion with their actual situation. This discussion did not strike us as in the least absurd, there in the midst of thousands of square miles of land, which any body who chose might occupy without the slightest possibility of his claim being disputed.

I would venture to predict that if some good fairy would come and tell us what the people in the ALERT and DISCOVERY talk most about during their long, winter night—for it is all night to them—we would be astonished to learn what absurdly irrevelant matters they choose for subjects of conversation ; not because they lack interest in what they are doing, but because their work is ever present with them, weighing upon them, and they are always glad to lay down the burden for a moment and soar away to another hemisphere.

We turned in at last, hoping the morning would bring us brighter prospects.

CHAPTER XXIV.

WAITING.

THE morrow came, but brought no change. The fog hung over and around us like a great, wet ragged fleece of wool that had got entangled in the PANDORA'S rigging, and hung from it in dripping masses. Here and there, through the ragged interstices, could be caught faint, spectral glimpses of ice floating around, which seemed to be equally thick in all directions.

Steam was kept up, and the ship was moved every half-hour or so; but, for my part, I cannot imagine how the Captain knew in which direction he was moving her. The island of La Roquette, although dangerously near, was invisible, as was the coast of North Somerset, and there was nothing else to serve as a land-mark. A seaman acquires, I imagine, another sense, a kind of instinct, which enables him to keep the points of the compass in his head like birds of passage. It must require a kind of intuition approaching instinct to have enabled Captain Young to save his ship amid the dangers which surrounded us in Peel Strait.

To make one completely miserable, wretched, disheartened, discouraged, misanthropic, and disgusted with life there is nothing, I think, equal to an Arctic fog.

It is cold, dank, and disagreeable. It searches and penetrates everywhere. The thickest, warmest clothing does not suffice to keep it out. It crawls through folds and unknown crevices of your dress, and wraps itself about your shrinking limbs like a snake trying to warm itself. Ugh! only those who have tried the cold-water cure can form any idea of it.

At noon the fog commenced to clear away, and by two o'clock the sky was bright again. But no change had occurred in the ice. We found ourselves a little to the north of La Roquette Island, and Captain Young started the screw going, and bore along the edge of the pack towards the western shore, rather with the object of moving about than in the hopes of finding a lead. It was too clearly evident that there was none.

In the course of the afternoon we came back towards the island, but loose ice prevented our approaching nearer than a mile. The Captain, however, decided to land, and he, Pirie, Beynen, De Wilde, and myself got into a boat and rowed off towards the island. We first landed on a floe, where Mr. De Wilde made a photograph of the island, and Mr. Pirie took observations for the dip of the needle, which he found to be here 89° 30′.

We then rowed on towards the island, but there was so much ice in the way that we only succeeded in reaching it with the greatest difficulty. We at last managed to get ashore between two pieces of ice, where the water was so shallow that we had to wade to land at the risk of getting our feet wet. We found the island to be, like the Cary Isles and North Somerset, a mere heap of huge boulders, worn for the most part round and smooth as if by the action of water. It was, perhaps, a mile and a half in diameter the longest way, and it rose from the shore in an irregular slope to a height of about two hundred feet above the water.

We hurriedly scrambled up to the top, anxious to have a look away to the south, from a standpoint a hundred feet higher than our look-out on board the ship. But, alas! the same white plain met our view we had seen the day before, the same snowy floor extending without a break to the sky. The only difference was that we perceived an iceberg far away to the south, which we had not remarked the day before. This iceberg Captain Young thinks a curious and important fact, bearing upon the movements of the ice, as no icebergs are formed in this part of the Arctic, and it must have come from a long distance.

Captain Young was here on familiar ground, and close to his old encampments when surveying these coasts in 1859. The land, the islands, the points, capes, headlands, and mountains, appeared familiar to him, engraved as they were on his memory during that fearful sledge journey, when he passed here scarcely able to drag one leg after another, wading through water up to his waist, and worn-out with the three months' continuous travel over ice and snow. Captain Young's sledge journeys while out in the Fox appear to me to be so interesting that I have thought it worth while to devote the next chapter to them, the more especially as he has never given a detailed account of them to the public.

We found here on the summit of the island a good deal of soft, thick moss, which had found a foothold somehow, but not a spear of grass, or other sign of vegetation. Captain Young had brought with him a tin tube, and a record, giving a short account of our voyage, which he proposed to leave on the island. We accordingly began to gather up stones to build a cairn, which proved to be no easy matter, as the summit, instead of being composed of a mass of huge boulders, as was the lower part of the island, was composed of great masses of rock, with very few small, detached pieces. We gathered up enough at last, however, and proceeded to build our cairn.

The construction of a cairn does not require any great degree of skill in masonry. It was only necessary to heap up a quantity of stones to the desired height,—about six feet, or higher if required, to be seen from a great distance, and the cairn is complete. The tube containing the record, sealed up with white lead, was then stuck in a chink between the stones, where it will stay until the next ship goes down Peel Strait.

As there was nothing more to be done here, we descended to our boat and put off for the ship. The loose ice, under the pressure of a light breeze, had commenced moving, and opened an easier passage than we had found when going ashore.

The sun was now setting, young ice had begun to form while we were on the island, and it was already a quarter of an inch thick, though very soft. It was strong enough, however, to make rowing very warm work, and we were very glad to get back to the ship, where a warm supper was awaiting us.

CHAPTER XXV.

ALLEN YOUNG'S SLEDGE JOURNEYS.

THE voyage of the Fox under McClintock, and the details of the wonderful sledge journeys performed by him and Hobson, with the dramatic incidents that attended the finding of the relics of Sir John Franklin, are familiar to English readers.

But I think that Captain Young's sledge journeys performed at the same time, an account of which he has never yet given the world, are equally full of interest. He came out with McClintock as navigating officer, having resigned the command of his own ship to accept that position, and contributed besides, to the expenses of the expedition. His work was allotted him, the region he was to explore marked out by his commander, and he performed that work with thoroughness and zeal, contending with the most frightful difficulties; but as he found no relics of Sir John Franklin, which was the grand object of the expedition, he has always thought that the story of his own adventures could not have the slightest interest for the public. It was only upon my earnest request, that he at last consented I should embody in the present chapter, his journal kept at the time, together with many incidents I picked up in conversation with him.

For my own part, I think that these journeys performed in the simple execution of an appointed task, with no hope of fame or reward, and with no results but the exploration of the country, are scarcely surpassed in interest by the more brilliant and successful feats of McClintock and Hobson.   But the reader shall judge.

It will be remembered that the Fox, the first summer out, was beset in Melville Bay, and drifted during the winter down through Davis' Straits, where she was only released the following spring. As soon as he got free, McClintock returned again to the charge, and this time—the summer of 1859 —succeeded in passing down Regent Inlet, and through Bellot's Straits to its western entrance, where he was stopped by ice about ten miles from the present position of the PANDORA. He went into winter-quarters on the east side of Bellot's Straits, and determined to prosecute the search for the missing ships of Franklin by sledge journeys round King William's Land to the mouth of the Fish River, and also to the west to explore Prince of Wales' Land.

It was not then known whether the latter

was part of Victoria Land, or whether they were divided by a channel, whose existence was afterwards proved by Young's sledge journeys. It had then been pretty well ascertained that Franklin's expedition had perished on the shores of King William's Island, and about the mouth of the Great Fish River; but in order that the whole of the unexplored region in which Franklin had disappeared might be included in the search, Young willingly undertook the exploration of the unknown tract where was the least probability of finding any traces of the lost expedition. It was arranged, therefore, that three travelling parties should engage in the search.

The first, commanded by Captain McClintock, was to push directly for the Fish River, and examine Montreal Island at its mouth, where he hoped to find the lost records, and then return to the ship by the west side of King William's Land. The second exploring party was under the command of Lieutenant Hobson, and its object was to proceed by the west side of King William's Land as far south as possible towards Fish River. The third party, led by Allen Young, was to cross Peel Strait to Prince of Wales' Land, and go southwards, if possible, to Victoria Land, as far as Collinson's winter-quarters. In the event of finding a channel to exist, he was to proceed to the north-west, and connect his discoveries with those of Captain Sherard Osborn.

During the winter, while awaiting the coming of spring to commence the projected sledge journeys, an account of the provisions was taken, and it was found that some very necessary articles were running short. This being reported to Captain McClintock, Young volunteered to proceed to Fury Beach, where Parry had landed stores from the ship FURY in 1825, which it was hoped would still be found there. Failing to find these, he was to go to Port Leopold, where Sir James Ross had left provisions, and endeavour to procure the necessary articles, returning to the ship in time to commence his long spring journey. Owing to the fact that the rest of the available sledging force was exhausted by earlier journeys, Young went on this desolate and uncertain exploring tour, accompanied only by the ship's cook, two Eskimos, and a few dogs. He started on March 18, and succeeded in reaching Fury Beach, eighty miles distant, after a severe struggle with the dreaded north-west gales.

Arrived at the place where he expected to see the store-house containing the provisions, he could find nothing. An even, unbroken line of snow met his gaze on every side, without the slightest indication to mark the spot.

The only guides he had to show him where the stores on Fury Beach lay hid were his sextant and chronometer; these had led him here to this smooth, level plain, where a rabbit could not have found hiding, and there was nothing to be seen.

This was a bitter disappointment; for if he found no supplies here, he would have to go on to Port Leopold, a hundred and fifty miles farther, with no assurance that he would find anything when he arrived there.

He had almost made up his mind to proceed to Port Leopold, when he was surprised to hear, a short distance away, the report of a fowling-piece. He looked, and saw that one of his Eskimo companions had fired at some small, dark object on the snow, about the size of a rabbit.

When an Eskimo perceives any object on the snow, he always fires, without waiting to see what it is, as it is impossible to distinguish, in the glare of the sun, whether it is ptarmigan, hare, or only a stone. Upon going to the object in question, the Eskimo perceived that, instead of a partridge, it was the top of a flag-staff, which barely came through the snow. Young then knew the store-house was near.

In fact, it proved to be directly beneath them, as the flag-staff, a very short one, was nailed to the house. They had therefore to open a mine, and bore down through the snow until they found the door, and it was not without considerable difficulty that they succeeded in hoisting the supplies they were in search of to the surface.

He commenced his return journey with two loaded

sledges, the whole weight being about 1200 pounds. In recrossing Cresswell Bay, one of the sledges broke down, and the whole of its burden had to be placed on the other.   This one was now so heavy that in places where the way became rough the load had to be taken off and transported in parts, thus necessitating double labour.   This involved such exhausting work and fatigue that Young became snow-blind.

But finding it would be dangerous to delay, he ordered the rest of the party to proceed, and leave him alone in his sleeping-bag, to recover.   This they accordingly did, and he remained here two days lying in the snow, in the midst of the dreary plain, blind and utterly helpless, far removed from human aid.   He had with him nothing to eat but a little frozen pemmican; nothing to drink but snow, which he melted in his mouth, and he was thirty miles from the land, in a locality frequented by bears!

The snow, however, drifted over him, and he remarks that he passed the time in tolerable comfort, listening, when not asleep, to the wind howling around, and feeling the warm coverlet of snow gradually thickening over him.

But these two days did not pass without some fearful emotions. Once during the time—he could not tell whether it was night or day—he heard steps approaching; thinking it was a relief party that had been sent out for him, he cried out, to let them know where he was, for fear the snow had completely buried him. The steps suddenly stopped, and there was a long silence. Then he heard them approaching, slowly crunching over the snow with a sound he knew could not be human. Then they receded; again approached; then went all round him, evidently reconnoitring.

This continued for what to the blind man appeared an age. Finally the steps began to approach cautiously, and at last he felt a great muzzle rooting at him, with a low, querulous sort of growl, as though asking him what he meant by it. He could even feel the breath of the animal through a crevice beneath the flap that closed the bag over his head. It was a bear!

But Bruin only seemed to be remonstrating with him for sleeping out in that reckless manner, and, having expressed his disapprobation by a few nudges and growls, walked away.

At the end of the second day his sight returned, and he therefore proceeded to overtake his party, and found their encampment about twenty-five miles distant. One of the Eskimos was completely snow-blind, the other had been away twelve hours, out to seaward, with three dogs, in chase of a bear, and had not returned; and the cook was in despair. On the following night the hunter returned, having killed the bear, as he thought, twenty miles away; and, having had a good meal, was greatly disgusted because Young would not allow him time to fetch in the carcase.

The party finally rejoined the ship on March 29, and prepared to start on the long spring journey — the real expedition — which they calculated would extend over a period of seventy-five to eighty days.

The travelling parties were each to consist of four men, drawing one sledge, and six dogs with a second sledge, besides the officer in charge, and the dog-driver. By the aid of depôts, already carried out, the extreme care with which Captain McClintock had prepared the travelling equipment, and reduced every ounce of unnecessary weight, they expected to be able to extend the journey over periods of from seventy to eighty days, and, if necessary, even longer. The captain and Hobson both started on the 2nd of April, and Young got away upon the 7th. The Fox was left in charge of Dr. Walker (surgeon) and three or four invalids, who were unfit for the fatigues of travelling.

Captain Young crossed Peel Strait, and found, as he proceeded, that the coast turned to the north-west, and led up, as was partly anticipated, towards the point which Sherard Osborn reached from the north.

In this outward journey, the ice was found to be exceedingly heavy for travelling, and constant fogs, gales, storms of sleet and snow, continually delayed the progress of the party. The difficulties of dragging the sledges, arising from the nature of the ice, and the deep snow, were such that a whole day's work did not sometimes advance them more than six miles. As they did not know which way the land might trend, and were on quite unknown ground, they were constantly making the circuit of deep bays in the land, where, if they had known it, they might have gone straight across, and thus saved many a weary day's march. Their progress was therefore very slow and fatiguing.

Their manner of camping at the end of the day was as follows :—They carried with them on their sledges a small tent of brown holland, a sleeping-bag for each man, and two or three large pieces of felt. As soon as they had decided to camp, they would instantly unharness their dogs, and set up the tent, which was then carpeted by means of a piece of felt laid down on the snow. The sleeping-bags were then thrown inside, and all, except the cook, instantly crept each into his own bag, drew it up close round head, neck, and ears, and waited impatiently for his supper.

This meal consisted of a pound of pemmican, and a pannikin of tea warmed over a spirit-lamp, and each man took his turn as cook. When the supper was despatched, and the dogs were fed, the cook crawled into his bag ; they stretched themselves out side by side, lying as close together as possible, drew the other piece of felt over them, and tucked it in all round. They were then prepared for the cold of an Arctic night.

The stuff of which the tent was made was so thin that the wind seemed to blow through it as through a net, with its force scarcely broken. After a few days, however, the thin canvas became permeated with ice, and it then afforded much better shelter.

The sleeping-bags were made of a thin kind of felt called duffle, and lined with a thick soft woollen blanket, which was found much more suitable than fur, for the reason that furs after a few days become a frozen mass of ice.

The dogs would lie down in a heap on the sheltered side of the tent; in a short time the snow would cover them over with a warm white blanket, and they were far better protected with their thick furry coats than their masters.

Captain Young's accounts of the nights passed in this manner are most interesting, and his sketches of the British Tar especially, are very amusing.

The men with him were, of course, all sailors. It might be supposed that living amid such conditions, so far away from home, and from human help or succour, they would form a band of brothers, among whom never a word of quarrel or dissension would be heard.

Not so the British Tar. No sooner were they comfortably tucked in for the night than some one of them would start a question which invariably resulted in a heated discussion. This question of " How about that grog ? " appears simple enough in itself, and one could hardly imagine the sinister meaning which was wrapped up in it.

These men were all old shipmates, and had known each other for years, and one of them about ten years before had been accused of making away with some grog which belonged to one of his messmates, a charge which, however, was never properly substantiated.

Now, Jack is not by any means a vindictive person. He might be persuaded perhaps, to shake hands with the murderer of his brother. But there is one crime he will not forgive nor forget, were he to live a thousand years, and that is, any sleight-of-hand where grog is concerned.

This grog was therefore a never-ceasing subject of recrimination, contention, and dispute. Never a night passed without some reference to it ; and one particularly cold night, when the thermometer was fifty degrees below zero, the quarrel waxed so hot that two of them, before Young knew what they were about, suddenly scrambled outside of the tent, with the intention of having it out by the light of an Arctic moon.

Then often after the affair had been adjusted for the night, and they had all gone to sleep, one of them would awaken in the night and imagine he heard a bear outside. Whereupon he would awaken his neighbour, who would arouse the next, and so on until all were awake, including the captain, who would, however, on these occasions generally feign sleep. Then a whispered discussion would ensue as to the advisability of awakening the " Old man "—who, by the way, was a good deal younger than any of them— mixed up with exclamations of " There he is ! "—"I hear the—sanguinary rascal ! "—" He's scratching the snow away under my head ! "—" Tell the ' Old man,' he has the gun beside him ! "—" Geordie, you go out and see ! "—" Oh, yes, of course I'll go out ! "—and so on until finally they would decide that there was no bear at all—a fact which they might have known from the first, because the dogs were quiet. Then the man who had first raised the alarm would get put down, and sat upon in the most ruthless manner.

Once, however, it would seem they really were visited by a bear during the night. This happened, however, to the party Young afterwards detached and sent home, which party were without dogs. Among them was the one who had been most persistent in stirring up discord on the question of the grog. His name was Tommy Florence, the same old Arctic veteran who was with us in the

PANDORA. They had a piece of bacon with them, which old Tommy used to put under his head every night for safety. One night a bear came, and, slipping his claw under the tent stole it, without awakening the tired sleeper.

The tables were then turned on Tommy, for he who had been accused of stealing the grog now affected to not believe in the bear, and pretended that Tommy had got up in the night and eaten the flitch of bacon himself. The result was a pitched battle then and there, the particulars of which Captain Young was never able to obtain.

But to the question of the grog was now added that of the bacon, which served as subjects of dispute until the Fox returned.

The difficulty of dragging the heavily-laden sledges over the hummocks of ice became so great that Young resolved to adopt the plan of sending all his men back, excepting one, rather than incur the risk of not completing the search of the area which had been assigned to him. Accordingly, when twenty-one days from the ship, he sent his men all back but one, George Hobday, giving them the tent, and then proceeded on the dreary journey accompanied by a single companion.

As they were now without a tent, they were obliged at the end of each day's march to build themselves a snow-house—not the scientific Eskimo dome-shaped structure built of blocks of snow, each cut with the precision of a geometrical figure, the proper size and shape for forming an arched vault; but a mere hole in the frozen snow, large enough to crawl into with their sleeping-bags. Then, having warmed some pemmican, and fed themselves and the dogs, they would throw their bags into the hole, struggle into them, and draw over them a brown-holland sheet, which was really the only thing they retained in the way of shelter, and leave it to the wind and snow to cover them in. In a very short time they would be buried beneath a thick deposit of drift-snow, and were thus literally entombed during their sleep. Travelling under such circumstances was never done before; and yet for days and days they proceeded northwards, camping in this manner.

Once they were attacked by snow-blindness. They hastily encamped, a gale came on, they were buried completely, and slept for many hours beyond their time without awaking. They were only aroused by the dogs, who scraped down to them through the snow to see if they were alive or dead. On Captain Young exerting himself to get rid of the pressure of snow, he found his sight quite restored. But in the meantime his chronometer had run down, and it was impossible at first to tell whether they had been encamped one night or a week.

This was a very serious mishap, for, unless he

could recover his lost reckoning it would be impossible to continue the survey, and even difficult, without astronomical observations, to find his way back to the ship. The problem was rendered all the more complicated because for several days he had not, owing to cloudy weather, been able to obtain a single altitude of any heavenly body. Fortunately it turned out a brilliant morning, and the sun and moon were both visible. He measured the angular distance between them, and ascertained the day and hour at which that distance would be found to be correct, and he then discovered that they had slept in their snowy tomb forty hours.

Those only who know what it is to be exposed to a temperature of frozen mercury, accompanied with wind, can form any idea of the discomforts of dragging a sledge over the ice, upon an unknown track, day after day, and for eight or ten consecutive hours, without a meal or drink, the hands and face constantly frostbitten, and boots full of ice; to be attacked with snow-blindness; to encamp and start in the dark, and spend sixteen hours upon the snow, in the hastily-erected snow-house, listening to the wind, the snow-drift, and the howling of the dogs outside, and trying to wrap the frozen blanket closer round the shivering frame. The exhaustion to the system is so great, and the thirst so intense, that the evening pannikin of tea and the allowance of pemmican would not be given up were it possible to receive the whole world in exchange; and woe to the unlucky cook if he capsized the kettle!

Captain Young eventually reached the desired point, viz., Sherard Osborn's farthest, having thus completed the entire coast of Prince of Wales' Land, which he thus proved to be an island. He then attempted to cross from that point the wide channel which he had discovered, now called McClintock Channel, and succeeded in proceeding about forty miles. But the ice was broken up, and the fissures full of snow, into which he and his companion frequently fell headlong, so that there was no alternative but to commence the return journey.

They were now about 270 miles from the ship, and for sustenance during the homeward journey had to trust to the small *caches* of provisions they had dropped on the outward route. On again reaching the land, and verifying the results of his previous observations by the interval of time elapsed, and ascertaining beyond doubt that he had overlapped Sherard Osborn, Young pushed on with all haste to reach the ship before his strength should finally break down. But, on arriving at one of the *caches* a few days afterwards, he found, to his consternation, that the pemmican had been eaten by the bears, and, still worse, that one of them had put a claw through the tin containing the concentrated spirit, the only fuel available, and that the whole had boen lost.

There was now not a moment to lose, for, by the ordinary calculations, there were not sufficient provisions for more than half-way to the ship, and should the next *cache*, which could not be reached under a week, fail, complete starvation would inevitably result.

This was perhaps the most trying period of the whole journey, for they had scarcely anything to eat, and there was nothing for the dogs except the merest scraps of pemmican.

They were obliged to make forced marches, which so enfeebled both men and dogs that the mere act of moving could only be performed with difficulty, and the travellers could not summon enough strength to even dig a hole in the snow for their night encampment, but had to content themselves with lying down beside the sledge, without any further shelter than that of the dogs, who would come and lie down upon them. Finally, the poor brutes all succumbed, and Young was compelled to ask his companion if he thought he could manage to eat the flesh of their faithful canine friends; to which Hobday replied that he could eat dog if his commander could.

They frequently had fainting fits, and, to save time, agreed that they should not wait for each other, but let the stricken man overtake his companion as he best could, on recovering.

They were now on the very verge of starvation, and Young was convinced, that unless game of some kind should fall in their way, they would never reach the ship.

To keep up the energy of his companion, Young from time to time told him that they would arrive next day. Finally, Hobday completely lost his reason, and Young had the greatest difficulty in preventing him wandering away and getting lost. But his delirium seems to have strangely sharpened his vision, for one day he kept exclaiming that he saw a man on a floe far out to sea, when Young himself could see nothing, and he was so persistent in this declaration that Young, to humour him, deviated from his course, and went in the direction indicated.

His surprise and joy were great when he perceived, not a man, but an enormous bear, that was following them. The animal kept a long way off, however, and occasionally stood up on a hummock, with his paws stretched out, looking something like a man. He had probably been following them for days.

Here was a chance to get food sufficient to last until the ship was reached; it was, too, their last hope, and they halted, lay down behind the sledge, and waited with anxiety for the bear to come up.

Then ensued one of those terribly dramatic scenes in which Nature, our cruel step-mother, so much delights. Not a fierce hand-to-hand struggle which would have ended in a minute, but a period of that intense suspense, and alternate ebb of hope and fear, that racks and shatters the strongest nerves.

Contrary to the general supposition, the polar bear is the most prudent and circumspect of animals, and never approaches any unknown object boldly and unhesitatingly. The movements of this one were of the most tortuous and uncertain kind. He would approach within two or three hundred yards, then retreat to the distance of half a mile; again approach, make a wide circuit around them, and then retire a long distance, as if going away for good.

The two travellers knew well that, unless they could kill him and get a meal of his warm flesh and blood, they would never reach the ship—that they must inevitably perish of starvation. Would the bear approach near enough to allow them to shoot him, or would he suspect the danger and go off? This was the question on which their lives depended.

The bear wandered about over the plain apparently without aim or object, alternately approaching and receding, circling around them in the most exasperating manner. Sometimes he would stand up on his hind legs and watch them with outstretched paws for half an hour, as motionless as a statue. Then he would lie down and apparently take a nap for another half-hour, at the end of which time he would probably walk off a distance of a mile or two.

Young had determined, in order not to miss his shot, to wait until his prey should approach within five yards; and he was so well acquainted with the habits of the polar bear that he knew the animal would come even closer, if time were given him, and he were not in the meantime frightened away.

But here was the difficulty. Hobday was delirious, and he insisted on Young shooting when the animal was still two or three hundred yards away. This would have been folly, but Hobday was almost uncontrollable. Young had to watch him as well as the bear, and at one time he became so clamorous that Young had to threaten him to keep him quiet. A silent, desperate struggle for the mastery ensued between these starving men, while the hungry bear was circling around them. Not a physical struggle—for the slightest movement would probably have frightened the animal away, and thus have proved fatal—but a struggle of will against will—of a sane man keeping the mastery over a madman by the mere force of will and eye.

And this scene—with the two haggard, starving, freezing men watching with burning eyes the huge beast that was likewise starving and waiting to feed upon them—lasted for five hours!

It is only in the Arctic that Nature offers us such tragedies as this.

At length the bear approached slowly—very slowly, with many a long pause, until he was within fifteen feet; then, and not till then, the thunderbolt was launched. The huge beast dropped dead in his tracks, and in a moment the two men were feasting on the warm blood that gushed from the wound.

They soon prepared a warm meal, cooked by means of the bear's own grease; then they slept, and when Hobday awoke he was perfectly sane; but he could scarcely remember anything that had happened for the last two or three days.

After a long rest, during which time they ate three or four hearty meals, they packed up enough of the delicious food to last them to the ship, where they arrived without further incident.

Allen Young, although he found no traces of the Franklin expedition during this journey, walked 800 miles, discovered the broad channel since named McClintock's Channel, proved the Prince of Wales Land to be an island, and explored and laid down 400 miles of new coast-line.

CHAPTER XXVI.

THE LAST MAN.

THE results of McClintock's and Hobson's most successful sledge journeys are too well known to the English public to require more than the briefest summary here. They pursued their journey together as far as Cape Victoria, on the east coast of King William's Land, and then separated. Hobson went around the north and west side of the island, which he was to explore as far as he should be able to travel; while McClintock himself went around the east and south side, with the intention of travelling until he should meet Hobson, or reach the point where the latter should have turned back. In this way the circuit of the whole island, or peninsula as it was then supposed to be, would be made.

Hobson, upon arriving at Cape Felix, the northern extremity of King William's Land, found numerous relics of the missing expedition. He discovered a cairn, around which was heaped a great quantity of warm clothing and blankets, that had probably been left there as a depôt by some of Franklin's men, in case they should be obliged to abandon their ships. But, although he made a very thorough search, he found not a line of writing.

He continued his march around the coast to Point Victory, and there he found a cairn, in which was placed a record, containing the only direct information ever obtained of the Franklin expedition. It was a scrap of paper, on which there were about ten lines of writing, resuming the progress and condition of the expedition up to the moment when the record was deposited. Even these few lines were written at two different dates, nearly a year apart, and in two different handwritings, that were readily recognized.

This showed that the record had first been left by a party of Franklin's men, and that nearly a year after, the cairn in which the record was placed, had been visited by another party, who had added the writing under the second date.

The first part of the record simply stated in the briefest words that the ERERUS and TERROR had passed the winter, 1845-6, at Beechey Island; that sailing from thence they were beset in the ice, September 12, fifteen miles N.W. from Cape Felix, the northern extremity of King William's Land, and that all was well with the expedition. This part of the record was written in May of 1847.

The second part was dated April 25, 1848, and

stated that Sir John Franklin had died June 11, 1847, that there had been, all told, twenty-four deaths in the expedition, and that at the date of the writing, 106 men, under the command of Captain Crozier, had landed at Point Victory, with the intention of starting the next day for the Great Fish River.

This record is the only scrap of writing ever found of the Franklin expedition, althoguh thirty voyages have been made in the search, and the whole region around King William's Island has been thoroughly explored. It is a strange circumstance that the expedition left not the slightest trace behind it in the shape of writing.

It has always been the custom of Arctic ships to build cairns in prominent positions, where they can be seen from a long distance, and to place in them records, stating where the ship has been, and in which direction she is bound, together with other details of the voyage. But here, although all the coast-lines along which Franklin must have sailed were searched in the most thorough manner, not the slightest trace of him was ever discovered. The only marks he ever left behind were the three graves at Beechey Island! It seemed as though some mysterious fatality had driven the doomed ships into the network of this great Archipelago, far beyond the point that any ship has since been able to reach, then had swept away all traces of them, and with a wall of ice cut them off from the outside world.

As to the fate of the 106 men who had landed at Point Victory, Hobson soon discovered evidence that showed only too clearly what that fate had been. Proceeding south along the coast, he discovered marks of their passage; not graves this time, but skeletons. At Cape Crozier he discovered a boat, by means of a stanchion, which just showed above the snow, very much as Allen Young had found the house at Fury Beach. Clearing away the snow, he found in the boat a heap of clothing and two skeletons. One of these was lying down, under the clothing, the other sitting in a half-recumbent position, and two rifles, loaded and cocked, were leaning against the boat, within easy reach.

This huntsman had been sitting here waiting for game, with cocked rifle, eleven years!

Hobson found many other relics of the lost expedition here—heaps of clothing, cooking utensils, watches, astronomical instruments, silver spoons, Bibles, Prayer-books, and a great variety of things that had been brought from the ship. But there was not a scrap of anything to eat, but a little tea and chocolate, neither of which would support life in such a climate. The truth was only too evident; the poor fellows had perished of cold and starvation.

Although one of the Bibles was underlined in

almost every verse, not a single line of writing was found to throw further light on the history of the retreating parties.

Hobson had during the latter part of the journey been suffering severely from the scurvy. He was now so bad that he decided to return. But he did not have Young's iron constitution, and his strength soon broke down completely; he became so weak that for forty days he had not only to be dragged on the sledge, but to be carried from the sledge to the tent when camping for the night. The men who were with him were common sailors, and they treated him during the whole of this time with the greatest tenderness and care.

Among them was Toms, the same who had shipped with us in the PANDORA as gunner—a man of Herculean frame and strength. He it was who used to pick Hobson up in his arms, and carry him back and forth from the sledge to the tent morning and evening. Hobson relates that the jolting of the sledge over the rough places in the ice caused him such intense suffering, and he dreaded so much being lifted about, that he often begged Toms to leave him behind, to let him lie there and die. But they used to all gather around him, before starting of a morning, cheer him up, and do their best to keep up his spirits during the long, weary march; and in this they succeeded so well that they brought him safely home to the ship, where he soon recovered.

Jack loves his grog, but he is by no means a bad sort of person for a travelling companion.

McClintock had in the meantime proceeded south, along the coast of King William's Land, to prosecute the search in that direction. He found that King William's Land, which up to that time was thought to be a peninsula, was in reality an island, separated from North America by the narrow channel of water called Simpson Strait.

On the Southern shore of the island he met with Eskimos, who were very friendly and communicative. He found them in possession of a number of relics, that had evidently belonged to the missing expedition, such as silver spoons and forks, with the names of some of Franklin's officers engraved on them, which they readily exchanged for knives and needles. They had obtained them, they said, from a ship that had gone ashore on the west side of the island; and they further informed him that the white men from the ship had all died, that "they dropped down and died as they walked along," but that some of them had reached Montreal Island in the mouth of the Great Fish River.

Thither McClintock continued his march. He crossed Simpson Strait, searched Montreal Island, and the neighbouring shores of the river, without finding anything but a few bits of iron and copper. Then he continued the exploration westward, along the southern shore of the strait, which he finally again recrossed to King William's Island.

There he soon began to come upon the traces of the lost expedition. He found near Cape Herschel a skeleton lying in the snow, face downwards, and near it a note-book with writing, which has never yet been deciphered. Further north he came to the boat Hobson had already discovered, and from there he followed in Hobson's track back to the ship, which he reached after an absence of nearly three months.

He had obtained in the paper found by Hobson the only direct information ever procured of the lost expedition. There could be no doubt now of the fate of the 106 men who had landed at Point Victory, and of the fearful catastrophe in which the expedition had ended.

They had all perished. But not until they had accomplished the great object of their voyage— the discovery of the NORTH-WEST PASSAGE; and the poor skeletons lying along the bleak, forbidding shores of King William's Island bore melancholy evidence of their success.

We of the PANDORA were now within one hundred and twenty miles of the place where these men met their fate. From the top of La Roquette Island we strained our eyes southward, in anxious longing, towards the melancholy spot. What would we not have given for some means of getting over this icy plain that interposed like a ghostly wall between us and the mysterious island ? It seemed to us that we were almost there. From our elevated position we had a view to the south that appeared to extend a hundred miles, and we almost thought we could sometimes distinguish far away on the southern horizon a dark, low-lying coast-line—the shores of the fateful isle.

If the ice would break up and open a passage, we might be there to-morrow ! We could easily make the run in twenty-four hours; and once there, with the ground bare of snow as it is now, what might we not find in the way of relics ! Papers and journals, the log-books of the EREBUS and TERROR, the private journal of Sir John himself.

One could not help thinking of those 106 men who landed on King William's Island twenty-eight years ago, starving and freezing to death. We were so near the spot that the fearful tragedy began to wear an aspect of reality it had never worn before. The imagination is seized upon by it, and in spite of you, goes, on picturing the last moments of these men with fearful distinctness, and constructing whole scenes of the tragedy that are full of a terrible fascination. You follow them, in spite of yourself, along that bleak shore, where " they dropped down as they walked along," wondering who died last, and how they finally met their fate when they saw it was inevitable.

Among these 106 men, there would be a few who would make a gallant fight for life ; two or three at least, strong in frame and stout of heart, who would survive when all their companions had perished, and the imagination is drawn towards these last survivors by a fascination that is irresistible.

You cannot help thinking, for instance, that one of them kept a journal to the end, and that this man was the last to die ; that his skeleton would be found somewhere in the same position in which he sat down the last time, resigned to freeze to death, with note-book and pencil still clinging to the bony fingers.

One sees this man, after the death of his last remaining companion, all alone in that terrible world, gazing round him in mute, voiceless despair, the sole living thing in that dark, frozen universe !

There is no hope for him—none. He knows that within a few hours, he will be as stark and cold as his companion who is lying there in the snow, his stony eyes gazing reproachfully at the relentless sky.

He shivers and shuts his eyes ; his mind wanders far away to the sunny south, and he sees a great city with its lighted streets, its crowds of people, its tall domes and spires and steeples, that rise like Titanic pillars to support the warm, soft blanket of smoke that hangs over it.

He sees its theatres, and balls, and clubs, brilliant with light and overflowing with heat; its bright, comfortable, English homes, with their blazing coal-fires and cozy rooms. He looks into the theatres; a flood of light flashes upon him, and he sees, in a confused picture, the great chandelier, the stage, the rows of faces that are so snugly enfolded by the warm red upholstery. But it is not the stage, nor the actors, nor the ballet, nor the people, that attract him. It is the great chandelier throwing down its beneficent flood of light and heat that he looks at; it is the warm, soft atmosphere that flows over him like a hot shower-bath that he enjoys.

He looks in at a ball, where he would be a welcome and honoured guest; he sees people whom he knows, his own friends dancing, moving about, talking, laughing, chatting gaily. Ah! if he could only speak to them; if he could only let them know; if he could only make his voice heard.

He looks into his club. He sees there many of his friends. They greet each other as they come in, and say, "How do you do, old man? awfully hot, isn't it?" and they go and dine, two or three of them, at the same table where he always dines, in a snug corner, and they complain of the heat and open the window. How can they think of such a thing? He hears what they order for dinner—juicy beef-steaks, new potatoes, green peas, asparagus, fruit —things he has not tasted for three years. And then they have coffee and cigars, and one of them wonders as he lights a Havana, where *he* is by this time. Ah! if they could only know where he is !

He looks in upon his own home, and sees wife, mother, sister, with dreaming eyes that are trying to pierce the darkness around the Pole; that are trying to find him out, wondering where he is, hoping he may soon return, praying he may yet be safe. But now he is glad they do not know where he is this winter night. He goes through the streets, looking in at the windows upon snug, cozy drawing-rooms, with steaming tea-urns, bright blazing coal-fires, with comfortable old gentlemen around them, lying back in easy chairs, blissfully toasting slippered feet, smoking and reading the newspapers. Everywhere thousands of lights gleaming bright, thousands of fires glowing hot—a world teeming, overflowing with light, warmth, heat, life !

He alone of all this multitude is cold. These fires do not warm, these lights do not cheer him. He is freezing to death.

Ah ! it is like a horrible nightmare. He opens his eyes, and instead of the great city with its lights and fires, beholds this stern, dark, frozen world.

The sun has set and the darkness gathers and thickens. The sky is sombre with dull, heavy clouds; but the earth is whitened with a cold, glittering whiteness that chills the heart. His clothing is covered with frozen snow, his face is lean and haggard, his beard a cluster of icicles, his boots two lumps of ice. But his feet are not cold, and he knows they will never feel the cold again.

He sits down in the snow, takes out his note-book and pencil, and scrawls a few lines, as he has done every day since he left England.

But a deadly torpor is crawling over his limbs, a drowsy stupor over his senses. It will be so sweet to sleep, and he will sleep well now—not that shivering, half-waking sleep he has slept so many nights, but a sound, sweet sleep, untroubled by dreams of cold and hunger.

Suddenly there appears a red flash of light low down on the western horizon, that gleams through a rift in the clouds like an angry, bloodshot eye glaring out from behind a sable curtain.

Nature is pitiless, and will glut her thirst for cruelty to the last.

From her throne in the western sky she looks back to earth to see her last wretched victim die.

He turns and meets her sinister gaze with a

steady eye, in which a fiery gleam is reflected, as though he were bidding her defiance.

For a few minutes they glare at each other, this man and this spectre, and then the curtain is drawn, and all is dark.

LA ROQUETTE ISLAND.

[Page 301.

CHAPTER XXVII.

A RACE OUT OF PEEL STRAIT.

WE remained here, cruising about La Roquette Island three days, vainly hoping the pack would break up, and open us a passage.

It was a period of excited, anxious waiting. We were in a most critical position—one in which we might be beset at any moment and imprisoned for the winter.

We could not even be sure that the mouth of Peel Strait had not already closed, and thus cut off our retreat. There was no harbour here into which we could put the ship for safety. And we were waiting with the knowledge that the delay of an hour might result in our staying here all winter, in a place the most unfavourable for wintering that can be imagined. For besides the danger of getting beset, and the probability of not escaping again next summer, there was the fact that it would be utterly useless and purposeless to pass a winter here.

There was absolutely nothing for us to do, no

work to occupy us during the ten long months of
a forced imprisonment. We could only remain
in the ship and waste away with scurvy and in-
action.

At length, on the afternoon of September 2nd,
there came a change. A light breeze sprang up
from the south, which soon commenced to move
the ice. This was a change, but a most unfavourable one; for all this mass of ice was moving
right towards us.

It should be remembered that we were here,
not trying to get north, but south. We had been
running south ever since we left Beechey Island,
and would have continued to do so for 200 miles
farther, had we not been stopped by this pack.
It was Captain Young's intention, had we reached
King William's Island, to attempt the passage
east and south of that island, through Victoria
and Dease and Simpson Straits.

As Sir Leopold McClintock has clearly shown,
Sir John Franklin, owing to the fact that King
William's Land was then supposed to be a peninsula,
attempted the passage west of that island instead
of east. This mistake, unavoidable on his part
at that time, was probably the principal cause of
the disaster, which ended in the loss of the
expedition. For to the best of our knowledge,
McClintock Channel is always closed, summer as
well as winter, by an impassable barrier of heavy
floe-ice, which, driven down from the north, heaps

itself against the western shore of King William's Island, and completely closes the way. While on the other side McClintock ascertained to a certainty that Victoria and Simpson Straits are always open in the summer. Had Franklin only attempted the passage on the east, instead of on the west side of this little island, he would have made the North-West Passage the same season, and the disaster which cost him his life and the lives of his party would not have occurred. Such are the chances of Arctic navigation.

It now became necessary for us to decide what we were going to do; for if we lingered much longer, it would not remain in our power to choose. Captain Young decided to go ashore on La Roquette Island, and have one more look at the prospect. There was no change for the better.

Away to the south-east could be seen the perpendicular cliffs, that form the gigantic gateway to Bellot's Straits; beyond, the coast of Boothia Felix, stretching away to the south until it was lost in the horizon; on the western side, but far away to the south, a bold, high promontory, the south-eastern extremity of the Prince of Wales Land; and all between these two coasts, the same unbroken plain of rugged ice reaching to the horizon.

The iceberg we had seen the day before was considerably nearer, and it was clear that this immense plain of ice was in motion; that it was advancing upon us in a solid mass like a mighty army. Divided in the middle by La Roquette Island, it sheered off right and left, and had already begun to creep up both shores of Peel Strait, leaving an open passage, however, in the middle. In two hours more these two wings would unite; we would be surrounded, and our retreat cut off.

Reluctantly Captain Young decided to withdraw while there was yet time.

As some surprise was expressed at our early return, it may be well to state here Captain Young's reasons for turning back.

With regard to the primary object of our expedition—the navigation of the North-West Passage—it was only too clear that its accomplishment was impossible this season. The spring tides, on which he had counted to a certain extent to break up the ice, had culminated during the three days we were waiting here, and now began to ebb without producing the slightest effect. New ice was rapidly forming everywhere, and the winter had in reality set in. Had the ice been moving south instead of north, we might have followed it as far as Bellot's Straits at least; but as it was advancing upon us, we could only flee before it.

As to remaining here all winter, and attempting to get through next summer, that formed no part of our plans. A North-West Passage that required two seasons for its navigation, would clearly be impracticable and useless. As to our second object—the discovery of some more relics of Sir John Franklin—it should be remembered that our hope had been to reach King William's Island in the summer. A search when the ground was bare of snow, might, it was thought, reveal many things that had escaped the very thorough and successful search of McClintock, made when the snow was on the ground. But from our present position it was impossible to reach King William's Island during the summer; nothing human could have got over that moving pack. We could only have gone into winter quarters and waited for the snow, that would enable us to make the journey by sledging. But a winter search had already been made by McClintock, and we could certainly hope for no further results by merely following in the footsteps of that veteran explorer.

Reluctantly we gave up all hope of prosecuting the voyage, and our last look south was a sad one.

The disappointment was rendered all the more bitter by the fact that the barrier which stopped us was a mere nothing, when compared to the whole distance of 8000 miles, which, but for this impediment, would be easy of navigation. It was, perhaps, not more than fifty miles in extent; and had we been able to pass it, we felt very confident of making the whole distance from Southampton to San Francisco. But this fifty miles of ice was as effectual a barrier to a ship as fifty miles of granite.

We returned to the ship, not without difficulty, for the loose pieces of ice were in rapid motion, and it was no easy matter to work through them.

Captain Young then gave the order to turn the PANDORA's head to the north; she swung round at the word of command, and was soon ploughing her way at full speed up Peel Strait, through a narrow channel of water that was rapidly closing up. In half an hour we had outstripped the ice, and our speed was slackened.

By nightfall we had left it far behind, and we hove to, partly to see if it was still following, partly on account of the danger of proceeding in the darkness.

Daylight came, and showed ice in every direction that had drifted after us during the night. The light breeze which had started it still kept blowing from the south, and we knew that as long as it continued from that direction the ice would keep moving after us.

We again proceeded north, with the pack close at our heels. It was now evident that summer had gone, and that the winter was beginning in earnest. We had squalls of snow and sleet, that rattled over the decks like hail, and the temperature went down to 26°, then to 24°. The rigging became covered with a thin coating of ice; and as the sails would soon have become so stiff as to be unmanageable, the Captain ordered the top-gallant-sails to be furled, and the topsails to be reefed down close, thus avoiding the necessity of going aloft on the icy rigging.

By the evening of the 4th we were again in sight of Limestone Island. As we approached it an enormous pack became visible, which, stretching across the mouth of Peel Strait, seemed to completely close it up and bar the way. It was the same pack we had passed with so much difficulty when entering the Strait, and it still lay there in wait for us.

As we neared it, there could be distinguished at intervals between the snow squalls a narrow thread of open water, along the shore of North Somerset, and through this Captain Young decided to attempt a passage. It was dangerous to run so near the shore, with the on-coming darkness, but it was our only chance of getting out of the Strait ; for had we hesitated, or attempted to turn the pack on the south-west, we would, in all probability, have been caught for the winter. Should this lead of open water reach as far as Cape Rennel, the most northerly point of North Somerset, and enable us to pass that cape, we had little doubt of finding open water beyond, as Barrow Strait and Lancaster Sound were almost certain to be clear.

So we pushed on with the fast-increasing darkness. It was a fearful night. The wind increased to a gale, bringing hail and sleet, which it dashed over us in blinding squalls. We threaded our way through the darkness, guided only by the gleam of the pack on one side, and glimpses of the ghostly, snow-clad land on the other. Once only during the night a solitary star shone out for half an hour, giving the man at the wheel for a short time a fixed point to steer by. The temperature fell to 18° Fahrenheit, and the spray that dashed over the ship froze as it fell.

By three o'clock in the morning we were, as nearly as could be judged, just off Cape Rennel; but although daylight was breaking, there was such a fierce squall of snow that nothing was visible beyond a hundred yards. Suddenly the storm abated and disclosed, close on our starboard beam, the high, precipitous cliffs of Cape Rennel hanging almost over us. The dark, horizontal strata and ledges, with the snow lying upon them, looked like the huge bars of some gigantic iron cage, enclosing a mountain of snow, and presented, close to it as we were, a most threatening spectacle.

The pack was close on the other side, and, looking ahead, we saw it extending right across our path until it met the foot of the cliff. The lead of open water we had been following was completely closed, and our escape in this direction was clearly impossible. We had hardly time to put the ship about when another snow squall beat down on us, and again hid everything from view.

It now looked as though we were to be jammed

against the rocks by the pack, which was slowly closing the narrow lane of open water in which we found ourselves. We ran back rapidly along the edge of this pack, looking for some opening, which proved to be a most difficult thing to find, with the air full of the whirling, driving snow.

Fortunately these snow squalls were of short duration, and when this one ceased, we perceived open water beyond the pack, which was scarcely more than a mile wide at this point. We had evidently passed the main body of ice in the night, and this was only a border stretching along the coast. It was, however, formidable enough to crush us against the rocks, had we not escaped in time.

We fortunately soon found a weak place in it; into this we dashed, and commenced boring our way through. The pack here consisted of old floes, welded together by young ice which was rapidly forming. We met a considerable swell as we advanced, and the young ice rose and fell on the waves without breaking, presenting a curious spectacle, as though the water had been covered an inch thick with oil. Finally, there was only a narrow neck of ice between us and the open sea beyond. This we charged with a full head of steam, and the sharp, iron-clad stem of the PANDORA angrily tore its way through this last barrier like a wild beast breaking out of a cage. Then the good ship dashed into the open waters of Barrow Strait, and we were free.

The Pandora now presented a curious and beautiful sight. As though the dangers of this night had been too much for her, she had turned quite white, as a man's hair may do sometimes under similar circumstances.

Her sides were covered with a heavy casing of ice, her decks were heaped full of snow; great masses of snow and ice covered her yards, and hundreds of icy stalactites hung pendant from yards, rigging, and shrouds. The Pandora, in short, had turned into a large and magnificent icicle.

It was well for us that the top-gallant-sails had been previously furled and the topsails close-reefed, as it would have been impossible to do anything with them in their present condition.

Three days later we had got through Barrow Strait, and out into the north water of Hudson's Bay.

We had failed in the principal objects of our expedition, but we determined to at least make another trial to obtain news of the Alert and Discovery.

The attempt would be attended with considerable risk, for it was now the 6th of September; ice was rapidly forming in all the little bays and inlets wherever sheltered from the wind, and winter was fast setting in.

Captain Young, however, decided to run up to the Cary Isles, search them all thoroughly, and if he found nothing there, to make a dash

for Littleton Island, at the entrance to Smith
Sound.

He was strengthened in this resolution by the
despondent views of our crew with regard to the
Government expedition, who expressed it as their
opinion that the ALERT and DISCOVERY had got
caught in Melville Bay and "droov down the
coontry."

Had we gone home without news these fears
would have grown into a fixed belief, which they
would, upon our return, have spread throughout
the country, and have thus caused unfounded
anxiety and alarm.

There are always people only too ready, not
only to circulate but to fabricate, through pure
perverseness, the most alarming reports about anything that may occupy the public mind. We
learned upon our return that an instance of this
kind had already occurred. Some imbecile, as
ignorant as he was malicious, actually went to the
trouble of writing a letter purporting to be from
somebody in the ALERT or DISCOVERY, and stating
that one of the ships had been sunk; this letter
he sealed up in a bottle and cast into the sea, to
be picked up, read, and published in the papers!

Captain Young knew that if we returned without news such reports would be kept in circula-
tion until next year, and he determined to nip
them in the bud.

The PANDORA's head was therefore once more

turned to the north, against a strong breeze which was blowing at the time, and which soon freshened into a gale. It took us four days, hard work, to reach the Cary Isles, beating up the whole distance in the teeth of this gale, which lulled and freshened alternately, but continued blowing steadily from the north.

At length, on the forenoon of September 10th, we arrived off the S.E. island of the group, and soon made out a cairn on its summit. The ship was hove to, and Lieutenants Lillingston and Beynen put off in a boat, to land and make the search.

The islands were now covered with snow, and the unsightly heaps of stones of which they are composed had been transformed into huge silvery cones, that rose up out of the sea to a height of 800 feet, like gigantic sugar-loaves.

Lieutenants Lillingston and Beynen mounted the steep ascent by means of the snow, and upon examining the cairn found the tube containing Captain Nares' despatch, and many private letters from the officers and crews of the ALERT and DISCOVERY.

It was fortunate that we happened to hit upon the right island this time, for the boat had scarcely returned to the ship when we were assailed by a violent snowstorm, which was so dense as to hide everything at a distance of a hundred yards. Had the boat's crew been a few minutes later they

could not have found the ship, and would have
been obliged to wait on the island until the storm
abated—perhaps all night. It would have besides
been impossible to search the other islands while
the storm lasted; the ship would have been
obliged to put out to sea to avoid the danger of
going ashore, and we might thus have been de-
tained here for several days.

As it was, everything happened for the best, and
having obtained the news we sought we turned
our ship's head to the south with light hearts. We
had not been successful in the grand objects of our
voyage, but we were nevertheless not altogether
dissatisfied with the results of our summer cruise
in the Arctic.

In conclusion, I would say that, although I
have here and there made a little sport of my
messmates, the reader will, I am sure, have read
between the lines, and perceived that this was
not done through any want of respect and
esteem. In truth, although no two of us had
ever seen each other, before stepping on board
the PANDORA, there existed nothing but the best
of good feeling in our little mess-room. This
was so true, that the Captain good-humouredly
complained of the fact, and pretended there was
so much good-fellowship, that it resulted in
our sitting around the table smoking and talking when we ought to have been at work. Nevertheless I believe the work was done well and

thoroughly, if not in the most regular and methodic manner.

Lieutenant Lillingston, with his experience as a naval officer, managed the internal economy of the ship in the most satisfactory and efficient manner.

The position of Lieutenant Pirie, our navigating officer, was a very trying one, for he, as well as the Captain, was responsible for the safety of the ship. There are only two or three officers now living who have navigated a ship under such difficult circumstances; for it is only in the direct neighbourhood of the Magnetic Pole that navigation becomes so dangerous. The escape of the PANDORA from the dangers which beset her in Peel Strait is the best evidence of his skill, as of Captain Young's ready presence of mind.

Dr. Horner was indefatigable in collecting botanical specimens, of which he found seventy-one varieties; in taking barometric and thermometric observations, in the midst of difficulties; and he displayed an exemplary equanimity under the vituperation and abuse that, as caterer of the mess, was heaped upon his devoted head.

Lieutenant Beynen was a very hard worker, and has made a most interesting and valuable report to his Government on ice navigation. He is the first Dutchman I ever met, and my acquaintance with him has convinced me that the old Dutch spirit which waged an eighty years' war for liberty is as vigorous as ever, and that now, as then, the love of country is for the Dutchman, and especially the Dutch officer, a kind of religion.

CHAPTER XXVIII.

A TRAGEDY.

I FIND that I shall have to close my book with the recital of a tragedy.

In a previous chapter I have spoken of the dogs, and incidentally referred to the one we had named "King." It is a well-known fact that in every Arctic dog team there is always one dog who rules the rest, and whose sway is undisputed. Indeed, the driver of the team depends to a considerable extent upon the assistance of the "King Dog" to maintain his authority over the others, and keep them in proper subjection.

Our King Dog was a magnificent specimen of the race, and with his great size, his grave intelligent face, and his heavy fur collar, that almost approached the dimensions of a mane, had a leonine appearance that was very impressive.

He was very intelligent. It is said to be difficult to teach an old dog new tricks, and there is even a proverb which flatly affirms that this cannot be done.

Our " King," however, evidently formed an exception to the rule. Although the custom of shaking hands is unknown to the Eskimo dogs, he had not been on board our ship a week before he learned it, and he liked this mark of friendship so well that he used to follow one about offering to shake hands, when there was no occasion for it at all. He was very plucky, and was ready at any moment to fight the bear, whom he evidently regarded as a superfluous and useless animal.

KING.

Bruin used to have a very disagreeable way, when chained up on the deck, of jumping at the dogs if they passed near him, with a savage roar. which was enough to shake the stoutest nerves. The other dogs were very much in dread of Bruin, and got out of his way without the slightest regard for appearances. The King, however, scorned to be frightened by mere noise, and when the bear leaped the length of his chain at him, refused to budge an inch. It is true he generally kept just out of reach of Bruin, and he often must have measured the distance with an accurate eye. Once, however, he missed his calculation, came a little too close, and the bear got a mouthful of his fur. Nothing daunted, the old fellow summoned the other dogs with a yelp, and was about making a general onslaught with his whole army, when Joe interfered and drove him off.

Afterwards, when we had put the bear in a cage, King lay down beside it, and Bruin caught his ear through the bars, and held it until obliged to let go by a blow over the snout. Two or three days afterwards the dogs were all playing upon the deck in the greatest good humour possible, the King with the rest, when he was suddenly seen to fly at the cage, and seize the bear by the ear. Bruin had lain down against the side of the cage to take a nap; his ear had come through between the bars, and the old monarch had seized the opportunity to be revenged.

He was a veritable old tyrant, and ruled the other dogs with a rod of iron. He had only to look at one of them and lift his bristles to bring the delinquent crouching at his feet begging for mercy, and fawning upon him in the most abject manner. To tell the truth, however, his authority, although most despotic, was exercised with a great deal of moderation. He never robbed his subjects of their food, for instance; but if they ran against him or annoyed him by any other breach of canine etiquette, the punishment was sure, swift, and summary.

In spite of his tyrannical disposition he was very fond of his subjects, as appeared afterwards. When we touched at Disko on the homeward passage, it was thought necessary to get rid of some of the dogs. Captain Young decided to keep King, and Lieutenant Lillingston took Snarley, because they were the finest specimens of the Eskimo dog. But nobody wanted poor Port and Starboard, and they were sold back to the Eskimos. I pitied the poor brutes with all my heart. The first night they were on shore they stood down at the water's edge and howled all night, while old King, with his fore paws up on the taffrail, answered them with the most dismal wailing. The old fellow seemed quite heart-broken, and refused to be comforted.

When we went on shore next morning the two dogs leaped all over us with their muddy paws, and indulged in the most extravagant manifestations of delight. And when we finally put off to the ship, the last night before weighing anchor, their howling was so utterly wretched and despairing that I put my hands to my ears to shut it out.

Curiously enough, the despair of the young dogs

was caused, I think, more by their separation from us than from the King, while he clung to them rather than to us, and, if any choice had been left him, would have followed them ashore. Such is the difference between the old and the young.

Snarley, however, was rather delighted than otherwise at the departure of the others, and was gayer than ever. And although he made a hypocritical pretence of sorrow by occasionally joining in a weakly howl, to please the old King, his delight was too apparent to be concealed. The King was never quite himself again, and when upon arriving at Southampton everybody he knew left the ship, and Snarley, his last subject, was taken from him, his cup of bitterness was full to overflowing. He walked about the ship for days, refusing to eat, and howling in the most dismal manner.

Existence under such conditions became intolerable; life was a mere blank, a thing not to be accepted as a gift. He determined to fly, probably in hopes of regaining his kingdom and rejoining his well-beloved subjects in the far-off Greenland. He escaped from the ship one day, and wandered forth into the streets of Southampton. Here he was beset by a crowd of men and boys, who, instead of trying to make friends with the poor bewildered, harmless brute, ran after him, shouting and hooting. All the curs of Southampton recognizing in him a fugitive king, joined in the hue and cry, and literally drove him out of the place.

He had lost his master, he was abandoned by his friends, deprived of his well-beloved subjects, and hunted down like a wild beast. He determined to become a wild dog, and he fled to the woods.

He completely disappeared, and for some weeks nothing more was heard of him. Then throughout all the country of Hampshire there arose a cry of terror. A strange animal was seen by many different people in a great number of places, flitting through the woods and along the roads in the dusk of the evening. Some thought it was an escaped lioness, others believed it to be a panther, and many good people of Hampshire maintained that it was the Evil One himself. There were paragraphs in all the Hampshire papers about this strange apparition. Finally it was decided to be a wolf, and hunts were organized all over the country.

In the meantime Captain Young, who was having a search made for his favourite dog in Southampton, heard of the "Wolf," and immediately telegraphed to several people in Hampshire that it was his Eskimo "King dog," asking them to try and prevent the poor animal from being killed.

It was all in vain. The good people of Hampshire wanted a wolf, and a wolf they would have. They hunted the poor brute down on horseback, and shot him.

The affectionate, harmless animal might have been led by a child ; if they had called to him and offered him something to eat, he would have come and held up his paw, and licked their hands !

His body was brought into the town in triumph, and the mighty Nimrod who had shot him added the last insult to this fallen and unhappy monarch by exhibiting his remains at sixpence a head !

The circumstance reminds me of a French account I remember reading somewhere, of the fearful death of the man who attempted to descend, or, more properly speaking, who did descend from a balloon in an inverted parachute. He fell into the garden of a public-house, and the proprietor exhibited the mangled body to the public, exacting the charge of a shilling a head ; *" triste exemple "*—as the Frenchman put it—*" de l'esprit commerçant des Anglais."*

Snarley, after a day or two passed in howling, became reconciled to his separation from King. Now, although he displays a certain weakness for butcher-shops, and cannot see why he should not step in and walk off with a piece of the meat displayed there in such profusion, he has gradually adopted the ways of civilization, and does not seem to regret the change.

Two younger dogs that Lieutenant Pirie brought home have become great favourites in the country where they are living, in spite of the fact that they mistake chickens, geese, and ducks for burgo-master gulls, eider ducks, and little auks, and are disposed to treat them as they used to treat poor Mr. Hogan.

APPENDIX.

No. 1.

LETTER FROM ADMIRAL RICHARDS.

(To the Editor of the *Times*.)

Sir,—When the Pandora left Portsmouth, in June last, the object of her voyage was to a great extent shrouded in mystery. Little more could be gathered than that she was provisioned and equipped to pass a winter in the ice, and that she was receiving letters for the Polar Expedition which had preceded her a month.

It was known, of course, that Captain Allen Young was an experienced Arctic navigator; that he had some able naval and other officers under his command, and that he was accompanied by a staff of talented correspondents, naturalists, artists, &c., with a small but picked crew, equal to any service they might be called on to perform. Under these circumstances, and without any display, he quietly sailed out of Portsmouth harbour on the 20th of June last for the Arctic regions.

But Captain Young's aims were not purposeless, and he did not leave England without confiding to a few of his Arctic friends what his hopes and intentions were. I confess I was among those who believed that he displayed a wise discretion in his reticence.

The Pandora has returned, probably, before many expected

her, and though the incidents of her voyage have been ably and graphically depicted by the talented special correspondent, it has not appeared very clearly or authoritatively what were the precise objects of her cruise or why she returned. A few words in your columns, therefore, from one who has no personal interest in the matter, and who does not overstep the bounds of confidence in writing them, may not be unfitting at the present time.

It is generally known that the late Lady Franklin entertained to the end of her life an unalterable conviction that some records of her husband's expedition still lay buried on King William's Land, off the shores of which his ships were abandoned in 1848. However much Arctic authorities may have differed as to the utility of a further search for those documents, Captain Allen Young was always anxious to gratify this natural desire, and, indeed, was the only one interested in the subject whose private means would permit him to do so.

More than once he went so far as to purchase a vessel, with a view of carrying out this object, though from one cause or another his efforts were frustrated. Last year, however, he succeeded in obtaining a suitable vessel in the PANDORA, and with the assistance of one or two associates who joined him in the enterprise, he strengthened and completely equipped her for Arctic service, himself assuming the command; and although he was probably encouraged by the change which had been gradually coming over public opinion in regard to Polar exploration, and by the decision of the Government to send out an expedition, it is pretty certain that he would have carried out his favourite project irrespective of either of these considerations.

The PANDORA then left England, and passed by the usual route through Davis Strait and Lancaster Sound, but instead of sailing down Prince Regent Inlet and trying Bellot Strait, where McClintock had been arrested in the Fox, Captain Young pushed down Peel Sound to the westward, which had scarcely before been attempted by ship, but which was very generally believed to be the true gateway to the north-west passage along the coast of America, which Collinson, in the ENTERPRISE, so nearly effected from Behring Strait.

Could the PANDORA have passed the barrier of ice which choked the narrow throat of this Sound about 120 miles within it entrance, the northern edge of which she reached, there is little doubt in my mind that Captain Young would have accomplished the north-west passage, and he would at the same time have had an opportunity of re-examining the western shores of King William's Land under favourable circumstances; but when he had reached this barrier, and saw from an eminence the western entrance of Bellot Strait, with firm ice stretching right across Peel Sound, he saw that there was little or no hope of effecting the passage during the present season. It was manifest, then, that he must either return or adopt the alternative course of seeking winter quarters, the nearest shelter being forty miles to the northward. In the latter case the PANDORA would not have been so advantageously placed for travelling as the FOX was under McClintock when he discovered the fate of Franklin, and all that could have been done would have been, in the summer of 1876, to have re-examined under less favourable circumstances, a portion of the ground traversed by McClintock, Hobson, and himself, fifteen years before. It must be admitted, then, I think, that a sound judgment was exercised in the course which was adopted.

But if Captain Young failed to accomplish with his little vessel what has never yet been achieved with greater means— viz., the passing by ship from one ocean to another—he has rendered good service to the Government expedition, which deserves to be recorded.

The last intelligence received from the ALERT and DISCOVERY was dated from Disco, the 17th of July, and we had no reason to expect anything further, unless from Upernavik—a short distance to the north—until their return in 1876 or 1877. Now, from Disco to the entrance of Smith Sound, a distance of about 600 miles, is the most difficult and critical portion of an outward Polar voyage, and through Captain Young's perseverance we now know that the ships arrived safely at the Carey Isles, within 100 miles of Smith Sound, after a remarkably successful run of nine days from Disco, includiug stoppages. It is true that Captain Young had promised the commander of the Polar expedition that he would endeavour to communicate with the Carey Isles, but the chances against his being able to do so were considerable, and were perfectly understood to be so by Captain Nares. Not only did Captain Young go considerably out of his way to fulfil his promise on his outward voyage, when he was late in the season, and had an important object of his own in view in another direction, but, failing then to find the records, he made a second attempt late in the year, when his own enterprise was at an end, and against a heavy northerly gale and very severe weather again fetched the Carey Isles on the 10th of September, and discovered and brought away the intelligence which must have been alike satisfactory to the Government and comforting to all who have friends in the expedition.

From this information we learn that the ships left Upernavik, the northernmost Danish post in Greenland, on the 22nd of July, and that Captain Nares, by boldly pushing out into the middle ice, had achieved in five days what formerly occupied more than as many weeks to accomplish, with harassing labour, in sailing vessels, along the land ice of Melville Bay. In a short note to myself from Carey Isles, dated July 27, Captain Nares describes the season as most favourable, and their prospects bright beyond anything they could have hoped for; and an extract from a private letter which has been put at my disposal, and which you may, perhaps, think will be of interest to your readers, speaks also more hopefully of their prospects. It is from Commander Markham, of the ALERT. No doubt the season had been favourable; but I am inclined to believe that unfavourable seasons were more impressed upon us formerly from the absence of steam power.

There can be no question but that the prospect from the Carey Isles was very promising. Northerly winds and a current of a mile and a half an hour had apparently cleared out the ice to the north, and no doubt existed in Captain Nares' mind but that they would be within the Sound in less than two days. This fair prospect was corroborated by Captain Young, who observed the same favourable state of things on the 18th of August, and again on the 10th of September.

Humanly speaking, therefore, the programme, so far as it could be laid down with any degree of certainty, has probably been accomplished, and less than 300 miles from the entrance of Smith Sound would place the DISCOVERY in the position hoped for. What lies beyond the 82nd deg. parallel we must wait to learn. In the meantime there is much cause for hope and confidence. Most people will probably agree that Captain Young has more than fulfilled his promise—a promise spontaneously and generously made and carried out at some sacrifice.

The PANDORA would gladly have followed the Polar explorers on the 10th of September, tempestuous, though promising, as the prospect was then to her; but those who know Captain Allen Young will best understand the delicacy which forbade him to seek a share of the honours where he could not add to the resources, and where possible disaster might have caused him and his gallant companions to become an extra burden upon them.

I am, sir, your obedient servant,

GEORGE HENRY RICHARDS,

Rear-Admiral.

Athenæum Club, Oct. 23.

No. 2.

LETTER FROM ADMIRAL COLLINSON.

DEAR MISS CRACROFT,—I enclose Allen Young's letters to McClintock, sent from Disco.

The PANDORA'S outward passage has been so long, that I have no doubt the loss of daylight will prevent their attempting Peel Sound this season. It would be madness to winter in the neighbourhood of Bellot Strait on that side. I do not believe there is one indentation either on North Somerset, west side, or Prince of Wales Land, that the ice does not move in during the winter, and it will not do to expose the PANDORA to a second edition of what the TERROR underwent in Hudson's Bay. The tide will be the means by which the passage will be made, but that tide must be encountered with the advantage of daylight and a higher temperature. I shall not be surprised to see them in England before the end of the month.

Very sincerely yours,

R. COLLINSON.

The Haven, Ealing, Oct. 12, 1875.

No. 3.

LETTER FROM ADMIRAL SIR LEOPOLD McCLINTOCK.

Portsmouth, England, Nov. 3, 1875.

JAMES GORDON BENNETT, Esq.

DEAR SIR,—You call for my ideas upon the subject of Allen Young's recent voyage into Peel Strait, and you call for it as being yourself deeply interested in Arctic exploration, and in all matters relating to the practicability of the North-west Passage. I can have no sort of hesitation in complying with your wish.

Young was with me in the Fox when we attempted to pass down Peel Strait in August, 1858. We were stopped by fixed ice, after a run down of only twenty-five miles. Without wasting time in waiting there, we attempted to pass through Bellot Strait ; and although we succeeded in this, yet our further progress was stopped by fixed ice across its western outlet. You will remember that my object was to reach King William's Island. From my position, at this western outlet of Bellot Strait, I could see that all to the north, as far as the horizon, was covered with unbroken ice, while all to the south was water, with the exception of the belt of fixed ice, some three or four miles wide, which so effectually barred my way.

Subsequent sledging explorations to the Great Fish River, and all round King William's Island, convinced me that we actually saw in that narrow barrier of ice the only impediment to our progress to and beyond King William's Island. It also convinced me that Franklin's ships passed down Peel Strait, thus proving that seasons do occur when it is navigable.

And now to sum up. We know of one year (Franklin's) when Peel Strait was navigable ; of another year (McClintock's) when it was not navigable, and of a third year (Allen Young's) when it was partially navigable. In my opinion, this Strait, together with its southern continuation, is probably navigable once in four or five years ; and if a steamer could then make her way through it before the close of the month of August, she would be able to complete the passage from the one ocean to the other before the navigable season was over.

Here let me refer you to my narrative of the voyage of the Fox (later editions, pages 265—267) for my own opinions, as they were written down at the time.

Young's attempt to accomplish the North-west Passage was as bold and skilful a one as was ever made. He persevered, not only after all hope seemed extinguished, but until further perseverance would have rendered his retreat impossible ; and here, at the most critical moment of his voyage, I consider that he exercised the soundest judgment and discretion in effecting his escape. Had his attempt been successful, he would not only have accomplished the North-west Passage, but would also have achieved another object which he had in view— namely, that of searching the shores of King William's Island, at the only season when they are free from snow, for further relics of Sir John Franklin's expedition, which perished there in 1848.

But, although baffled in the main objects of his voyage, other important and useful work remained for him to do, and well he has done it. He has brought us intelligence of our Arctic expedition of very great interest. By it we know that they had surmounted all the difficulties of Baffin's Bay navigation, had crossed the dreaded Melville Bay with hardly a check, and that as early as July 26th they were within 100 miles of Smith Sound, where their work of exploration was to begin, and that they were favoured with an unusually good season.

But for Allen Young, in the PANDORA, this good news could not have reached us for another year at the least. The country has been spared a year's doubts and misgivings, and I trust that Mr. Young has received from official quarters an acknowledgment commensurate with the great public service he has thus rendered, at so much personal hazard and cost.

I remain, dear sir, faithfully yours,
F. L. McClintock.

No. 4.

LETTER FROM ALLEN YOUNG.

St. James's Street, London, Oct. 26, 1875.

My dear Bennett,—You will doubtless ere this have gathered some idea of our Arctic cruise in the yacht PANDORA, toward the expenses of which, as an act of friendship toward Lady Franklin, as well as to myself, and with that interest in the work of exploration which you have always shown, you so generously contributed. Your representative, Mr. MacGahan, who accompanied me, and who was of the greatest assistance to us, apart from the special duties he had to perform in his capacity as an officer of the PANDORA, will have informed you already of what we accomplished. I fear that the results attained will not have come up to your anticipations, but you are too well aware that the chances of navigating the Polar Seas are so uncertain that it was scarcely possible to reckon seriously on carrying out all our cherished plans. One can only try to do one's best. It is unnecessary for me now to go into the details

of our voyage, but I take great pleasure in sending you with
this letter copies of passages from my private journal, which
will give you some idea of both the hardships and pleasures of
an Arctic cruise.

You will remember that the objects of our voyage as arranged
before starting were, first, to ascertain the practicability
of the North-west Passage, and by taking advantage of
the experience gained by previous explorers, to sail through
in one summer season ; and secondly, as in the accomplishment of an undertaking of such universal interest we should be
led past that sadly romantic region about King William's
Island, in which may yet be locked up the mystery still hanging
about the journals of the EREBUS and TERROR, we might be
enabled to search for further relics and papers of the lost expedition.

As to the first object of our expedition, our hopes were
founded upon the following grounds :—

It is well known that during August and September there
is generally open water along the whole northern coast of
America, from Behring Strait to King William's Island. Captain Collinson, now Admiral, made nearly this whole distance
in a sailing vessel in 1852-53 when in search of Franklin, and
wintered within 100 miles of that place. Simpson likewise
sailed through Dease and Simpson Straits in boats, finding open
water all the way along the south coast of King William's
Island, and many ships have sailed from Behring Strait as far
as Point Barrow, on the west, while on this side the passage
is known to be open as far as Bellot Strait, in Regent Inlet.

There is therefore only the short distance, about 120 miles,
from Bellot Strait to King William's Island, of doubtful navigation. Through this no ship has ever been able to pass,
owing to a barrier of ice that has hitherto baffled every effort
to penetrate it. Were it not for this one barrier the North-west
Passage would be practicable, and could be sailed through in a
single season. The first ships that attempted the passage by
this route, although whether by Peel Strait or McClintock
Channel is not known, were the EREBUS and TERROR, of Sir John
Franklin, and they were arrested and beset on the north-west

shore of King William's Island, and, as is well known, abandoned after eighteen months' imprisonment in the ice, having drifted in that time only nineteen miles. It is now thought that had Sir John Franklin passed to the east of King William's Island, instead of attempting to sail around the west side, he would have avoided the Polar pack which descends McClintock Channel and impinges on the west coast of that island, completely closing the passage, and he might possibly or probably have passed through James Ross Strait with little difficulty and through Dease and Simpson Straits into the open waters along the northern coast of America. Unfortunately, it was not known at that time that King William's Island was in reality an island. The existence of this channel was unsuspected by Franklin, and the charts then showed the island to be a peninsula. The only way open to him, as he supposed, was that through Victoria Channel, and it was this route which he probably attempted.

In the year 1858 the Fox tried to follow the lost ships by passing through Peel Strait, but only succeeded in penetrating twenty-five miles, when she was stopped by the ice and obliged to return out of it. She then attempted a passage by way of Regent Inlet and Bellot Strait, the existence of Bellot Strait being even uncertain.

In this most successful voyage McClintock actually passed through Bellot Strait and arrived in Peel Strait, but was there again arrested by a barrier of fixed ice, which prevented any further advance to the south-west. My reasons for supposing that this barrier might not always prove to be an impenetrable one were, first, that Franklin is supposed to have passed down Peel Strait in order to reach the position where we know his ships were finally beset. This would seem to indicate that Peel Strait and the bottom of McClintock Channel are, in some seasons at least, open enough to allow navigation. Secondly, when the Fox was finally stopped by this pack, an expanse of open water was seen beyond, which, if she could have reached, she would probably have been enabled to arrive at King William's Island. My hope was that I would find this pack broken up, as it must have been the season that Sir John

Franklin passed through ; and thence, by passing around the eastern side of the island instead of the western, I would have avoided the danger of being beset where Franklin was, and have sailed through Dease and Simpson Straits, and so on along the coast to Behring Strait. Thus it will be seen that the only doubtful and intricate navigation of the North-west Passage is reduced to a distance of about 120 miles. It is now known that the latitude of Bellot Strait, 72 deg. north, may be reached by proceeding down Peel Strait as well as by Regent Inlet, and as for the prospect of any future attempt, we need scarcely take into account any further obstacles than might be met between the limits of that point and the northern shore of King William's Island.

Unfortunately, we were stopped by the same pack which arrested the progress of the Fox, although by navigating the whole length of Peel Strait, hitherto found impassable for ships, we had approached it from a different side. We had chosen this route in preference to that of Bellot Strait as offering greater chances of getting through the pack, because we would have had better opportunities of reaching any lead that might have offered, or, perhaps. of penetrating between the pack and the shore of Prince of Wales Land. The result, then, of our expedition has not proved the impracticability of the North-west Passage. A more favourable season might permit of success. The pack alone prevented our further progress. Our ship was perfectly equipped and in better condition than when she left England. We had still ninety-five tons of coal on board, everybody in good health and spirits and very anxious to proceed. It was only the obstacles offered by nature that prevented the accomplishment of our enterprise.

I do not, therefore, wish to protest against the possibility of making the North-west Passage. On the contrary, I believe it will yet be done.

As to the second object of our expedition, our hope was to reach King William's Island in time for a summer search for the books and papers of the EREBUS and TERROR, which recorded scientific observations extending over a period of four years, and would have been probably deposited in some place on the land in or near the vicinity of the imprisoned ships, there to await another expedition, which would certainly have been sent for the purpose of recovering them had any of the party succeeded in reaching home.

This supposition is confirmed by reports brought home by that enterprising and gallant American explorer, Captain Hall, who gathered from conversations with the Esquimaux that a tradition existed of such deposit.

When that great Arctic explorer, Sir Leopold McClintock, made his most exhaustive search in his extraordinary sledge journey from Bellot Strait down the east coast of King William's Island to the mouth of the Great Fish River and Montreal Island, thence round the south and west coast, and thus circumtravelling the whole island, the ground was covered with deep snow, and it is possible that many objects were concealed that might, when the ground was bare, have been revealed, and on this supposition our project was founded; but the same obstacle that prevented our making the North-west Passage also rendered it impossible to obtain any further information regarding the manner in which those brave men died who gave their lives for the noble cause of science and their country's honour, but not without having been the first to discover the North-west Passage.

In closing my letter, let me again thank you for the generous and disinterested way in which you have assisted my undertaking, and the liberal spirit you displayed when you thus showed that the cause of science is of no nationality, and that you were as ready to aid an English expedition as you would, I feel sure, be equally ready to aid one organized and sent out by your own countrymen.

On our way back we decided to make another attempt to obtain news of the progress of the English Arctic expedition, sent out under Captain Nares, by searching the Carey Isles, and if necessary, even to proceed as far north as Littleton Island, where also the POLARIS passed her second winter. You will see by the English papers the good news we brought home, and which have, I trust, at least given some satisfaction to the friends of the members of the Government expedition,